THE HAUNTING OF AUTUMN

THE
HAUNTING
OF
AUTUMN

William

Panzarella

THE HAUNTING OF AUTUMN

© 2008 By William Panzarella

ISBN: 978-0-578-00541-6

Dedicated To:

*The tens of thousands of children
that are abducted each year.*

*As well as all those – family members,
law enforcement and volunteers –
who are dedicated to finding them.*

TABLE OF CONTENTS

PREFACE

By all accounts Autumn Grace appears to be a normal sixteen year-old. She is preoccupied with the same things as many girls her age: boys, school, having fun with her friends. Brought up as an only child, Autumn has a good relationship with her parents and despite partying on the weekends and getting into occasional mischief, she keeps good grades and never gets into any real trouble. About to finish her junior year of high school, the soon-to-be seventeen year-old should be eagerly waiting the long summer ahead and then entering her senior year. However, everything becomes derailed when Autumn starts learning about a secret. In fact, this secret is about to turn her life upside-down and take her on a harrowing journey through the darkest regions of mankind.

Autumn's secret starts off with a little girl in the woods. However, like ghostly pieces to a macabre puzzle, only parts of this secret are exposed, little by little. But the more Autumn learns, the more the mystery seems to deepen. Why was this secret even revealed to her? What does it mean? How can she even possibly know the things she does? Is it real? Where will it all lead? These are all questions Autumn must answer in order to solve this haunting puzzle and free herself from its sinister grasp. But this is far from just a case of deciphering some riddle. This mystery will take Autumn places that she never knew existed – even in her darkest nightmares. It will make her question her own sanity, question reality. It will take her face to face with evil in its purest form. It will stretch her bounds of fear and sorrow beyond their breaking points. And even if she finds all the answers, she will never be the same again.

1

The foreboding darkness of the starless night stretched into infinity. The only light: the ominous glow of a crescent moon that hung above like a beckoning sign of doom. There was no mistaking that evil lived here. It lurked within the coldness of the air and in the damp scent of the ground. It howled in the cries of the wind that brushed against the hollow trees. It suffocated any last lingering thoughts of hope.

Just below the bare, brittle branches of the trees stood the faceless silhouette of a little girl that could not have been more than ten years old. Draped in a dirt-covered nightgown she stood there silently, her small, bare feet against the hard, cold ground of the woods. Who was she? What was she doing there? Was she oblivious to the monsters that surely lurked, waiting in the darkness? Clearly she must have been lost, but how could such a young girl wander so far from innocence into a world, which knew none. As her ghostly silhouette slowly came into focus, it appeared that the dirt that covered her nightgown was not dirt at all... it was blood! It was smeared all over and looked to be still wet and dripping.

Suddenly, a piercing scream echoed through the darkened woods like the sound of a thousand last breaths. Oh, what a hideous noise! Where could it have come from? It was hard to tell, because it reverberated from every direction, as if it came from the trees themselves. But it was a human scream. Someone was out there in the nearby distance meeting a most torturous fate. But it was too dangerous to try to find whoever it was. It was too perilous to venture any further into the waiting jaws of the woods. Was this some kind of test? Was it to see if someone would risk their own life to save another? Perhaps any good person would, but standing there, it was not such an easy decision. Evil never felt so evil. Hope never felt so hopeless. Hell never felt so real.

Covered in cold sweat, Autumn lunged straight up in her bed in a moment of panic. After taking a few seconds to gather her composure and look around, she realized it was just a bad dream – a nightmare. Still out of breath, the sixteen year-old used her arm to wipe the sweat from her forehead. Yet it still dripped down the rest of her body. The red glowing numbers on the small clock that sat on the nightstand read 6:15am. Wanting to do anything but fall back to sleep, Autumn turned off the alarm that was set for 6:45 and decided to get ready for school.

After a long, hot shower Autumn finished getting ready and headed downstairs. While going into the kitchen for a glass of juice, the high school junior was stopped by her mother, Joanne. "Autumn Grace, didn't I ask you twice yesterday to take out the garbage?" She squawked in a stern, but controlled voice.

Autumn let out an exasperated sigh. "Sorry, I forgot."

Mrs. Grace, who was already dressed and ready for work, crossed her arms. "Well I guess that makes it ok then, doesn't it?"

"C'mon mom, it's no big deal. I'll just take it out now. I didn't hear the garbage truck come by yet."

"It's too late, I already took it out." With her day already off to a dismal start, Autumn waited for what was coming next. "You know Autumn, if you can't even remember to take out the garbage how can your father and I feel confident about leaving you alone next month when we go away?"

Since her parents booked their cruise over two months ago, they had been hounding her about being responsible and taking care of the house. It was the first time Autumn would have the house to herself. As any sixteen year-old would, she was looking forward to it, but was fed up with the way her parents – especially her mother – dangled it over her head. "Ok mom, I said I was sorry. My God, it's not the end of the world or anything."

Realizing there was no use in pressing the issue any further, Mrs. Grace changed the subject as she walked over to the refrigerator. "Did you study for your history test?"

"Yessss," Autumn replied while grabbing a glass from the cabinet.

"I still can't believe they're making you take tests so close to finals."

Autumn held out the glass as her mother filled it with orange juice. "Well it's kinda like trial tests to prepare us for finals. I'll tell ya' though, by the time school is finished I don't think I'll ever want to see another test again as long as I live."

Her mother smiled. "We all had to go though it Autumn."

"I know."

Before heading off to work, Joanne gave her daughter a kiss on the forehead and wished her good luck on the test. It was then time for Autumn to finish her juice and stand in front of the mirror one last time before catching her ride to school. With great concentration she made sure that her long, brown hair was perfectly in place and that the subtle make-up she wore was precise. The bangs had to hang just right. The mascara couldn't be too thick. Everything had to be perfect. After all, where was appearance more important than in high school? Autumn might not have been conceited, but she *was* a sixteen year-old girl.

Suddenly, a car horn broke the silence of the house. It was Kelly. After grabbing her faded black, backpack and turning off the bathroom lights, Autumn rushed outside. The bright, blue

Arizona sky seemed a drastic contrast to the dark and ominous world she had awaken from only an hour earlier. Ready for the long day ahead, the brown-eyed teen threw her backpack in the back of the 1986 Ford Mustang and jumped into the front seat. "Hey Kell," she said with a smile.

"Ready for another day?"

"I guess so," Autumn replied. "Thank god there's not too many left before summer." With that, the two teens were off under the already hot May Sun.

Autumn and Kelly had been best friends since sixth grade. Although in high school, their social circle expanded, the two remained inseparable. As freshmen they even dated two guys who were also best friends. They were not the most popular girls in school, but were far from being loners or outcasts. In fact most people knew who they were and most guys would have jumped at the opportunity to go out with them. However, Kelly was stuck in an on again, off again relationship with some guy she had been seeing for over a year. Autumn, who had dated several guys over the past two years, never seemed to find a lasting relationship. Two of the guys cheated on her and the other one – well they just weren't compatible. For all their misfortunes in finding true love though, the girls still had each other. They were a team. They looked out for each other.

As Led Zeppelin played on the radio, Kelly weaved in and out of the sporadic traffic that lined the open Arizona roads. "So what are we doin' tomorrow?" Kelly asked as she unknowingly cut-off a car.

"I don't know," Autumn answered nonchalantly.

"I can't believe its Thursday already and we don't even have any plans yet. Usually we have the weekend all planned out by Wednesday afternoon." As a car drove by with two guys hanging out the windows whistling, Kelly gave them a flirtatious wave. Then it was back to mapping out the weekend. "Hey, you know Jason Krull is having a party tomorrow night. We can go there. Whatdya' think? There should be at least a few cute guys there." Kelly paused to let Autumn respond, but there was no reply. "Hey Autumn, are you even listening to me?" There was still nothing. "Autumn," Kelly nearly shouted.

Finally Autumn turned her head. "What?"

"You didn't hear a word I said did you? What were you zoning out or something?"

Autumn lowered the volume on the radio. "No, I'm sorry," she replied in a drab voice. "It's just that I haven't gotten much sleep the last couple of days. I've been having these fucking nightmares about this little girl in the woods."

Stopping for a red light, Kelly turned to her friend. "A little girl in the woods?"

"Yeah," Autumn answered in a serious voice. "I've been having them for the last couple of days. The other night I woke up in the middle of the night and it took me an hour to get back to sleep."

"Well what's so freaky about a little girl in the woods," Kelly asked in a voice that was more inquisitive than mocking.

Autumn stared aimlessly out the windshield as she recalled the reoccurring dreams that had never plagued her before. In fact she rarely even remembered her dreams, let alone had ones that kept her up at night. "I don't know. It's kinda' hard to explain. I guess it's more of a feeling than anything else. It just seems like such a spooky place. You know, it's all dark and gloomy and the trees feel like they're watching you."

"What about the little girl?"

"Most of the time she's just walking around like she's lost or something. The other night she kept pointing to something, but when I went to look all I remember is waking-up, covered in sweat. I don't remember seeing anything, but something must have scared the shit out of me. And then this morning I had a dream that her nightgown was covered in blood. Then I think I remember this person screaming." Autumn paused. "I guess though the freakiest thing about the dreams is that they feel so real."

"You know what? I betchya' this is all because of those two girls that were abducted. It's been all over the fucking news. I betchya that's what it is. I mean it is scary shit when you think about it."

Autumn shook her head. "Yeah, maybe you're right."

Two weeks earlier, in Payson Arizona – 83 miles from where Autumn and Kelly lived, in Chandler – two girls, age 12 and 13, were abducted while walking home from a park. The younger girl's parents were out of town, so she was staying at the thirteen year-old's house (both families were close). When neither of the girls showed-up for dinner, the thirteen year-old's mother started calling around to see if they were at a friend's house. After several phone calls, a neighborhood boy, when asked if he had seen the girls, explained that he had last seen them a few blocks away from the park, talking to "some guy" standing next to a parked, brown van. Immediately the police were called and the worst was feared. Those fears grew as the night wore on and still no word from either of the girls. Then, in the morning, when the police went public with the suspected abduction, several other people came forward to say that they had seen the same suspicious van, "trolling" as one person put it, around the park. Yet another eyewitness said that she had seen a brown van – that she had never seen before – driving slowly around the elementary school a day earlier.

By the afternoon after their disappearance, the story was all over the local and state media – from Payson to Phoenix to Tucson. Soon, even the national media would get involved, as news crews stormed the small, suburban city. This was no ordinary abduction, if there was such a thing. For one, two girls had vanished – at the same time. Secondly, it happened it broad daylight. Thirdly, Payson, Arizona was a quiet, uneventful city – if you could even call it a city – where something like murder or kidnapping just didn't happen.

Though the neighborhood boy had seen the girls talking to a stranger by a van, he could not give a detailed description; only that it was a white man, wearing jeans, t-shirt and a black baseball cap. He never saw the man's face and apparently neither did anyone else. There were no ransom calls (though neither of the girls' families – the other girl's parents' naturally came home from their vacation when they were notified what happened – were wealthy). Hundreds of leads poured in, but at least initially, none seemed to pan out. But the authorities had to investigate each one. Local and state police, as well as the FBI, who was called in to assist, interviewed neighbors, schoolmates and family associates. Within a few days it seemed like they had talked to nearly everyone who lived in Payson. They scoured DMV records, trying to find the elusive brown van; criminal records to see if any sex offenders lived in the area; and missing persons reports and crime blotters of the surrounding areas to see if they had some kind of serial killer on the loose. They even had both sets of parents take lie detector tests, to which they all agreed to and passed.

Naturally – and sadly – with each day that passed without any definitive clues as to the girls' whereabouts, the hope of finding them alive dwindled. On the third day, both sets of parents each made their own televised, heartfelt pleas to the perpetrator, who they hoped was listening: "Please, we just want our daughter back." "Please, Amy is just an innocent little girl. She's never done you any harm. Please just let her go. We're begging you." "Whatever you do, please, please don't hurt our little girl." And, in total desperation, also to the girls themselves: "Amy, if you can hear this honey, mommy and daddy love you." "Cassy baby, please come home safe."

The town of Chandler is not far from Tempe, which is home to Arizona State University. It was mostly a residential community and did not see the growth in the early 1990s as other places in the same county – Maricopa – did, such as Scottsdale or

Paradise Valley. Most of the people that relocated to Arizona didn't go to Chandler. Neither did the tourists, most of who came during the winter and were known as "Snowbirds". It didn't have any of the extravagant resorts or golf courses as Scottsdale or Phoenix. It also didn't have the immense, lavish houses as some of its northern neighbors. Chandler was a blue-collar community, but that didn't mean it was not nice. To the contrary, it was for the most part a peaceful place, with plenty of wide-open spaces. It was a place where you could breathe easy and raise your children. It was a different world than Los Angeles or New York.

It was here in Chandler that Autumn Grace lived; a place that she had known her whole life.

The Grace's were a middle class family. Autumn was an only child. Bill Grace worked for the Department of Planning and Development. What exactly he did there his daughter had absolutely no idea, nor was she was dying to find out. Autumn's mother, Joanne, worked as a travel agent. The family was able to afford a nice three-bedroom house and two cars. They were even able to put money aside for their daughter's college education. They were not rich, but lived comfortably.

The Grace's weren't perfect, as is no family. They had their share of arguments, but it was never anything too serious; Autumn would come home with a bad grade or forget to do something she was supposed to do or Bill and Joanne would quarrel about directions on their way somewhere. Sometimes Bill would come home from a hard day at work and bitch about his boss. Sometimes Joanne would do the same. But for the most part they were a "happy" or at least a "normal" family. There was never any abuse, physical or verbal. Bill and Joanne had several friends and would sometimes indulge in a few drinks, but they were in no stretch of the imagination either socialites or drunks. Despite the normal strains of having a teenage daughter, Joanne, who was in her early forties – Bill was two years older than her – always had a good relationship with Autumn. Even though Autumn was now almost seventeen, she still sometimes went to the mall with her mother.

The high school halls were teeming with teenagers from all kinds of social circles. Like most high schools across the country, there were jocks and nerds and stoners. There was the "in crowd" and the outcasts. There were the posers and the Goths and the preppies. Some of the groups intermingled with each other, some did not. However, unlike many of the high schools on the east coast and in big cities, the schools in Arizona were spread out and open. None were more than three floors – most were only two – and didn't resemble decaying prisons, like some of their big city cousins.

Having surprisingly arrived at school ten minutes before the first bell rang, Autumn and Kelly waded through the sea of kids to their lockers. Once there, they were greeted by a girl and two boys. "Hey guys, only one more day to go before Friday," said the girl.

"Thank God," Kelly acknowledged as she opened up her locker.

"Kelly, you're looking good today," said one of the guys, whose eyes were bouncing between her hazel eyes and firm, perky breasts.

Kelly gave a sarcastic smile as she brushed the blonde hair from her face. "I don't think so Toby."

Shot down, he moved on to the next target. "Autumn, you're looking quite sexy yourself."

"In your dreams Toby," she politely replied.

Kelly then changed the subject. "I can't believe we have less than two weeks to go."

"I know," replied Dawn, the other girl. "Summer vacation!" Everyone shook their heads in enthusiastic agreement.

"Hey what are you guys doing Saturday night?" asked the other young man, who was built like a jock, but had long hair and was wearing a Metallica shirt. "A friend of mine's parent's are out of town and he's throwing party. He's supposed to have two kegs there. And it's a really nice house. It's in Scottsdale."

Autumn and Kelly looked at each other and then looked back at Tom. "That sounds pretty cool," Kelly answered for the both of them.

The group talked another five minutes about the party before finally dispersing to class. Autumn walked with Dawn, since the two had the same first class together. Along the way they bumped into various friends and associates.

Right before third period was about to be over, a boy walked into the classroom and handed the teacher a note before leaving. The teacher looked straight at Autumn but said nothing. Apprehensively, Autumn would have to wait another three minutes to find out what it was all about. As the end of class bell rang, the teacher did not have to call Autumn forward; she practically ran to the front of the room. "You're supposed to call your mother at work in between periods," said Mrs. Bumble.

Only a few seconds elapsed before Autumn's paranoia set in. There had to be something wrong, she convinced herself while walking blindly to the front office. What was so important that it couldn't wait? Suddenly, dire thoughts started running through the sixteen year-old's mind. She thought about her reoccurring nightmares. Were they foretelling that something terrible was going to happen? Did something happen to her father? The scenarios were overwhelming. With a racing heart and bated breath Autumn reached the front office. "I… I got a note that I'm supposed to call my mother," she nervously stuttered to the receptionist, while holding the note in her shaking hand.

"You can use that phone over there," she replied, pointing to a desk where nobody was sitting. "Just dial a nine first."

Fully excepting some tragic news, Autumn went to the desk and dialed the number. "Mom, what happened?" she asked in a low, but frantic tone.

Mrs. Grace laughed. "Calm down honey, nothing happened."

"Nothing happened? Why'd you want me to call then? You know you almost gave me a heart attack. I thought that something happened to you or dad." Joanne let out another laugh. "Oh I'm glad you're so amused mother."

"I'm sorry. It's nice to see that you still care about me and your father so much though."

At this point, Autumn was annoyed more than anything else. "So what did you want?"

"I want you to make sure to come home right after school today. Your father found out today that he just got a promotion and we're going out to dinner to celebrate."

"Mom, I'm really happy for dad, but I was going to go over Kelly's and study tonight."

"Autumn. This is a big deal for your father. For all of us. You can…"

Autumn cut her mother off. "Ok, ok. I'll go. Jeeze."

That evening, the Graces' went to their favorite local restaurant – El Paso's. Obviously serving Mexican food, it was somewhere between an upscale and family restaurant. It catered to all groups. Senior citizens ate there. Families ate there. Young people ate there and indulged in their famous pitchers of frozen Margaritas. The place was always packed, but fortunately it was set-up so that tables were not right on top of each other.

Over fresh nachos and a cheese crisp – a tortilla with melted cheddar and monetary jack – Bill talked about his promotion. He would now be a supervisor in his division. As he explained what that meant, Autumn tried to listen and appear interested. She was in fact excited; not only because it would mean more money for the family, but she was genuinely happy for her father. However, she just couldn't get engrossed in the details of what *either* of her parents did for a living.

As joyous as the occasion was, eventually the conversation – as it usually did – focused on Autumn. "So, are you thinking about getting a job this summer, Autumn?"

"Daddd," Autumn whined, as she wished that they were still talking about her father's boring job.

"What? Sixteen is when most kids get their first real job. And you'll be seventeen next month. I'm not talking about anything too serious – maybe just a part time job as a cashier or something."

Autumn turned to her mother for help. "Mom." Seeing that her mother was not going to bail her out, she turned back to her father. "I haven't even finished with school yet. Besides, I thought we were here to talk about you."

Joanne finished chewing on a nacho. "Look, nobody said you have to look for something the day after school gets out. Besides, like your father said, we're just talking about a part time job – and a summer job. I think it'd be good for you."

Just then, the waiter came with the main course. As the subject was quickly put to the side, Autumn breathed a sigh of relief. After comments about how delicious everything looked, it was time for silence as the family of three indulged in their meals. There was time for chatter and time for eating and before stomachs were satisfied, the two never mixed.

"So mom," Autumn said, finally breaking the quiet, "is it all right if I stay over Kelly's Saturday night?"

Joanne gave her daughter a disheartening look. "I don't know Autumn. Are you guys going to be going out?"

Autumn looked shocked that her mother did not give an automatic stamp of approval. "I guess we'll go out. I mean it' is Saturday night. Why? What's the difference?"

"I just don't think it's a good idea for you two girls to be running around with this psycho on the loose."

Autumn was taken aback. "What are you talking about? What psycho?"

"Maybe you've seen on the news," Mrs. Grace answered almost sarcastically, "those two poor girls that were kidnapped up in Payson."

"Mom, they were twelve years old. And that was in Payson."

"But they don't know where – or who – this guy is. What if he's some serial killer? What…"

"Mom, please," Autumn cut her mother off.

Bill's head popped up from his plate of enchiladas. "I think all your mother is trying to say is that we worry about you. And even if it's not this sicko… there's a lot of sicko's running around out there. I mean this happened in broad daylight."

"Those poor girls," Joanne repeated.

"Even though you're older, you can't let your guard down," Mr. Grace continued. "These people are predators."

Autumn felt terrible about the two girls that were abducted, but she had more practical concerns at the moment – like going out with Kelly Saturday night and partying. "I promise we'll be careful, "she pleaded. "Dawn's gonna be with us too. Besides, if we go anywhere it'll only be to some one's house. I promise. C'mon."

Somewhat reluctantly, Autumn's parents gave in. In reality, they were never really going to say no to her staying at Kelly's. They – especially Joanne – were just on edge about the two young girls that were taken. No parent could watch the constant, heart-wrenching news coverage and not help but think *what if that was my child?*

2

Autumn was a B student, who did not let partying get in the way of her schoolwork. She had never been arrested and tried to stay away from trouble. But she *was* a sixteen – almost seventeen – year-old girl. She went out on the weekends, got drunk and even smoked an occasional joint. She had even tried cocaine once (but didn't like it).

Autumn had lost her virginity in the beginning of the school year to a boy named Dave that she had been going out with for several months. However, soon afterwards Autumn broke off the relationship after she found out he had cheated on her. Autumn went out with another boy for a few weeks after Dave, but although they fooled around, they never slept together. In fact to date, Dave had been Autumn's only "one". She tried to pretend that she didn't care what other people thought about her, but it was just a thin façade. And Autumn certainly didn't want to be known as a slut. However, as any other teenage girl, she was always on the look-out for that "right" guy, that knight in shining armor.

Also, like nearly every other teenager – girl or boy – Autumn was always up for a good time.

It was Saturday night; a time to go out, get wild and maybe even get lucky. It was a time to throw all caution to the wind and do nothing more than enjoy oneself. Add to that the fact that the school year was almost over and it was already feeling like summer outside.

Autumn, Kelly, their friend Dawn and two guys from school that they knew were on their way to a party in Scottsdale, about a half hour away. One of the guys, Tom, who was a senior, was driving. They had stopped at a nearby supermarket where Tom's older brother, who had followed them there in his own car, went in to purchase them beer. Tom had also gone into the store, but to use the restroom.

As the girls and the other boy, Justin, waited for their beer, they congregated outside Tom's Nissan Pathfinder. They weren't expecting to be there for more than ten minutes, but it was nice outside and they were like four puppies that didn't want to be caged in. Besides, Dawn was smoking a cigarette and Tom did not like people smoking in his car (though he probably would have made an exception for a pretty girl).

As Kelly was talking to Dawn and Justin, she noticed Autumn standing by herself near the back of the Pathfinder, looking across the parking lot. "What are you looking at?" she almost shouted.

There was no answer. Kelly was about to ask again, but finally, Autumn answered. "You see that guy sitting in that car over there"

Kelly, Dawn and Justin turned their undivided attention to Autumn, as the mood suddenly shifted. It was not what Autumn said as much as the solemn tone she said it in. It was definitely not *see that guy over there, he's cute.* Or, *look at that guy, look what he's wearing.* "What, what guy?" Kelly eagerly asked as she scanned the parking lot. Autumn inconspicuously pointed – at least she tried to be inconspicuous – at an old Fort LTD parked somewhat by itself on the outskirt of the parking lot. It was about fifteen yards away, close enough to see a scraggly-looking man, who appeared to be – at least from the distance – in his early or mid thirties, sitting in the driver's seat with the window rolled down.

"He was staring at me," Autumn said in a nervous voice.

"So?" Dawn casually replied. "He's just some dirty old man. Get used to it. It's no crime to look."

"But I think I've seen him before," Autumn said as her sober words drifted ominously into the night. "I think I saw him this afternoon when I was walking to your house. He was staring at me."

Kelly's face dropped. "What?!"

"He's looking right at us," Dawn remarked simultaneously.

Now it was Justin's turn to get into the mix; his turn to play the hero. "Fuck that," he barked as he began to march towards the car.

"No Justin," Kelly pleaded as she grabbed the seventeen year-old's arm. But it was no use, as he easily broke free from her feeble grip and continued to storm towards the car.

"Hey what the fuck are you looking at?!" Justin yelled as he approached the car.

The girls stood by Tom's Pathfinder, almost frozen, as they watched the stranger open the door and leap up from his seat to confront Justin.

Justin, a high school senior, was on the wrestling team and at 5'8", well built. He weighed about 170 pounds, of which hardly any was fat. He was usually not a trouble-maker and didn't get into too many fights – though he had been in one or two – but he saw this as his perfect opportunity to score some points with the girls. It also obviously would have been a dent in his teenage bravado if he stood around doing nothing while the three girls he was with talked about how this guy was stalking them. When Justin first stormed off towards the car he was filled with confidence and adrenaline. He was still pumping with adrenaline, but when the stranger defiantly lunged from his idling car to meet him, Justin could not help but think *what have I gotten myself into?* The scruffy-looking stranger, who was wearing faded jeans and a yellow tank top that revealed his colorful, tattoo-covered arms, was about 6'2" and lanky. He wasn't muscular, but nevertheless looked menacing. But Justin couldn't back down now – especially not with the girls watching. Besides, despite the tattoos, age and hardened look, Justin figured he could take him. And after all, Tom and his brother would be out of the store any minute to back him up. *Where were those guys anyway*, Justin wondered. "What are you some kind of pervert?!"

"Who the fuck do you think you're talking to?" The stranger replied in a stern, but under-control voice. "You got some kind of problem?"

"Yeah, you staring at my girl over there!" Justin barked as he pointed towards the girls.

For a second, the stranger just stood there. Then, a sinister smile stretched on his, oily, unshaven face. "Oh yeah, they're little firecrackers, ain't they. That pussy's so fresh and juicy you probably need to put on a bib to eat it."

"What the fuck did you say?!"

"A boy like you probably don't even know what to do with pussy like that. I'd tap that ass until…" Before he could finish, Justin shoved him hard against his own car. The stranger didn't say anything further – he just landed a hard, right hook to Justin's jaw, knocking him helplessly to the ground. Justin was still conscious, but dazed.

"Oh my god!" Dawn screamed as she looked on with horror.

"Do something!" Autumn shouted to no one in particular.

Right at that moment, Tom and his brother approached the scene, unaware of what had been going on. However, as soon as they saw the girls, in concert, they both looked over to what the girls were looking at. After taking a split second for everything to register, Tom and his brother ran to Justin's aide (first, Tom's brother threw the beer in the open Pathfinder).

As soon as the stranger knocked Justin to the ground, he jumped back in his car. By the time Tom and his brother arrived, the stranger had thrown the LTD into Drive and hit the gas. Tom was able to kick the right-rear panel of the car as he fled, but nothing more. They didn't even have anything to throw at the car.

Now Tom, his brother and all three girls – who had run over – were hovering over Justin, who was now sitting up on the asphalt. "Dude, you ok," Tom asked his best friend.

"Yeah, yeah," Justin replied in a disappointed voice as he held his lip.

"Who was that guy?" Tom's brother asked.

"We should call the cops" Autumn frantically suggested before Justin could answer.

"I should take the beer out of your car first," Tom's brother wisely replied.

At this point, Justin was getting up. "The cops? No, no. I'm all right. That guy just got a lucky punch," he went on, trying to build back his ego. "I'll be all right. Besides we got a party to go to. Let's just get the fuck outta here."

Listening to Justin, the group scurried back to their cars – Tom's brother to his Camero and everyone else to the Pathfinder – and went on their way before the cops came anyway. After all, there were other people in the parking lot that probably witnessed the incident. Once in the Pathfinder and back on the road, Justin and the girls explained – everyone was talking at once – to Tom what happened. Justin spared the girls the exact, crude words that the stranger had used, though he did get the general point across. Then, Kelly explained that Autumn had seen the same guy watching her earlier that day. "What?!" Tom looked over, taking his eyes off the road for a second.

"Well I don't know. Now that I had a better look at him, maybe it wasn't the same guy."

"What about the car?" Dawn asked. "I though you said it was the same car."

Autumn hesitated for a second before answering. She realized – everyone realized – that if she hadn't had made such an accusation in the first place that Justin would not have gone over there. But the truth was, now that Autumn thought about it, she wasn't so sure anymore. And her honesty just naturally came out. "I don't know. It was a similar car. Maybe... I don't know... I just feel so bad. I'm so sorry Justin."

"That's all right," he quickly replied.

Though they now had a story to talk about, they went to the party as planned and had a good time. Though Justin, who had a slightly swollen lip and minor discoloration on the lower, left side of his face, obviously was not happy about being punched-out, he took some solace in the way Autumn, Dawn and Kelly were coddling him.

If it wasn't hell, it could not have been far from it. Fear and anguish permeated the darkness, which strangled like a noose. Everything about it – the starless night, the coldness of the air, the wind howling through the trees – was meant to terrify. It was a place that seemingly, even God had forsaken. Yet there she was, the little girl in the woods. Out of the darkened haze, her face eerily started to come into detail. It was so sad, so frightened. It was as if she had stared into the eyes of the devil himself. She said nothing, pointing to the woods as her blood-smeared nightgown waved gently in the breeze. What was she pointing to? Who was out there? Or better yet, *what* was out there?

Walking barefoot along the hardened ground, she slowly ventured further into the looming woods. With each floating step, the silent terror that seized the air grew ever so more. Only the dim glow from a quarter moon a million miles away, showed the way. There was no path, no clearing. As the wind picked-up, it made a harrowing sound that spewed out into the night. Still, the young girl pressed on. Every sense foretold that she was walking further into danger, but she seemed on a mission. Was it a trap? Was she some kind of illusion?

From out of nowhere, a faint illumination splintered through the empty trees. It was towards this light that the girl was going. Following the glow, it appeared that something was hiding through the branches. Its hazy image peeked from behind the trees. A few more steps revealed the ghostly façade of a house. As the woods parted, the house became clearer. Even from a distance, it resonated with fear. Everything about it said, "stay away!" But the young girl seemed undeterred. With her long, straight blonde hair blowing in the cold wind, she kept walking. Then suddenly, as the two-story house grew larger, she stopped and turned around. Her distant eyes filled with tears as she pointed towards the foreboding structure. It looked abandoned, except for a light protruding from one of the downstairs windows. That must have been the faint glow that could be seen through the trees. Someone must have been living there, but it was hard to imagine. It looked – it felt – so void of living touch. There were no other houses. There were no foreseeable roads. There was no dog barking in the backyard. Its tall, slender chimney did not puff with smoke.

Suddenly, there was a bright flash and not only was the little girl gone, but the surrounding woods had transformed into the inside of the house. It must have been the downstairs, because there was the light – a floor lamp, standing next to a yellow couch. The walls of the room seemed to be closing in, like the jaws of hell trying to devour its prey. Before the rest of the room could reveal itself there was another flash. Now, all that could be seen was blood splattering against a white wall as a gargled, helpless scream rang out through the air. It was not clear from whom it was coming. There was no body, no face – only the thick, red blood splattering against the wall. But the pain was overwhelming. The torment could not only be heard in the scream, but also felt. It besieged the air and lept from the wall and grew more overpowering with each streak of blood that splashed against its white surface.

Breathing like she had just run a marathon, Autumn jumped straight up in the bed. Trying to catch her breath, she nervously looked around the room and realized it was just another nightmare. To her elation, she was safe inside Kelly's bedroom, with Kelly still sleeping on the other edge of the bed.

The early morning sun was seeping through the closed Venetian blinds. Still shaken by the dream, she breathed a sigh of relief. The wholesome, familiar surroundings were a welcomed contrast to the unworldly woods and that godforsaken house.

Feeling more relaxed by the second Autumn glanced at her friend who looked so peaceful. Then suddenly, she noticed the doorknob slowly turning. Kelly's parent's usually knocked before entering, so she thought it was probably Kelly's twelve year-old brother, Ryan. He also was supposed to knock, but sometimes didn't. Not thinking much of it, Autumn continued to watch as the door gradually cracked open. However, instead of Kelly's brother, in walked the little girl from the woods! As terror sucked the air from the room, Autumn tried to scream, but no sound came out. There was only a terrible silence as the little girl, still dressed in her bloodstained nightgown, leisurely walked towards the bed. With ghostly eyes, she pointed towards a petrified Autumn. As an unmistakable evil pulsated through the room, the longhaired little girl mumbled something that ended with the word "dead".

In a feverish panic Autumn lunged up in bed, pulling off the covers in one quick motion. The little girl was gone and the light that splintered through the blinds now seemed much dimmer. Although she had been tricked before, Autumn instantly realized that this time she was indeed awake. However, that did little to quell her fright. Sweating and out of breath, she turned to notice that Kelly had been awaken by her furor.

"What's the matter?" asked Kelly in an exhausted, but alarmed voice.

Still shaken-up, Autumn tried to compose herself. "I... I just had another one of those dreams," she replied with a crackling tone.

"Are you all right?"

Autumn paused before answering. "Yeah... I guess so. It was just so real. I dreamt I was in the woods again with that little girl and I think someone was getting stabbed. I just remember there being all this blood." Autumn stopped to take another breath. "Then I thought I woke-up, but I was still dreaming."

"I hate when that happens," replied Kelly, who still looked half asleep.

"Yeah," Autumn agreed. "It was so freaky. I dreamt that I woke-up and I was right here in bed. Then your door opened and in walked the little girl, still covered in blood. She said something. I don't remember what it was, but it was something about being dead – maybe 'I'm dead' or 'we're all dead'. I don't know, but it fucking scared the shit out of me."

Through her dangling, blonde bangs, Kelly looked at the clock on the nightstand. "Well it's not even six thirty. Why don't you try to back to sleep for a while? Just try to think about pleasant things. Think about being on a beach or something."

"Yeah, you're probably right. After all, we were up 'till about two thirty last night. I'm sorry about wakening you up."

Kelly put her hand on Autumn's shoulder. "Don't worry about. Just try to get some rest. And remember… it's just a bad dream."

With that, Kelly rolled over and quickly drifted back off to sleep. Autumn tried to do the same, but could not. She was exhausted, but fear beat out exhaustion. She knew nightmares could not hurt her, but they certainly could terrify and terror was sometimes worse than any pain. For nearly four hours the sixteen year-old sat quietly in bed, being careful not to wake-up Kelly again. It was the longest hours of her young life.

Around noon, Kelly dropped Autumn back off at her house. To Autumn's delight, she found a note on the kitchen counter that read: *We went out looking for luggage, will be back in a while.* Autumn didn't know when her parents left or how much longer they would be gone, but for at least a while, she had the house to herself. She was exhausted and hung-over and more than anything, just didn't want to deal with talking to her parents – about anything.

After heating up some left over Chinese food in the microwave and pouring a glass of soda, Autumn adjourned to the couch and flipped on the TV. Food and relaxation, it was exactly what the doctor ordered. When Autumn first turned on the television, the news automatically came on. But the sixteen year-old was in no mood to hear about abductions, murders, or any other bad news. She just wanted – needed – some mindless entertainment. After flipping through a few channels, she happily settled on an episode on *The Brady Bunch*.

With a full belly, comfortable couch and mindless TV, Autumn soon started to doze off. However, before she even realized that she was sleeping, Autumn was awoken by the front door opening. And if that didn't wake her, her mother loudly announcing "Autmun, we're home", surely did.

Begrudgingly, Autumn lifted herself off the couch and went over to meet them, more out of curiosity than anything else. "So I see you guys actually got some luggage... and some other things too," she said, looking at the large Macy's bag her mother was carrying.

"You're mother finally settled on a bathing suit." Bill looked exactly like a guy that had just been dragged shopping by his wife for three hours.

"All right mom."

While putting their purchases in the living room – their temporary resting place – the light conversation continued. Autumn made her mother pull out the bathing suit, as well as a few shirts that she had bought. Then she made her father do the same with his two pairs of shorts. Everything seemed to be gliding along. Then it happened. "Autumn, there's something that your father and I want to talk to you about."

Autumn knew that nothing good ever followed those words. "What is it," she asked with a visibly perturbed look on her face.

"I know we had talked about you staying by yourself while we're gone, but..."

"No way! I'm going to be seventeen years old!"

"But," her mother calmly continued, "we think that two weeks is a long time and... well, we were thinking about having Aunt Margie stay with you."

If looks could kill, both Joanne and Bill would have been dead on the spot. "You have to be kidding me!" Autumn barked. "No, this cannot really be happening!"

"Just calm down," her mother pleaded.

"Dad!"

"We know you're almost seventeen," Mr. Grace replied, almost reluctantly, "but with everything going on..."

"What's going on?!"

"With those poor girls in Payson," answered Joanne.

Autumn gave her mother – who she knew was the culprit behind the sudden change of plans – a look of disbelief. "Again with those stupid girls?!"

"Autumn Grace!" her mother growled.

"Autumn," her father sternly added.

Autumn took a second to slow down. "I didn't mean that. You guys know I feel terrible about them. I have a heart. But this has gotten out of hand! I'm not a little girl! Besides, it makes no sense. Even when you guys are home, it's not like you follow me everywhere I go. I mean what happens when I go to the mall... or walk to Kelly's."

Autumn did have a point, so Joanne skipped over what her daughter said and tried a completely different angle. "And we don't want you having any parties."

Autumn looked like her usually pale, young face was about to explode. "Now all of a sudden you don't trust me! Arrgghh!" She shouted in frustration as she stormed off to her room, slamming the door behind her. At first Joanne was going to follow her, but Bill stopped her, figuring it would be best to just let their daughter cool off. Besides, he did feel a little guilty. After all, they *had* told Autumn that she could stay by herself.

Coiled-up on her bed and clutching a pillow, Autumn was so upset that she started to cry. She tried to fight off the tears, but could not. She was furious at her parents, especially her mother. She was disconsolate about the fact that at age sixteen – almost seventeen – she needed a babysitter. She was still hung over. She was still exhausted; not being able to sleep because of those damn nightmares. At the same time, Autumn wanted both to explode and to crawl up in a ball and sleep for two weeks. To her dismay though, she could do neither. All she could do was sit there on her bed, drowning in the quicksand of her thoughts.

After about an hour, Autumn, despite still being angry, upset and worn out, tried to find enough mental strength to study for her final exams. Autumn had always been a good student – and a practical person – and she was not about to let being drained or being mad at her parents affect her grades. Autumn was still somewhat undecided on a career – she volleyed between a veterinarian, psychologist, and TV producer – but she always planned on going to college and getting a good education. So, though disgruntled and fatigued, she retrieved a notebook and science textbook from her backpack. Still sitting on her bed, she then frustratingly flung open the textbook.

Sitting Indian-style on her twin-size bed, Autumn looked at the thick textbook by her feet. Next to it sat an open spiral notebook, with which she hoped to jot notes down in with the pencil she was holding. The high school junior really wanted to study, but after reading a few lines in the textbook she would space-out for a minute or so, only to have to read the same lines over again. Nothing was sinking in. Autumn just couldn't focus. Finally, alone in her lassitude, Autumn found herself mindlessly scribbling into the notebook as she stared out her window. After about a minute, Autumn looked down at the white piece of paper she had been doodling on. Instantly, her tired eyes opened as wide as they could as a cold, terrifying sensation shot through her entire body. Without consciously realizing it, Autumn had drawn a large, upside-down pentagram and under it, the words *He's*

Coming. In a frightened panic she violently shoved the notebook off the bed and onto the floor.

Autumn was petrified. She wanted to scream, but was too scared. She wanted to run to her mother, but was afraid that she would just think she was on drugs. After all, a sober person – a sane person – doesn't draw upside-down pentagrams without even knowing it. Autumn looked at her hand, as if she was waiting for it to something else she had no control over. But nothing happened. Then, against her better judgment, she slowly retrieved the notebook from the floor and thumbed through the pages. Maybe it was just in her mind. Maybe she was so exhausted that she was seeing things. But then came the page – it was still there – the pentagram and the ominously, mysterious message. Again, Autumn threw the book on to the floor, this time even farther away. She then grabbed her pillow as tight as she could and coiled-up in the corner of her bed. *What is going on?!* She cried in her mind. The little girl in the woods – those horrible nightmares – and now this! Autumn knew she had to get a grip on herself.

3

The room pulsated with evil. A faint light came from a floor lamp by the corner of the wall, but otherwise the house was draped in darkness. The hallways and the staircase led to certain, but unknowing peril. Everything seemed to be strangely untouched in what appeared to be the family room. The couch waited patiently for someone to sit on it. The coffee table had not an item on it. The dormant television set sat silently on its stand. Everything was quite, yet the tension spoke a thousand words.

Suddenly, if by magic, the young girl appeared at the base of the stairs. She was clothed in the same bloodstained nightgown and wore the same wretched look of despair. Yet she said nothing. She just stood there, with her long, blonde hair and ghostly presence. Slowly, she climbed the wooden stairs. They did not creek or make any noise at all. However, her steps warned not to follow. As the girl approached the top a cold darkness reached out like the hand of Satan himself. The air was thick and filled with fear. Still, she moved on, as if on a mission.

A narrow corridor ran the length of the upstairs, with rooms on each side and one at the end. All of the doors were opened, some barely, some all the way. As the little girl gravitated to the first doorway on the right, the narrow walls of the walkway seemed to constrict even more. Standing in the entranceway, the girl looked back before stepping into the room. Suddenly the air began palpitating like the pounding of a heart.

The room was dark, but the outline of a bed and dresser were visible. No one appeared to be in the bed, but the sheets and quilt were torn off and laid halfway on the floor. Something terrible had happened here, something unfathomable. Slowly, the room mysteriously illuminated just enough to get a glimpse of images that had been drawn on the walls. They were pentagrams – upside-down pentagrams – and a closer look revealed that they were drawn in blood. They were still dripping down the white-painted walls. Whose blood was it? Did it belong to the little girl? Now, the pulsating grew to a feverish pitch. The thumping kept growing and growing. The anxiety was tormenting.

Abruptly, the walls were replaced with hollow trees. The entire room had been transformed into the woods. The cold, windy air made it breathable again, but the forest was far from refuge. In fact there was a sinking feeling that refuge did not exist in this world. Beneath the long, skeletal branches of a lurching tree was the little girl, kneeling against the coarse, brittle ground. What was she doing? What was she looking at? A different angle exposed the horrid truth. She was kneeling besides a still and bludgeoned body of, at first glance, what looked to be a child.

Before the figure further identified itself, the scenery once again altered without notice. Only this time, it was a place unlike the darkened woods or menacing house. In fact it could not have been more opposite. The starless night had been replaced with a sun-soaked, azure sky. Under it laid a serene, grassy plane. Right off to the distance was a small, wooden steeple. However, the image was there for only a matter of seconds before it melted away.

Monday morning, just like clockwork, Kelly pulled-up in front of Autumn's house to pick her up from school. Usually, if

Autumn wasn't already waiting outside or peering through the window, Kelly would have to wait no more than a few minutes. Sometimes she would beep the horn, but never more than once. That is until this morning. Kelly waited impatiently outside in her idling Mustang for about ten minutes before pressing once on the horn. About two minutes later, she pressed on it again. Still no Autumn. Figuring that she was probably just being hassled by her mother – about anything – Kelly was about to go up to the house and rescue her friend. But as Kelly opened the driver's door, Autumn finally walked out of the house.

In complete languor, Autumn climbed into the front passenger seat, throwing her backpack in the back. "Damn, girl, you look like shit."

Autumn, who felt like shit, flashed her friend a sarcastic smile. "Thanks Kell."

"What's the matter?" Kelly asked as she drove away.

Autumn hesitated before answering. "I'm just exhausted. I just haven't been sleeping at all."

"Not the nightmares again?"

"Yeah," she sheepishly replied, somewhat embarrassed. "I don't know what it is. It's fuckin crazy. Maybe I saw some horror movie. Maybe it is these girls in the news – the ones that were kidnapped. I don't know. It's stupid, huh?" Autumn didn't mention the incident of her unconsciously drawing a pentagram or the bizarre message. It was the first time that Autumn had held anything back from Kelly. The two were best friends who had always confided in each other – without exception. But Autumn was afraid that if she told Kelly about it, even her best friend would think she was crazy.

"It's not stupid," Kelly replied, in an attempt to mollify her friend. "I had this nightmare a few months ago about this crazy werewolf-looking creature chasing me through my own house. It scared the shit outta me. I woke-up and I was covered in sweat."

"Yeah. But it's just I keep having them. I mean when is this gonna end? I need to get some sleep. And I have my first finals tomorrow."

Stopped at a red light, Kelly looked over to her weary friend. You know what you need," she said in an upbeat voice, "sleeping pills. You know – painkillers. My dad has a whole bottle of them."

For the first time that morning, Autumn's eyes opened wide. "Are you serious? He won't notice some are missing?"

"No. His doctor prescribes it to him because he gets back spasms sometimes, but he only takes them when it gets real bad – if he can't sleep at night. It's good shit too, Darvocetts. I took two pills once and it knocked me the fuck out. It'll put you in such a deep sleep you won't even have any dreams – or at least remember them. You'll be so out of I'll stop by the house and I'll grab a few for you. "

"You mean right now?"

"Yeah. It's alright. Besides, it's better to do it now, because no one's home." Kelly's father, who worked as a Super for a mid-sized construction company, sometimes came home before her (Kelly's mother also worked, but didn't get home until later).

So, backtracking a little bit, Kelly stopped by her house and ran inside. As she climbed back into the car, she handed Autumn three white, oblong tablets. Autumn thanked her and then the girls were off to school.

After school, Kelly and Autumn went to Autumn's house. Autumn's parents were still at work, so the girls would have the house to themselves for two hours or so. It was the second half of May and in central Arizona that meant the temperature was already pushing close to triple digits. So the girls decided to jump in the pool. Actually, it was something they had been planning since lunch. And when teenagers get something in their head, they go with it. In less than ten minutes, they parked the car, ran into the house, changed into their bathing suits – though the girls were the same build, Kelly had left-over one of her bathing suits – and were in the pool.

The cool water rejuvenated Autumn. Though she was still working on little sleep, it was the best she had felt in over a week. Laughing and screaming, the girls began to playfully splash each other. For a moment, Autumn was able to forget all about the little girl in the woods. For a moment it was all about just having fun; just being a sixteen year-old girl.

Eventually, no matter how much fun they were having, Autumn and Kelly started getting bored – and Autumn started getting tired again. After drying off, before heading home, Kelly sat with her friend on the living room couch to watch a little TV. The set was tuned to a news interview. A woman reporter was talking to a fit-looking middle-aged man wearing a suit. Right beneath the chair he was sitting on, was the caption: "Retired Phoenix Homicide Detective, Frank Roberts". It was apparent, even from the few words that Autumn and Kelly caught, that they were talking about the two girls who were abducted in Payson. Almost immediately, Kelly changed the channel. "No wait," Autumn pleaded, "turn it back."

"Come on, you don't want to see that. Especially with your nightmares."

"No, I do. Just turn it back for a second."

Taken aback a little by Autumn's stern demeanor, Kelly complied and flipped back three channels to the interview.

Now that it was back on, *both* girls watched intently as the female reporter attempted to lead the interviewee into guessing – and that's what it was, guessing – all the possible (and grave) scenarios that could have befell the two missing girls. "But certainly it doesn't bode well that there have been no ransom calls, no prime suspects… that we know about, at least."

"Well, unfortunately, statistically speaking, the more time that elapses the less likely it is for a happy ending. That's why the first forty-eight hours are so crucial in these types of cases." The ex-detective must have realized immediately how morbid his comment probably sounded – even if it was true – because he tried to backtrack a bit. "But of course, we don't know what happened. And there have been plenty of cases where, even after considerable time has elapsed, victims have been found alive. In fact just last year that fourteen year-old girl escaped from her abductor after being held captive for over a month."

"Yes, Lisa Yulick," the woman responded matter-of-factly as she nodded her head.

"Yes. In some ways it was a similar case. I mean, there were no ransom demands, no immediate suspects. After two weeks without any viable leads everyone – especially the media – started assuming the worse. But then low and behold, a month later, police happen to spot this girl running down the street in pajamas – and its Lisa Yulick. I mean obviously, she went through a very traumatic experience and will have to deal with the emotional scars that this sick bastard left her with, but she's alive. And there have certainly been other cases where victims have been found alive; some where the girl – or boy – wasn't even harmed… other than emotionally, of course."

"Yes, but wouldn't you say that is the exception to the rule?" Just like the media to cast the dark clouds of tragedy. "I mean obviously we're all hoping for a happy ending to this story. I mean our hearts go out to those two poor little girls and their families. But unfortunately, we see all too often in cases like this, a heartbreaking ending: this past winter with that poor girl in Albuquerque; the Molly Roland case last year; Toby Daniels, before that."

The retired detective slowly nodded his head, with the look of utter defeat on his face. "Yes."

"And then there are the cases where the victims are never found."

"Yes, unfortunately that happens more than you could imagine. I mean people – including children – go missing in this country every day and are never found."

"There's even been some high-profile cases," the reporter morbidly pressed-on, "Lisa Watson in Raleigh, North Carolina.

She was taken out of her upstairs bedroom in nineteen eighty-nine, and despite one of the largest missing persons investigations in the country at the time, has never been found. No one was ever even arrested in connection with her disappearance. Then of course, who could forget Dewey, Oregon in the mid-eighties."

The ex-detective moved almost uncomfortably in his chair. "Well Dewey was particularly bad, because one of the girls' entire family was murdered."

"That's it!" Kelly proclaimed as she changed the channel.

"Kell, I was watching..."

"I don't care. I'm sorry. How can you sit there and listen to that morbid shit. Dead and missing kids. Slaughtered families. No wonder why you have nightmares. I mean to watch and see what's going on is one thing, but enough's enough."

Autumn silently agreed.

That night, Autumn sat in her room with her stereo playing softly in the background. Autumn was exhausted and was going to take one and a half of the pills Kelly had given her to help her sleep. But before she did, Autumn figured she would at least try to study for her next finals. However, it was a useless cause. She just couldn't focus, at least not on studying. But there was something that Autumn could not seem to get out of her mind and she didn't understand why – it was the word Dewey. The whole conversation on the news, about the missing girls and other previous, notorious crimes, stayed with the sixteen year-old. But for whatever reason, it was the word – the mere word – Dewey that stood out. Autumn sifted through her teenage recollection, but did not remember ever hearing about the kidnapping and murders in Dewey, Oregon.

Finally, around eight o'clock, realizing that studying was futile and too tired to do anything else, Autumn swallowed one and a half tablets that Kelly had given her. About fifteen minutes after taking them, Autumn felt dizzy and flush, as if she had drank too much and began questioning if she should have taken the pills. But twenty minutes later, she was out cold.

When Autumn woke-up the next morning, she was groggy and felt like she could go back to sleep for another three or four hours. But for the first time in nearly two weeks, she didn't have any nightmares; none that she could remember anyway. And by about 11:00 am, Autumn not only felt wide-awake, but also rejuvenated. For the first time in what seemed like a while, Autumn felt "normal".

Since it was finals' week, juniors and seniors had an early dismissal – 12:15. With the buzz of summer already in the air – there was only seven days left of the school year – teenagers eagerly piled out of their classes to go hang out with their friends. Like everyday after school, Autumn was on her way to the Junior parking lot to meet Kelly. Walking hurriedly past one of the outdoor locker bays, she ran into Dawn and another girl she knew. "What are you and Kelly going to do?" Dawn asked excitedly.

Before Autumn could answer, a guy that they all knew – Dawn had gone out with him for several weeks the previous summer and had regretted it ever since – who had happened to overhear the girls conversation, jumped in. "Yeah, what are you guys going to do? You guy's going over Kelly's?"

"I didn't know you were part of the conversation," Dawn replied blatantly.

"I think I'm just going home," Autumn answered. Like her friends, she *did* want to hang out, but did not want him tagging along. None of them did.

Eventually, with some effort, the girls were able to ditch their unwanted hanger-on. After meeting Kelly in the parking lot, the four girls stood around discussing what they were going to do, before it was decided that they would all go to Dawn's house.

Dawn lived with her mother, but she wasn't supposed to be home for work until 6:00 pm. So the girls had the house to themselves for hours. The girls were there, just standing around the kitchen gossiping, for no more than fifteen minutes before the doorbell rang. It was Tom and Justin – and Tom had a 12-pack of Budweiser. (The girls had run into them in the school parking lot and Dawn had invited them over.) "Somebody order some beer?" Tom asked in a tone that was almost yelling, as he held the cardboard box of cans up in the air.

The girls' eyes lit up. They were expecting Tom and Justin, but the beer was a complete bonus. "All right!" Dawn proclaimed. "Now we can get started.

The front door was not even closed behind them before Tom began doling out the beers. And no one wasted any time in opening their can. "Hey, you guys hear the news?" Tom asked, before pausing to take a chug of his beer.

"What?" Kelly asked, while checking Tom over.

"They found out who took those girls up in Payson."

"What?"

"Yeah, it's all over the news," added Justin.

"They caught the guy?" Autumn asked in an excited voice. "Are the girl's alive?"

Tom took another chug of his beer. "No, I don't think they caught him yet, but they know who it is. I just saw a couple of seconds of it on the news when I stopped home to get the beer. My brother was watching it. I had to give him a couple of joints for the beer."

"You've got weed?" Dawn asked enthusiastically.

"Yeah," Tom replied with a smile. "It's some good shit too."

"It sure is" confirmed Justin.

"Dawn, put on the TV," Autumn asked, changing the subject back to more serious matters.

Kelly gave her friend a disgruntled look. "What is your fascination with this shit? It's morbid."

"No, put it on," Justin said as he started to walk towards the family room. "I want to see if they caught this sick fuck."

Dawn went over to the television set. "Yeah, don't you wanna know if the girls are ok?"

"Come on," Tom replied as he sat down on the couch. "You really think those girls are still alive? It's been like two weeks."

"How could you say something like that," the other girl shot back at him.

"I'm just sayin'. I mean don't get me wrong. I'm not a fuckin' monster or anything. I hope they're all right."

As the teens gathered in the family room, drinking their beers – and as Tom proceeded to roll a joint on the coffee table – they intently watched the news, trying to figure out exactly what had happened.

A combination of phoned-in tips and old fashion detective work led the authorities to their number one prime suspect, a 35 year-old career loser that one of the girl's parents had hired several months earlier to remove a dead tree. His name was Horace Delvin. Then came the big break in the case: their man was caught on a gas station surveillance camera, with what appeared to be the two girls in the back seat of his car, in Bullhead City, Arizona, which rests on the California border. The tape was taken three days after the girls had disappeared. The following day, the gas station attendant that had helped Horace, saw the pictures of the two girls on the news and recognized them – or at least thought he recognized them – as the girls that had been with Delvin. He called the hotline number that the news had given and told the operator that he was "ninety percent sure" that he had seen the missing girls.

By this point, receiving over a hundred tips a day – most well-intentioned, but off base and yet others, sick pranks – it took the authorities three more days before they paid the gas station a visit. By now, four days had passed since Delvin was at the gas station and seven days since the girls were abducted. And even then, the gas station lead was not seen as the smoking gun. The FBI agents took down the attendant's statement and looked over the surveillance tape, which would have been ordinarily recorded over had it not been purposely saved by the savvy attendant. However, though the tape showed two girls in the back seat and they appeared in likeness to missing girls, it was hard to tell with certainty. Also, the way the car was situated, the camera could not pick-up the license plate of the beat-up Dodge Impala. However, the camera did get a clear picture of Horace Delvin and a few days later, when through other independent leads, he became the prime suspect, the agents who had been out to the gas station immediately put two and two together.

Horace Delvin's picture – a mug shot from a year ago when he was arrested for drug possession – was plastered all over the media outlets. So was his full description and nuisances: such as his several tattoos; the fact that he walked with a slight limp; and that he chain smoked Camels. A description of his car – along with the license plate number, which they now had – was also given (they were still not sure – or at least saying – how he had come into possession of the van that was spotted when the girls were abducted). Now, there were Horace Delvin sightings everywhere and the task force had to check out each one.

Drinking their beers and passing a joint around, the teens watched the news. "Dude," Justin said, still holding in his hit, "you think those chicks are actually still alive?"

"I don't know man, but I hope they fry that fucker," Tom replied as he grabbed the joint from his friend.

"They should fuckin' castrate and torture him," Dawn emphatically added.

Tom handed off the half-gone joint to Kelly. "I just can't believe there's people like that roaming around," she said. "Sick fucks!"

"Hey, do you think Mr. Richards could be a rapist?" Dawn asked from out of nowhere.

Everyone laughed. Everyone except Autumn. "What the fuck are you talking about?" Tom replied, still laughing.

"I see the way he looks at me. The way he looks at all the girls; taking peeks at their breasts and trying to look up their skirts."

"Get outta here," Autumn finally chimed in.

"Yeah, and he's just all weird looking."

"Yeah, and he's not married," added Kelly. "He probably goes home and fantasizes about you Dawn. Goes in the bathroom and..."

"Eww! Stop it!" Dawn screeched, grossed out by the thought.

Tom nearly spit out his beer. "You guys are fucking sick," he chuckled.

"Hey Dawn, you got anything to munch on?" Justin asked, finally changing the subject.

When Autumn arrived back home later that evening, her parents were already there. The sixteen year-old had used Visine and gum to mask the fact that she had been smoking pot and drinking. Still, she went straight to her room, telling her parents that she had eaten dinner at Dawn's – which she did, if you consider popcorn, Doritos and microwavable potato skins dinner.

Still buzzed, Autumn propped herself up onto her bed and turned on the TV, trying to see if there were any new developments in the search for Horace Delvin and the two abducted girls. It was only around 7:00pm, but after two beers and several hits off the joint, Autumn started to doze off. She tried to fight it; not so much because she was afraid of having another nightmare, but she knew that if she went to bed at seven, she would probably wake up in the middle of the night and not be able to go back to sleep. However, when sleep really wants you, it gets you. Still fully-clothed, Autumn's eyes finally became too heavy to stay ajar. For the first fifteen minutes or so she would pry one eye open, just long enough to see a brief, splinter of a blurry image on the television set. But soon the images and sound of the TV, melded with the thoughts in her head until she became unable to decipher reality from dream.

About an hour later Autumn woke-up, still in a daze. After looking at her clock, she stretched and then turned her attention to the TV, which was still on. Within seconds, Autumn snapped to attention, as she watched the "Special Report". They had found Horace Delvin… and the girls. And they were both alive! All three were found in a roadside motel in Beatty, Nevada. Delvin had shaved his head and worn sunglasses in attempt to disguise his appearance, but the motel manager, who had just been watching the news, still recognized him. He also noticed that he had two young girls in the pick-up truck with him (somewhere along the line, Delvin had ditched his Impala and somehow acquired a pick-up truck). The manager immediately called the police and in less than ten minutes, authorities from several agencies swarmed the small motel.

Autumn listened to every word on the television with intense focus. She couldn't believe that the whole thing had actually come to an end. She couldn't believe that the girls were still alive. Sadly, it would soon come out that they had both been molested. But they were alive.

As anyone with even an ounce of humanity would be, Autumn was ecstatic that the girls had been found alive. And that the sick bastard who took them was in custody. But Autumn was also relieved for more personal reasons. She had been increasingly convinced that the nightmares that had been plaguing her were a result – direct or indirect – of the almost overbearing media coverage of the girls' abduction. Now that they had been found, now that it was over, Autumn hoped that the nightmares would stop – for good. And then there was also the issue with her mother being too nervous to leave Autumn alone for two weeks while she and her husband went on their cruise. Maybe now her mother's mind could be a little more at ease and would drop this nonsense about a "babysitter".

4

It was the final week of school. Four days left to be exact – and not even full days. It had been nearly a week since Autumn had had a dream about the little girl in the woods and was once again sleeping well (she attributed it to the Payson girls being found, assuming that their plight had been the cause of her nightmares). And to top it all off, her parents had changed their mind about having Bill's sister stay at the house with her while they were away. Feeling like a "normal" teenager again, Autumn was faced with a long summer and the house all to herself for two weeks. For a sixteen year-old, it was a dream come true. Everything was falling into place. Finally!

That morning, on their way to school, Kelly and Autumn talked about what they were going to do that afternoon – and what they were going to do that Thursday, the last day of class. When they arrived at school, their conversation continued with their other friends. Understandably, electricity was pulsating through the air, through the halls, locker bays and classrooms.

Autumn breezed through her first class – American History – barely paying attention to what the teacher was saying. No one was really paying attention. That is, until the last ten minutes or so when Ms. Turner handed out the graded finals that the class had taken the week before. It was obvious what students had done well, by the glowing look on their faces. And a few students, who surprised – almost shocked – themselves that they had done so well, even let out a triumphant "yesss!" Then, naturally, there were those long, glum faces of those who had not done as well as they had expected. Some kids just looked puzzled. Of course, there were also a few students who seemed indifferent; the same ones that had been indifferent about the class the entire year. Nervously, Autumn awaited her turn. It seemed that Ms. Turner had walked to every desk and plopped-down a graded test, everyone's except Autumn's. It was mere process of elimination; the more tests she handed out, the greater chance that Autumn would be next. Finally, with what looked like just two more tests left in her hand, Ms. Turner approached Autumn's desk. "Autumn, I'd like to talk to you about your test after class."

Immediately, Autumn felt an empty, sinking feeling in her stomach. *Could she have done that bad?* She wondered. But she had noticed the boy sitting across from her had gotten a "D" on his final. And the teacher hadn't asked to talk to *him* after class. *What the hell could this be about?* Autumn worried. But she did not have to ponder for long. A minute later, the bell rang. With some trepidation, Autumn went up to the teacher's desk. "You wanted to see me Ms. Turner."

Ms. Turner waited until the last student had left the classroom before answering. Then, the thirty-something year-old teacher peered through her glasses at Autumn with a look mixed with puzzlement and disappointment. "I don't understand Autumn. You were always such a good student... an 'A' student."

"I don't understand Ms. Turner," Autumn answered honestly.

The teacher then grabbed a packet of paper off the desk and showed it to Autumn. It was her History final – and it had a big red "C" on the top right corner. *Was this what this was all about?* Autumn asked herself. *All this over a "C"?!* She would have obviously liked to have done better, but it was far from the end of the world. Autumn knew that she had to have gotten either an "A" or "B" in the rest of the class, so at the very worst – the very worst – she would get a "C" for the semester. "I'm sorry Ms. Turner. I studied. I thought I did a lot better."

"Well you would have gotten an 'A' if it wasn't for the essay part of the exam." Even though Autumn knew that the essay question accounted for 25% of the test, she couldn't fathom how she could have done so poorly on it. "I just don't get it," Ms. Turner continued. "Do you think this is some kind of a joke?" Autumn didn't get it either.

Openly agitated at her student's oblivious response, Ms. Turner flipped to the last page of the test and held it right in front of Autumn's face. At the top of the page was a three part essay question about the Industrial Revolution. Autumn's answer: *It's dark in here. Please help me! Please! I'm sacred!* And then, right under it: *You have to stop him!*

Autumn, looked down, trying hard not to let Ms. Turner see how terrified she was. Autumn had absolutely no recollection of writing any of it.

"I don't know if this is some end of the year prank, but this is going to affect your overall grade. This isn't some joke." Ms. Turner's words fell on deaf ears as Autumn was still internally shuddering from what she had just seen.

Just then, students started to filter in for Ms. Turner's next class. "I...I'm sorry," Autumn offered in a nearly inaudible voice before fleeing the room. Detached from where she was, Autumn scurried through the crowded halls, knocking into people with every few steps she took. Then, fighting back tears, she made her way outside, by the side of the school. She would surely be late for her next class, but that was the furthest thing from Autumn's mind at the moment.

Catching her breath – she had nearly run through the halls – Autumn Grace tried to come to her senses. Hoping the fresh air would somehow calm her down, Autumn tried to wipe her mind clean. Trying not to think – about anything – she nonchalantly looked around at the open scenery. But within seconds her eyes caught a man standing across the street in front of a house, staring at her. At least he appeared to be staring at her. And on further inspection, he looked like the same guy who she had thought was stalking her a week earlier; the one she had mistaken for the guy who had knocked-out Justin in the parking lot. Or was he just some man standing in front of his house? Was there ever any guy watching her? Now the tears started to flow. Once again, Autumn could feel herself losing it.

After school, Autumn went straight home. Summer was already in the air and once again, Kelly tried to persuade her into hanging out. But Autumn said she wasn't feeling well, which was not an outright lie, and Kelly could clearly see that her friend did not look herself.

Autumn's parents were still at work, but she secluded herself in her room anyway. She wanted to tell some one what was going on – Kelly, her mother – but was afraid of what they might think. But more than that, Autumn was afraid that something was happening to her – something that she had no control over. And worse, she didn't even know what it was. Was it some kind of stress? Was it a brain tumor? Was she loosing her mind?

That night, Autumn took the one and a half tablets of Darvocet she had left from Kelly. About forty minutes later, she was out cold.

The fear of the dark. The fear of impending doom. The fear of the anticipation of pain. The fear of the finality of death: that you will never see another sunrise; never see your loved ones again; never speak another word; never get to see how it all unfolds. It was all there as Autumn laid motionless, staring up at a mercilessly black sky, which was speckled only by a few, faint flickering stars light years away. She could not see to either side of her; did not know where she was. She could not even see her own body, only that cold, night sky. But both pain and fear wrenched its way through every fiber of her being; a pain and fear that seemed almost incalculable to the human psyche. Suddenly, as she continued to look up, a faint silhouette of something moved its way into her line of sight. Before she could make out what it was, the darkness became even darker and nearly simultaneously she could feel something cold fall on her face. It was dirt – and the object was a shovel. Autumn was being buried alive!

As more dirt fell on her face, Autumn panicked to blow it away. But it was no use. More dirt – that cold, gritty looseness of earth – was coming. And Autumn didn't know why, but she couldn't move; not her legs, arms or even fingers. Dirt started to cover her eyes, transcending her into total blackness. And as it remorselessly found its way into her mouth and down her throat, Autumn futilely choked for air. This was it. This was the end. And how agonizing – how brutally terrorizing, it was.

But just as she was painfully fading into forever, Autumn could feel a hand taking hold of her arm. Then, as everything turned completely black, she could feel this powerful thrust. A split second later, she opened her eyes to find herself back in the forest and holding her hand was the little girl with the blood-stained nightgown. Autumn never imagined that she would be glad to be back in those foreboding woods and seeing that little girl again. But she was. Anything was better than being buried alive. Autumn bent down and tried to talk to the little girl. She wanted to thank her for rescuing her from certain death. Autumn also wanted to know – had wanted to know since the beginning – who she was… and what she wanted. But though Autumn could feel her mouth open, no words came out.

At first, the little girl just looked-up at Autumn with the saddest, most heart wrenching eyes. It was as if all the sorrow and suffering in the world had been encased in those eyes. Then, without saying a word – she never spoke – the girl slowly pointed towards something. Instinctively, Autumn looked towards where the little girl was pointing and by the foot of a tree saw a small, hunched-over body. Autumn could not see herself, but she could feel tears starting to flow down her face, as she cautiously walked towards the body. Its face was towards the ground, but she could tell it was that of a young boy – maybe eleven or twelve years old. And there was a pool of blackish-red blood surrounding him. Still holding Autumn's hand, the little girl then pointed in particular to the boy's bare back, which had a fist-sized, gaping hole in it. The tears were now pouring down Autumn's face like water from open faucets. The sorrow and anguish were unbearable.

Then, as if by some unforeseen force, the boy's body started to turn over. Autumn first focused on his chest, which was completely torn open, revealing his now inanimate insides. Oh the gore! The indescribable, graphic gore! Instinctively shunning away, Autumn turned her attention to his face. As she did, instead of the face of a young boy, the grainy portrait of a demon appeared. It was so evil, so ugly, so hauntingly terrifying: greenish black face with jagged teeth and red horns and eyes that could only have been forged in the deepest regions of hell. But she only saw this demon's face for a split second – a flash. For almost as soon as it appeared, Autumn's entire surroundings once again transformed.

In a fast, phantasmagoria-sequence Autumn was transported to the bedroom inside the house in the woods, watching as blood splattered on the walls; then to another, larger bedroom, where two motionless bodies lay on a blood covered bed; then to a red pentagram slowly dripping down a wall; then to a scene of a boy running through the opened front door; then to the vision of a young girl – not the same one as she always saw – with a man's hand over her mouth; to a picture of yet another girl, huddled in the corner of a darkened room; then to the contrast of an open, green field soaking under a bright sunny day, not far away, the image of a small church. But then, just as quickly, she finally found herself back in that hole – that tomb – having dirt shoveled on top of her.

Autumn awoke as her bedroom door flew open. It was her father. "What happened?!" he shouted in panic as he looked around the room.

Autumn, now propped-up in her bed, tried to catch her breath. "Wha... what? What do you mean?" she sputtered intuitively.

"You were screaming," Mr. Grace answered in a now calmer voice. Finally, Autumn, covered in sweat, realized exactly where she was. After pausing for a second to asses the situation, she told her father that she had just had a bad dream. Mr. Grace smiled. "I thought something happened. You screamed so loud that it sounded like you were being attacked or something."

At that point, Autumn's mother showed-up in the doorway. "What happened?!"

"Autumn just had a bad dream," Bill replied with a smile. It now seemed like he found the whole thing almost amusing.

"Are you all right?" Joanne asked. "It must have been a hell of a nightmare. What was it about?"

"Nothing," Autumn lied. Inside, she was still pulsating with fear, but also felt embarrassed. "It's all right. You can guys can go back to bed now." Autumn didn't really want to be alone, but what was she going to do? She was almost seventeen years old. Was she going to ask her parents if she could crawl into bed with them?

Autumn's parents retired back to their room. It was 3:00 am and Autumn was utterly exhausted. But she was terrified to go back to sleep. She was terrified period. Turning the TV on low, Autumn watched some infomercial – the only thing that seemed to be on network TV at that time.

On the way to school Autumn told Kelly about her latest dream. She didn't volunteer it, but Kelly prodded, easily seeing that something was wrong with her friend. Kelly said that she "might" be able to pilfer another couple of her father's

Darvocets, but Autumn told her not to bother – that it wouldn't help anyway. Other than that, Kelly really didn't know what to do, other than reassure her best friend, once again, that they were only bad dreams; that they would soon go away on their own. Of course, Kelly could not possibly put herself in Autumn's shoes. And she did not know about the eldritch message Autumn had put on her History final, or about the pentagrams she had unknowingly drawn. So Kelly nonchalantly changed the subject to the inevitable summer and how much fun they were going to have. Particularly, she talked about the last day of school, which was now only a day away. Kelly, in complete contrast to her friend, was thinking about the things any normal sixteen year-old would have been under the circumstances.

At school, Autumn was a complete wreck. Drowning in lassitude, the sixteen year-old couldn't focus on anything besides her reoccurring nightmares – and her recent bizarre behavior that seemed somehow related to them. Autumn's last final exam was that day, but she almost blindly went through the questions. Even if the little girl in the woods wasn't on her mind, she was too exhausted to concentrate.

Following her final, Autumn had what would be her last English class. After telling the class that their exams weren't all graded yet, the teacher gave a loose pep talk about how he wished everyone the best and what they could expect as seniors. As he did, Autumn half-listened as she doodled in her open notebook. But Autumn suddenly realized that she had been writing the word "Dewey". Not once, but twice. It only took a second for Autumn to realize where she had heard the name before; it was the town that was mentioned on the news; the town where a family had been murdered.

As soon as the dismissal bell rang, Autumn hurried through the hall to meet Kelly. Along the way, several people tried to stop and talk to her – one of them being a guy who she had gone out with – but she paid them no mind, walking right passed them as if they weren't even there. They all took offense; her ex-boyfriend uttered "bitch" underneath his breath. But

Autumn wasn't trying to be rude. She was on a mission to find Kelly.

Autumn was relieved to run into Kelly by herself. "Do you remember the other day, when that ex-detective guy was talking about Dewey," she blurted out in one breath.

Kelly looked puzzlingly at her friend. "What the hell are you talking about?"

Autumn grabbed Kelly's skinny arm and started to escort her towards the car. "Remember the other afternoon, before they caught the guy who took those two girls up in Payson," Autumn excitedly replied directly into Kelly's ear. "That reporter was talking to that retired detective guy and they were discussing past cases… you know, where kids were kidnapped and murdered."

Kelly stopped in her tracks and swung around so she was face-to-face with her friend. "Autumn, you're starting to scare me. "

Autumn paused for a second. She and Kelly had always been on the same wavelength. As best friends, they could usually finish one another's sentences. And they could always relate to what the other one was going through. But not this time. For whatever reason, something – something unworldly – was taking possession of Autumn. And how could she expect even her best friend to fully understand what she was going through? Hell, Autumn didn't understand herself. But Autumn needed someone to talk to about it, so she decided to completely come clean. "Just come on, let's go. I'll tell you about it in the car."

Once in the car, Autumn told Kelly everything: the nightmares, which Kelly already knew about; the pentagrams; the written, cryptic messages; the suspicion that someone was watching her; and this now, sudden, incomprehensible fascination with a town she knew nothing about. As Kelly listened, understandably, she first just tried to digest everything she was hearing. It sounded like the words of a crazy person. But this was Autumn – her best friend. Maybe she was just stressed about something, Kelly theorized. After all, stress can cause a person to do some bizarre things. As Kelly tried to rationalize, or at least downplay the situation, Autumn pressed on with her newfound obsession. "Hey, you have the internet at home."

"Yeah," Kelly replied, not knowing exactly where her friend was going.

"Well remember that Prodigy thing you were showing me... how you can put something in and it'll do a search for you... articles and news reports."

"Yeah."

Autumn looked at her friend with a look that said *don't you understand what I'm getting at?* "Well we can put in Dewey and see what it turns up."

Initially, Kelly was going to try to talk her friend out of it, but then figured that it seemed harmless. Maybe Autumn would actually find something to set her mind at ease; that would make her realize that this unheard of town had nothing to do with anything. There was also a part of Kelly that thought it might be interesting. After all, it is human nature to want to try to solve a mystery.

In 1992, not every kid had a computer in his or her room – especially with the internet. In fact, in 1992, many households still did not have the internet, as it was not the can't-live-without tool that it is today. Kelly's family had one computer in the house – in her father's study – and it was hooked up to the World Wide Web. And with Kelly's parents' still at work and her younger brother still at school, that's where the girls found themselves.

As Kelly sat in her father's black, leather chair, Autumn impatiently hovered over her, watching the small monitor. "Where is Dewey anyway?"

Autumn racked her brain, trying to remember the interview on the news. "I think Montana or Wyoming. No, I think it was Oregon... maybe. Can't you just put in Dewey or famous murders or something?"

"When did it happen?"

"I don't know. I don't know if they said. Oh wait," Autumn said excitedly. Kelly looked back at her friend. "You're not really making this easy."

Autumn shrugged her shoulders. "Sorry."

With little information, Kelly searched the World Wide Web. But it wasn't easy. Internet search engines were a new thing in 1992 – Google wouldn't be introduced for another eight years – and the information that was actually on the web was only a minute fraction of what it would be a decade later. Still, somehow, after about twenty minutes, Kelly found something. It was an article on modern unsolved murders. As Kelly scrolled down, one of the headings read <u>Dewey, Oregon</u>, and under it was the following blurb:

In October of 1985, in the small town of Dewey, Oregon, Peggy Glass, age 32, her husband John Glass, age 35, and their son John Jr., age 11 were found brutally murdered. The bodies were discovered by the mother of the Glass' daughter's friend when she went to the house to pick-up her own daughter, Lilly Flower, who had spent the night at the Glass'. April Glass and Lilly, both age 9, were nowhere to be found.

The murders of Peggy, John and their son were particularly grizzly. Each of their bodies, which were found in different rooms of the two-storey house, had been mutilated and partially dismembered. "It was like walking into hell," was how Sheriff Henry Foster put it. "There was blood and body parts everywhere." On the walls of the upstairs bedrooms were pentagrams drawn in blood, and the media instantly dubbed the case "The Pentagram Murders".

Because of the graphic manner in which the slayings took place – and in particular the pentagrams – rumors that the crime was the work of a satanic cult immediately ran rampant.

Seemingly, the only question was: were there devil worshippers living amongst the small-town population of 1,225 or was this done by outsiders?

In the ensuing weeks, local and state police, two dozen agents from the Federal Bureau of Investigation, as well as countless local volunteers scoured the surrounding woods for April Glass and Lilly Flowers. And in what was the largest missing persons search ever conducted in the state of Oregon, authorities followed thousands of leads. But they all turned out to be dead ends. Though sadistic rumors have lingered through the years that the two girls met their fate as some sort of satanic sacrifice, to date, their bodies have never been found. And no suspect has ever been charged in connection to the crime.

As Autumn read aloud with Kelly, she could feel a cold sensation traveling not only down her spine, but through her entire body.

"Wait, it say's click here to see pictures of the missing girls," Kelly announced.

With bone-crushing trepidation, Autumn watched as the cursor, which seemed to be moving in slow motion, scrolled over and clicked on the link. Then, after waiting a few seconds for the next screen to load - computers and internet connections were relatively slow in 1992 – the faces of the two girls appeared, side-by-side. Autumn instantly jumped back, knocking into a nearby bookshelf as several books and other trinkets loudly tumbled to the ground.

Kelly looked at her friend's terrified, pale face and already knew the answer, but asked anyway. "What is it?"

Autumn pointed to the monitor with her trembling hand as if she was pointing to a ghost – and perhaps she was. "That's her," her voice quivered with fear. "That's the girl... the girl from woods... in my nightmares... that's her."

"Which one," Kelly asked in her own shaky voice, having been completely spooked by Autumn's reaction.

"April" she replied, her trembling finger still pointed at the monitor. "April Glass. That's the girl that's been in my dreams."

What followed was the longest minute of silence that the two girls had ever endured. Autumn could not believe that she was actually staring at a picture of a girl she had always assumed existed only in her dreams. And if that wasn't surreal enough, she now knew the story of that little girl – and what an incomprehensibly haunting story it was. But as alarmed and scared as Autumn was, Kelly's initial reaction was similar. The way Autumn jumped back, the petrified look on her face, the distress that she permeated, freaked Kelly out. But after a minute, Kelly tried – tried for Autumn's sake as well as her own – to rationalize the situation. "Well, maybe you've heard about this whole Dewey thing before, but just don't remember it." Autumn didn't answer; she just kept gazing in terrified disbelief at April Glass' picture. "Yeah, that's probably it," Kelly pressed on. "You probably saw some show on this whole thing… what happened to the girl and her family… right before you started having these nightmares." Kelly had already convinced herself that that is what it had to be, but Autumn still stood there silently against the wall, staring at what she believed was a ghost. "Come on Autumn," she pleaded. "Say something!"

"I have to go to Dewey."

Kelly was no longer spooked, but rather afraid that her friend was loosing it. "What the hell are you talking about?! Have you completely lost your mind?! Think about what you're saying?! You can't go to Dewey – it's in Oregon! And… and… it's just crazy."

Autumn didn't expect her friend to understand. Ever since the day she first heard it, the name "Dewey" had stuck in her mind. But now that she was staring at a picture of April Glass, Autumn knew she had to go to Dewey, Oregon. She did not exactly know why; what she was going to find there or even look for. And Autumn had no idea of how she would get there. But she knew she had to go. "You don't understand," she said to Kelly in an almost trance-like voice.

"You're right, I don't understand. And I don't think you understand either."

Autumn grabbed her friend by the shoulders and stared straight into her eyes. "You're right, I don't understand. But that's why I have to go. I have to find out."

"Find out what?"

"What it all means."

"Autumn, will you listen to yourself. I told you, you probably just saw something on the news about this place... about this girl. That's all it is. Besides, how are you going to get to Oregon? And what are you going to tell your parents? They'll put you in a loony ward."

Autumn paused for a second before answering. "They'll be going on their cruise in four days. They'll be gone for two weeks."

Kelly shook her head in frustration, not believing that Autumn was actually serious about this whole thing. Now Kelly was feeling like *she* was in some bad dream. "Autumn, you just need some time to calm down and think straight. Have a beer, smoke a joint, get laid. But please get off this crazy – and that's what it is, crazy – obsession about this little girl. You read it yourself; this thing happened in nineteen eighty-five. That's seven years ago. What do you think – you're going to go there and find this girl? I mean really, say you do go to this town. Then what?"

Autumn looked towards the floor. "I don't know," she replied softly. But then the teen raised her head and in a defiant voice, continued "All I know is that I've never been so sure of anything in my entire life. I can't really explain it. I just know I have to go there. I just have to. I know now that that is what this is all about. For whatever reason, this April has been visiting me – I know this sounds crazy, but maybe from beyond the grave – for the sole purpose of getting me to go to Dewey."

At first, Kelly just looked at her friend with a blank, speechless face. The whole conversation was surreal to say the least, but now it was entering the completely bizarre. Was Autumn actually losing her mind, Kelly frighteningly pondered. "Autumn," Kelly said in a calm, but assertive voice, "you really think – you honestly believe – that April Glass' ghost has been haunting you?"

"Not necessarily haunting. She…"

Kelly cut her off. "Autumn – and I'm being totally serious here – I think that maybe you should talk to your parents about this. I mean maybe you're having some kind of a breakdown or something."

Autumn was aggravated by her best friend's suggestion and it visibly showed. "Do you remember when your appendix almost burst when you were ten and you had to be rushed to the hospital to get it removed? Remember when you told me that while you were laying on the hospital bed, before the operation, you could feel your grandfather's presence; that you said you could actually feel his hand and him telling you that everything was going to be ok?" (Kelly's grandfather had died a few months prior).

"Yeah, but that was different. I was probably just…"

"And do you remember when we watched that show on that real life haunted house last year and you said that you believed in ghosts."

"Yeah, but…"

"And you said that you didn't understand how people couldn't believe in them – that there was too much evidence that they existed?"

Kelly found herself in somewhat of a conundrum; she did believe in ghosts – at least she thought she had – but now she was calling her friend crazy for believing in the same thing. "But why would this girl be after you?"

"I don't know. But she is."

Autumn seemed so sure of herself that for the first time Kelly asked herself what if she was telling the truth? What if, for whatever reason, April Glass was trying to reach out to Autumn from beyond the grave? Kelly was torn. Part of her – most of her – still thought that Autumn had seen or read about the Pentagram Murders and April Glass, and was subconsciously affected by it and now it was coming back in the form of nightmares. Another part of her wondered if Autumn was seriously loosing it; if she was cracking under the pressure of an unknown stress. Or maybe she was just sick. Still, Kelly oddly now found yet another part of her wanting to believe. Taking a reluctant leap of faith – and also out of loyalty to their friendship – Kelly decided to help Autumn with her quest in any way she could.

5

The final day of school had arrived. Most teens were consumed with what parties they were going to and all the fun things they were going to do over the next three months. But as her peers were caught up in the electricity of the moment, Autumn was planning her trip to Dewey, Oregon. As her peers were ready to party, Autumn was ready to chase a ghost.

Autumn had cashed in several U.S. Savings Bonds that she had gotten over the years from her aunt and grandfather as birthday and Christmas presents. She had been hoping to put the money towards a car – her parents said that if she found a job they would also help her out – but plane tickets and trips cost money. Autumn walked away with $750. Kelly also tried giving Autumn $200 that she had saved-up, but Autumn wouldn't accept it, saying that she had enough.

Autumn had booked a flight for the day after her parents were to leave on vacation (she would return two days before them). However, Dewey was 128 miles from Oregon's Eugene Airport, which meant that Autumn had to take a train the rest of the way. Using the internet, the girls found and called the only motel actually located in Dewey. Not surprisingly, they had vacancies and Autumn reserved a room. She didn't even need a credit card. But Autumn didn't tell them that she was only sixteen. And of course, there was a real possibility that when she showed up, they wouldn't rent her a room. After brainstorming, the girls came up with a sketchy plan: Autumn would start sobbing, saying that her license and credit cards and had just been stolen (but she would still have the cash to pay for the room). There was certainly no assurance that it would work and there was still the not so minor detail that Autumn looked like a teenager. The thought of Autumn getting to this small, backwards town thousands of miles away and not having any place to stay was enough for Kelly to once again try to talk her friend out of the trip. But Autumn wouldn't budge. "I can pass for eighteen," she said, not believing it herself. "Besides, this isn't the Hilton or the Marriott we're talking about. I'm sure as long as you pay for the room, that's all they care about. Don't worry – they're not just gonna turn me away," she then went on, trying to convince herself as much as she was Kelly.

Though her parents were going to be away for two weeks and neither of them had cell phones, they would still no doubt be calling to check in on Autumn. But Autumn figured that they would only get a few chances to call home and would assume that they had just missed her. If they called Kelly's, Kelly would say that she had just been with their daughter and that everything was fine – and that she would tell Autumn that they called (of course, that was assuming Kelly answered the phone).

Then there was the question of what to tell their friends, as they were obviously going to realize that Autumn was not around. Autumn – or Kelly – didn't want anyone else to know that she was off somewhere in Oregon by herself chasing some dream – literally. The answer: Kelly would just tell them that at the last minute, her parents made her go on the cruise with them.

It was far from a perfect plan, but Autumn felt like she had no choice. In fact, instead of coming to her senses, with each passing day, the feeling that going to Dewey was the right thing to do cemented itself even more into her consciousness. Autumn felt almost relieved since she had made the decision. Ironically, it made her feel that she *wasn't* loosing her mind. Most importantly, though she was still unsure how, Autumn was convinced that going to Dewey would not only solve this unworldly puzzle but release her once and for all from the nightmares, the bizarre behavior… and what she was certain was the ghost of April Glass.

As for the nightmares, Autumn stopped having them. But that only helped convince her that it was because she was going to Dewey. She was doing what the little girl in the woods – what April Glass – had wanted her to do from the beginning.

Five days after Autumn finished her junior year in high school, her parents left for Florida, where they would stay for two nights before embarking on their 12 day-long long cruise. They left their daughter with a house full of groceries, a list of instructions and $200 in cash. The following afternoon, Kelly drove Autumn to the airport for her own voyage.

As Kelly dropped Autumn off at Sky Harbor International Airport in Phoenix, she couldn't help but feel that she was not only not doing the right thing, but that she was actually putting her friend in danger by facilitating her bizarre journey. In fact she tried one last time to talk Autumn out of it, but it was to no avail. Before parting ways, when Kelly realized that they had reached the point of no return, she pulled from her pocket a small plastic card and handed it to Autumn. "What's this?"

"It's a calling card," Kelly replied. "It's good from anywhere in the country. It has up to 500 minutes on it. I bought it for you so you wouldn't have an excuse not to call." Fighting back tears, Autumn took the card. "I want you to call me everyday to check in – you hear."

Autumn gave Kelly, her best friend since grade school, a tight, long hug. "I will. I promise." Now Autumn was staring to cry. "You've been such a good friend, Kell. I don't know what I would do without you. I really don't."

"You just take care of yourself, you hear. You be careful."

"I will."

With that, the two teary-eyed friends finally loosened their embrace. Then, for a few seconds, they just looked at each other, both with a reassuring, yet at the same time, melancholic smile. "Well, I guess I should be going. I don't want you to miss your plane." Autumn just answered with the same smile. Kelly then turned around and began to walk towards the exit, but after three steps, stopped and turned back to Autumn. "I hope you find what you're looking for."

"Thanks," was the only word Autumn could find to say.

What Autumn didn't tell Kelly was that *she* was now having second thoughts as well. They only really started on the car ride over, slowly webbing their way through her consciousness. Once she stepped foot inside that airport, those doubts only grew. However, it was not until Kelly tuned to walk away, leaving Autumn by herself, that she began to fully appreciate the reality of what she was about to do. In fact, for a second, Autumn almost ran to Kelly, almost called the whole thing off. But something inside of her – something deep inside and now embedded in her subconsciousness – made her turn the other way and walk towards the gate. She had to go to Dewey. She still wasn't sure exactly why or what she would find there. She just knew she had to go.

It was a two and a half hour flight from Phoenix to Eugene. Autumn was more than relieved when she found out that no one would be sitting next to her. She was in no mood to talk to strangers. She just wanted to sit there and zone out, maybe read a magazine.

Autumn had gone to Disney Land with her parents when she was 10. That was the only other time she had been on a plane. With all that was going through her head, she hadn't had time to be apprehensive about flying. Luckily however, though she clutched hard onto the armrest during take-off, once the plane had reached its cruising altitude, Autumn was completely at ease.

The flight was smooth and not crowded. Importantly, there were no screaming children. Autumn read the magazines in the seat pocket in front of her for a while before unwittingly dozing off. By the time she woke-up, the captain was announcing the plane's initial decent into Eugene. Autumn was elated. Not only had she slept through most of the flight, but she didn't have any nightmares.

With her one suitcase, Autumn made her way through the small, but unfamiliar airport. Following the directions of a kind pedestrian, the sixteen year-old found her way outside to the taxi stand.

As Autumn stepped outdoors, it was more evident than ever than ever that she was thousands of miles from home. *So this is Oregon*, she thought as she looked around at the green, open landscape. Perhaps Chandler Arizona – at least in 1992 – was no thriving metropolis, but this really looked like it was the middle of nowhere. As Autumn scanned the horizon and basked in a refreshing, cool breeze, the taxi attendant approached her. "Can I help you?" He asked in a polite voice.

"Yes, I need a cab to the Amtrak station."

The man, in his middle years, looked Autumn over. "Are you here with your parents?"

"No," she quickly replied. "It's just me. I'm visiting my aunt."

"Oh," was all he said as he motioned a waiting taxi to come. The truth was that Autumn was three weeks shy of turning seventeen and looked it. And there was nothing that suspicious about a seventeen year-old traveling on his or her own. Most importantly, Autumn didn't look in any kind of distress. To the contrary, she actually looked quite content.

After the attendant told the driver the destination, Autumn climbed in the car. As she looked at the white, middle-aged man's eyes looking back at her through the rearview mirror, she knew the question was coming. "So what brings you to Oregon?" The driver could tell by Autumn's voice – when she thanked him for putting her lone suitcase in the trunk – that she was not a native.

"Oh, I'm just visiting a friend," she replied, giving a different story than what she had told the attendant. Not that it mattered.

"Have you ever been to Oregon before?"

"No, this is my first time. But it looks quite lovely."

The driver nodded his head as he made a left turn. "So where does your friend live that you have to take the train?"

"Dewey."

"Ohhh," the driver replied in a slow, almost ominous voice.

Autumn was taken aback by the sudden change of tone at the mere mention of the word Dewey. "You know it?"

The driver deliberately paused before answering. "Oh yeah, I've heard of it."

"Have you ever been there?"

"No, no, no. I've never been there." He responded as if Autumn was accusing him of a crime.

Autumn was about to ask if he had known about the Pentagram Murders, but just then, the taxi's CB radio came to life. As the driver picked up the transmitter and began to talk, Autumn slouched back in her seat. After a few minutes, as the driver continued to jabber away with whoever was on the other end, Autumn began to feel that he was purposely trying to avoid any further conversation with her. And that made her understandably uncomfortable, even worried, because before she mentioned Dewey, it seemed like he wasn't going to shut up.

By the time Autumn's train left, it was 6:30pm. The sixteen year old was already beat from a long day of traveling and still had another hour and forty-five minutes before she would arrive in Dewey. Luckily, like the plane, the train was not crowded. After stowing her oblong suitcase in an open compartment near the doors, Autumn languidly walked down the narrow isle. Finding an empty row of three seats, about halfway down, she climbed into the one by the window.

As the train slowly, but loudly began to pull away from the station, Autumn gazed out the window at the nearby green, mountains. For once, she wasn't thinking about April Glass, her nightmares, or even her destination – Dewey. In fact, she was almost thoughtless, processing nothing more than the bounteous landscape in which her eyes swallowed. Everything seemed so open and free, so peaceful. She was mesmerized by its green grandeur. After about fifteen minutes, as the pulchritudinous scenery rolled placidly by, Autumn faded into sleep.

Slowly opening her eyes, Autumn instinctively began to stretch and wondered how long she had been asleep. After a drawn-out yawn, she went to look at her watch. But before her eyes caught her wrist, they saw something else: the little girl from the woods. The girl Autumn now knew to be April Glass, still wearing her dirty, blood-smeared nightgown, was sitting in the middle seat, right next to her. And in her lap was a severed, human head; a head of a woman. While clutching with all her strength onto the armrest, Autumn pushed back in her seat, trying to distance herself as much as possible from the devilish scene. But she was cornered; the locked window to her left – the train was moving too fast to jump out of it even if it could open – a row of seats in front and back of her and the little girl to her right… with that ungodly head in her lap. Still pushing as hard back in her seat as humanly possible, Autumn tried to scream. Her mouth opened, but no words came out. Autumn watched in excruciating horror as the little girl – April Glass – slowly reached out her small hand and touched Autumn's trembling shoulder.

Autumn then felt the hand gently shaking her, followed by a faint voice. Was the girl finally going to speak her first words? But suddenly, as the voice grew slightly clearer, it sounded like that of a man. What the hell was he – or she – saying? Autumn could feel the hand on her shoulder even more now. It was almost moving her back and forth.

"Miss. Miss." As the words finally became definitive, Autumn opened her eyes and let out a panic-ridden gasp. Gone was April Glass, but sitting in the isle seat was a slender, tall, balding man who looked to be in his fifties. And he had his outstretched hand on Autumn's shoulder. "Miss, are you ok," he asked in quasi-drawl.

Autumn looked frightfully at his big, rough hand, which he quickly drew away. "Yeah… yeah. I'm ok," she replied out of breath.

"I'm sorry. I didn't mean to touch you, but you looked like you were having one heck of a bad dream." Still flustered, Autumn continued to catch her breath. "I mean you were squirmin' and breathin' real hard and finally I thought you were going to scream."

Autumn realized that the man was still talking; still trying to apologize for waking her up, especially by shaking her shoulder. "No, no… It's ok… It's ok… thanks… you're right, I was just having some nightmare. I don't remember about what," she lied, not wanting to get into the whole ordeal.

After waiting a few seconds for Autumn to finish gaining her composure, the stranger stretched out his hand once more, this time in the gesture of a handshake. "Well my name's Roy Dunn."

Now feeling like she had completely made an ass out of herself, Autumn shook the man's hand, taking note of what a strong grip he had. "My name's Autumn."

"That's a pretty name," he replied while releasing his grasp.

"Thank you." Autumn then paused for a second. "And I'm sorry. I feel so stupid."

A slight smile stretched on the stranger's, dry, coarse face. "Don't worry – everyone has bad dreams."

"Yeah, I guess," Autumn sheepishly replied.

"I got on at the last stop, while you were sleeping." Autumn simply replied with a half-smile and nod of the head. "So where you headin'?"

"Dewey."

The stranger's leathery face suddenly grew glum. In fact his entire demeanor appeared to change. "Dewey?"

"Yeah," Autumn answered apprehensively.

For what was probably only a second, but felt much longer – at least to Autumn – the man looked Autumn over with what now seemed like cold, brown eyes. "What's a young, pretty girl like you going to a place like Dewey for?"

For the first time since leaving Arizona, Autumn actually felt scared. Was the complete stranger sitting next to her a harmless old man, or some kind of pervert – or worse? The reality was that she had no way to know. But as cautiously as she now thought about her chance riding companion, Autumn was becoming even more concerned about her destination. "I'm visiting a friend."

"Oh," he responded in a noticeably doubtful tone.

"Why, what's wrong with Dewey? Every time I just mention the word to some one it seems like they get spooked. Is it about those murders that happened there?"

The man who had introduced himself as Roy Dunn leaned back in his seat. "That was bad. Very bad. That poor family… and those poor little girls." That he showed feelings for what happened eased Autumn's mind, at least with regards to her uneasiness about him. "But a crime like that, unfortunately, could happen anywhere. That was of course particularly gruesome and troubling, but people get murdered and go missing everyday, all over America."

Autumn digested his words for a second, not sure what to make of them. "Then what's so bad about Dewey. I mean after all, all that happened almost ten years ago."

Mr. Dunn's large hands glided along his blue-jean pants' legs as he looked uncomfortable by the question. "They say strange things happen in that town; stories of devil worshipping in the woods and animals being sacrificed. And it goes back to before what happened to the Glasses. There's always been something just not right with that place." The stranger, who had been looking straight ahead, now turned to look at Autumn and let out an uneasy smile. "But I don't wanna spook ya'. Besides, you said your friend lives there. You tellin' me that she never told you about what goes on there... the stories?"

"Nah, not really," Autumn replied sheepishly, feeling like that she was beginning to be caught in a lie.

"How long has your friend been living there? You've never been there before?"

Autumn didn't know how to respond. She just sat there for a second, fiddling with her fingers, feeling extremely uncomfortable. But in an ironic twist of fate, just then, the train's intercom came alive to announce that they were approaching the Dewey station. "Well I guess I should go," Autumn gladly pronounced.

Her neighbor smiled. "Well good luck," he said before slowly getting up so Autumn, who was sitting near the window, could get by.

"It was a pleasure meeting you."

"Likewise," he replied as Autumn climbed out of the row of seats past him. "And don't forget your luggage."

"I won't. Thank you."

With her back now towards him, Autumn was about to leave the stranger for good. But after a few steps, he stopped her. "Oh and Autumn..." She stopped and turned around to look. "Be careful. Don't go looking for something that you're not prepared to find."

For a second, Autumn just stood there frozen, looking at the slender, six foot-plus tall stranger standing in the narrow isle. Her first inclination was a natural one – to ask what he meant. But then surmised that maybe she didn't want to know the answer. Besides, she did not want to miss her stop. So without saying anything further, Autumn simply turned back around and kept walking down the isle towards the exit.

As Autumn stood by the door, holding her lone suitcase, waiting for the train to pull into the station, all she could think about was the stranger's mysterious warning. How did he know she was looking for something? Was he somehow a part of this eldritch puzzle in which she had become unwittingly entangled? Should she take heed of his warning? Maybe he's just a crazy old man? As all these thoughts ping-ponged through her already cluttered head, the train began to grind to a halt. "Dewey. This is Dewey." The doors slid open and Autumn walked out onto the awaiting platform.

As the train pulled away, Autumn quickly realized that she had been the only one to exit at the small station. In fact no one else was on the platform at all and the stationhouse appeared closed. As a darkening sky swallowed the last remnants of the day, a cold feeling of complete vulnerability ran through the sixteen year-old's body. "What have you gotten yourself into?" she asked herself out loud. Of course, her words carried into nothingness; for there was no one around to hear them.

Autumn had been so certain of going to Dewey. It was something she convinced herself that she *had* to do. But now, standing alone on that platform, in the middle of nowhere, all she wanted to do was go home. *What the hell was I thinking?!* She cussed herself. There were no awaiting taxis; no cars or people at all. There were no stores or houses nearby – just woods and a narrow road that led to god knows where. How close was the town, the motel? Was it in walking distance? And what if Autumn went the wrong way? She had no map, no directions. Lost, alone and defenseless, Autumn Grace started to cry. And she couldn't stop. And even if she could, she didn't know what else to do. But as mascara-laced tears streaked down her soft, young face, Autumn made herself a promise: that if she made it through the night, in the morning she would get a seat on the next flight back to Phoenix. (Money wasn't that much of an object, because besides the $750 she had after cashing in the bonds, her parents left her with $200. So even after spending $275 on the plane tickets and $50 on the train, Autumn still had $650 in cash left.)

After about ten minutes of just standing there trembling and crying, Autumn figured that she had to do *something*. After trying to clean her tear-streaked face, Autumn pulled her suitcase around the outside of the station and happened upon a payphone. *Saved!* She thought. It had no phonebook, but Autumn figured she would just call information for a number to a cab service. But her elation quickly turned into dread. The phone didn't work. There wasn't even any dial tone. Starting to cry again, Autumn frustratingly smashed the black, plastic receiver into the base with all her might, finally breaking it in half.

With no other choice, Autumn rolled her suitcase onto the road, blindly picked a direction and started walking. Obviously though, she did so with great trepidation. By now the day had completely disappeared and although the station had several lampposts, the road had none. It didn't even have sidewalks and on top of everything else, Autumn now had to worry about being run-over. Her only saving grace was that it was a starry night and the moon was half-full, providing at least some illumination.

After only about thirty yards, however, a car going in the same direction pulled up beside Autumn. It was a dusty, black 1970's Roadrunner and inside was a neatly-groomed male who looked to be in his mid-twenties. "You need a ride miss?" he asked through the open driver's side window, over the loud idling of the car.

"I just got off the train," she replied, leaning towards, but not too close, to the open window. "I didn't realize that the station would be closed. I'm going to the Davison Motel."

"That's about four miles up the road. I'm actually going that way. I can give you a lift."

Now Autumn was faced with yet another dilemma. Somehow she had chosen the right direction to walk in. But four miles was a considerable distance, especially in the dark while pulling a big suitcase. But it might be a much better fate than jumping into a car with a complete stranger. What if he was a rapist or murderer? Maybe another car, one with a woman or even a family, would pass. After all, Autumn only walked thirty yards before this guy had stopped. So it definitely didn't seem like an isolated road. But what if another car didn't pass? Or what if another car came barreling down the road and plowed into her? Or what if this guy was actually "normal" and she didn't accept the ride, only to have some sicko stop further down the road and snatch her? After all the scenarios flashed through her mind in fractions of seconds, it was probably her exhaustion coupled with the stranger's appearance – young, shaven, neatly dressed, seemingly not intoxicated – and polite, country tone that made Autumn climb into the car.

"So where you from?" he asked as he hit the gas.

"Arizona," Autumn replied instinctively.

"What brings you to Dewey?" Autumn didn't answer. "Are you some kind of runaway or something?"

"No." Autumn was now having second thoughts about accepting the ride.

Dividing his attention to the road ahead, the young man looked over at the apparent teenage girl now sitting next to him. "Are you in some kind of trouble or something? I mean Dewey isn't exactly a big tourist town."

"No... I'm just... how far did you say the hotel was?"

The stranger could clearly see – and hear – that he was making his passenger uncomfortable. "I'm sorry. It's none of my business. I mean it's cool; everybody's got secrets. We're almost there," he then added, as he made a turn onto a street that had some stores on it.

The next few, long, minutes were shrouded in overbearing unnerving silence, at least from Autumn's point of view. She just sat there in the passenger seat, her body stiff as a statute, counting each passing second.

Finally, after about four miles, just as the driver had said, they pulled into the parking lot of a small, somewhat dilapidated motel. "Well this is it."

Autumn never felt so relieved before. "Thank you. I really appreciate it," she said as she started to open the door.

"Hey, listen, do you need any money?"

"Oh no, thank you," she answered without really thinking about it.

Then, as Autumn was beginning to climb out of the car, the young man grabbed her arm. "Wait." Feeling like something terrible was about to happen, Autumn looked back. "Just wait a second," he said, still gripping onto her frail arm. "I'm sure you could use some money. I know we can work something out."

"Please let me go," Autumn pleaded in a quivering voice.

The stranger let go. "Ok, ok. I didn't mean to scare you. I just thought... I mean a girl like you... I mean come on, I got forty bucks."

Tears started to once again roll down Autumn's face. "Please, you've got it all wrong. Please, I just want my suitcase. Please."

The young man looked at Autumn and could tell that she was completely terrified. "Ok, ok. It's all right." With that, he let Autumn get her suitcase from the backseat and walk away.

Relieved to have been able to escape, yet still understandably unnerved, Autumn hurriedly dragged her bag into the small office of the motel. The red-headed woman behind the desk – who looked to be in her mid thirties – carefully looked Autumn over, realizing instantly that she was far way from home – wherever that was. She could also tell that this strange young girl had been crying. "Can I help you? Are you in some kind of trouble?"

"No, I'm ok," Autumn answered with bated breath. Then, after a pause, "I have a reservation."

The woman chuckled. "I didn't know we took reservations."

"My name's Autumn Grace. I called about a week ago. I talked to a woman named Gayle."

"Oh yes, Gayle," the woman answered in a dry, cigarette-induced voice. "She works the day shift."

"Don't tell me you don't have my name. You don't have any vacancies?"

The woman half-smiled. "No, we have rooms available."

Autumn let out an animated sigh of relief. "Oh thank God!"

The clerk sized-up Autumn once more, this time with even more suspicious eyes. "How old are you?"

With all that she had been through – the vision of April Glass and the strange man on the train, being abandoned at the station and the guy that she thought for sure was going to rape her – Autumn hadn't had time to worry about checking into the motel; what their policy would be on renting out a room to a sixteen year-old girl. But now the possibility that she was going to have to spend the night on the street was the only thing she could think about? How could she not? "Listen, I have cash," Autumn desperately pleaded as she took out a roll of twenty and hundred dollar bills. "I've traveled a long way and…"

"Ok," the clerk interrupted. The woman was convinced that Autumn was on the run, hiding from either an abusive boyfriend, father or stepfather. She certainly looked traumatized. And unbeknownst to Autumn, the woman had been in her own abusive relationship – a husband that had beat her regularly – so she had compassion for Autumn's perceived situation. She certainly was not going to kick her out to the curb. "I'll get you a room."

"Thank you," Autumn replied, as she fought back yet another round of tears.

Seeing Autumn's response, how grateful she was, made the woman almost start to cry, especially that she now had in her head that she and this young girl shared a certain bond. Before getting the keys, the woman then extended her hand towards Autumn. "My name is Molly."

For what seemed like the first time in a long time, Autumn smiled as she shook Molly's hand. "I'm Autumn," she said… again.

Molly then grabbed a set of keys off the wall. But right before giving them to Autumn, asked "Are you sure you don't want me to call the police for you?"

"Oh no, please. I'm fine. Really."

The woman paused for a moment and then handed Autumn the keys. Then, after making Autumn sign the registry – Molly figured that Grace was just a pseudonym – she walked out from behind the counter through an open doorway. "Here, I'll walk you out front and show you where it is."

When Autumn walked into the small, but clean motel room, she was utterly exhausted. The digital clock on the nightstand glowed 9:20pm. Autumn couldn't believe it, because to her, it felt more like three in the morning. Falling – nearly collapsing – onto the twin bed, she just lied there for a few minutes staring up at the speckled ceiling. Half of her brain was running rampant with a thousand thoughts at once. The other half was too tired to think and tried to shoo them away.

6

S lowly and wearily Autumn opened her heavy eyes. For a second – either out of routine or wishful thinking – the sixteen year-old thought that she was in her bedroom, back home in Arizona. But after a quick look around that sense of security faded as Autumn realized that she was literally thousands of miles from home. Gingerly pushing herself up on the bed – Autumn was lying on top of the covers – she also realized that she had fallen asleep with all her clothes on. As the partially opened curtains let in a slender ray of almost blinding light into the otherwise darkened room, Autumn looked to the clock on the nightstand. It read 9:45 a.m.

To distract herself from the reality of the situation more than anything else, Autumn flipped on the small TV. After closing the blinds completely and turning on the lights, she then undressed and jumped in the shower. Trying not to think of anything, the soon-to-be high school senior stood under the showerhead, staring aimlessly at the basin of the tub. Autumn exhaled deeply as hot water poured on her head and down her body, slowly bringing her back to life. After a few minutes, soothing steam blanketed the entire room, which she exhilaratingly breathed through her mouth and nose. It all felt so revitalizing: the steam, the hot water on her skin. Autumn could have stood in the shower all day. But after about twenty-five minutes, she grudgingly shut off the water.

After getting dressed, Autumn decided to venture outside. Used to the blistering June heat of Chandler, the almost spring-like weather of Dewey was refreshing. It must have been in the high-seventies and a comfortable breeze was subtly blowing from the east. Dressed in shorts and a t-shirt, Autumn stood in front of her motel-room door for a few minutes, just soaking under the bright sun and taking in the scenery of the vast, majestic mountains that stood in the background.

Even though she had slept in her clothes, it was a good sleep, a long sleep. And although she could not fully stave-off the reality that she was in the middle of nowhere, in a town most people had never heard of, chasing some bizarre mystery, Autumn felt content. She definitely felt much better than she had the previous evening. After a long stretch and deep breath of fresh, crisp air, Autumn started walking. She did not have any particular destination, she just started walking.

After about four blocks, Autumn came to what appeared to be the center of town. There were several stores and eateries, all lined on the same narrow street. No structure was over three stories tall. But rather than being quaint, the town had a rundown look to it. It wasn't particularly dirty, but just unkempt. The sidewalks were cracked and in some places uneven, from long, roots pushing up from underneath the ground. Even the road looked like it had not been worked on in quite sometime, as if it was a back street; it's grainy, black asphalt pock-marked and yellow lines faded almost to oblivion. The brick facades on all of the buildings looked weathered and in some places chipped. The wooden planks on several of the benches that sat in front of stores were cracked and looked like if you sat on them, at the very least you would come up with some splinters. A lonely payphone had its receiver ripped off, its silver chord, dangling helplessly for all to see.

As Autumn strolled down the main street – which was yes, actually called Main Street – she was hit by an overpowering sense of déjà vu. In fact it was haunting. But then again, what about the past month, in particular the past 24 hours, was not she wondered?

As Autumn passed a small diner, she realized that she had not eaten in nearly twenty four hours. At first she thought that that couldn't be right. Despite being slender, Autumn always had three meals a day and was never one to turn down snacks. Surely the undersized sandwich and crackers that they served on the flight from Phoenix to Eugene could not have been the last thing she had eaten. But backtracking through her mind, she realized that that was indeed the case. Only her strange, emotionally-straining voyage could have taken her mind off the hole in her stomach. But now, as she looked though a window at people sitting down eating, as if someone had flipped on a switch, that hole suddenly began burning her insides.

Autumn was thinking only of stuffing her stomach with as much food as possible when she opened the front door. But as soon as she took one step inside the diner, everyone stopped what they were doing and looked up at her. Feeling the cold eyes of every patron, waitress and even the cook behind the counter fixated on her, Autumn contemplated walking right back out the door. But she had to eat. Feeling uncomfortable to say the least, she found a booth by a window and sat down, hoping that now everyone would go back to what they were doing before she walked in. *At least the place isn't that crowded,* she thought.

A slender, but weathered waitress approached slowly, with cat-like curiosity. "How are you doin today?" she asked as she handed Autumn a one page, laminated menu.

"OK," Autumn replied in a coarse voice; it was the first time she had spoken that day.

Eventually, Autumn settled on a ham and cheese omelet with hash browns, sausage and toast. And she planned to eat every last morsel. While she waited for the food to arrive, she just sat in the booth, staring aimlessly out the window. But she couldn't help feeling that people – if not all, at least some – were still glaring at her. There was absolutely no doubt that she was a stranger in a strange land. But she could not figure out if the townspeople were just curious or if this was a place where outsiders were not welcomed. She tried to convince herself that it was merely curiosity. True, the guy that had given her a ride to the motel had nearly accosted her, but creeps like that existed in every town. And he probably did the same thing with the local girls, Autumn surmised. The only other two people she had talked with, the waitress and Molly the hotel clerk, were friendly.

When the food arrived Autumn put aside her thoughts and immediately dug in. She wasn't sure if it was just because she was starving or if the food was really that good. When the waitress came around again for a refill of orange juice, Autumn commented how delicious everything was; it seemed to make the waitress happy, as if *she* had cooked the food.

Completely stuffed – only a lone sausage and two pieces of toast were left – Autumn left the diner. As she walked out, just as when she entered, people looked up and watched. But already, Autumn was almost accustomed to their stares.

Full and well rested Autumn was now faced with what to do next. She had already withdrawn the promise she made to herself to get a ticket on the next flight back to Phoenix. She no longer felt in danger. In fact, for a few moments, as she stood there outside the diner looking around at the landscape, Autumn almost felt like she was on vacation. But that feeling soon subsided; replaced with the reality that this was no pleasure trip. She was brought to Dewey under duress. She was brought there – by her own troubled mind – to chase the ghost of April Glass.

Feeling like she at least needed to burn off some of her meal, Autumn simply started walking. After just one block, she happened upon a small store, which had a white, cardboard sign in the window that read: *Palm Reading. Only $10.* Autumn didn't really believe in psychics or palm readers, but then again, she had never believed in ghosts before, either.

Cautiously opening the front, glass door, like a child about to climb aboard a rollercoaster for the first time, Autumn was immediately greeted by a middle-aged woman dressed like a medieval gypsy. "Come in my dear," she said with a welcoming smile, while standing next to a small, round table.

"Thank you," Autumn replied sheepishly, as the door swung closed behind her. Autumn was fighting herself not to stare at the woman, who was wearing a thin, long, flowing purple and black gown and multi-colored scarf atop her long, frizzy brownish-red hair. Several, thick silver bracelets, probably fake, dangled from both of her wrists. And around her neck, on a silver chain, hung a miniature, black claw holding a marble-size crystal ball. The woman was definitely dressed for the occasion.

"My name is Rosie," she said, extending her hand towards Autumn.

"My name is Autumn," she replied as she loosely shook the woman's hand.

"You've come to get your palm read? Please, sit down," Rosie said with the same comforting smile as she motioned Autumn to a chair at the round table.

"Thank you." It was not until this point that Autumn realized that the self-proclaimed palm reader was the first person that didn't look at her like such an outsider. Even the hotel clerk and waitress, who had been friendly, gazed at her with curious eyes. But Rosie treated her like just another customer. Of course maybe that was just because Autumn was the first person to give her business in a long time, she realized.

Autumn now found herself sitting at this small, wooden table, across from some woman who looked like she could win first prize at a Halloween contest. Two months ago, Autumn would have found the situation strange, to say the least. But for her, strange had now become normal.

"So tell me, what is it that you are looking for?"

"What makes you think I'm looking for something?"

Rosie smiled once again. "Everyone's looking for something."

OK, fair enough Autumn thought. "I was just walking by and…"

"Your eyes," Rosie interrupted, before pausing.

She was now staring straight into Autumn's eyes, which made Autumn a little uncomfortable. "What about my eyes?"

"They look like they hide so much," she answered in a deliberate, almost sad voice. "There is so much mystery in them." Autumn didn't know how to respond, so she just sat there, bouncing her eyes between Rosie and the table. "Well its ten dollars for a simple palm reading and for thirty five I can look into my crystal ball for you."

Instantly, Autumn was snapped back into reality. This woman wasn't some psychic; she was just a low-level con-artist trying to make a quick buck, Autumn assured herself. In fact she laughed at herself – obviously not out loud – for even being there. But she *was* there and did not want to be rude. "I think I'll just start with the palm reading." What was ten bucks anyway she thought as she pulled it out of her shorts and handed it to Rosie.

The atmosphere now actually seemed lighthearted as Autumn gave the woman her right hand for examination. "You have such soft hands."

"Thank you."

"You must use a very good lotion. Then again, you're young. Young people have nice everything." Autumn let out a fleeting laugh. "Now let's see… this my dear," she said pointing to a line on Autumn's palm, "is your love line. At your age that's probably what you're most concerned about." Autumn blushed. "It says here that there was someone who you cared about, but never really loved and don't really see him anymore. You want to find that special some one, but lately you've been too distracted to think about boys. But don't worry, you'll…." Suddenly Rosie stopped in her tracks as a pale look of terror besieged her face.

Autumn pulled her hand away. "What?! What is it?!"

"Please, give me your hand." Autumn extended her hand, as slowly and apprehensively as if she was giving a biscuit to a giant pit bull. Rosie grabbed hold of her trembling hand and stared at it with the look of petrified disbelief; her friendly, welcoming demeanor long gone. "This," she said in a slow, ominous voice as she pointed to Autumn's palm, "is your life line… According to this you are already dead."

A freezing, cold rush shot through Autumn's body, as she once again pulled her hand from Rosie's grasp. "What are you talking about?! What are you trying to do?!" Autumn paused, trying to overcome the initial shock of Rosie's assertion. "Obviously I'm still alive!" She yelled defiantly, as she shot up from the chair, knocking it over.

Still sitting down, Rosie stared at Autumn as if she was looking at a ghost. "I'm sorry dear," she said in a slow crackling voice. "But the palms don't lie."

"You're crazy!" Autumn shouted before storming out of the small store. Once outside, however, she felt like she was going to faint. Breathing heavy, as if she had just run several blocks, Autumn leaned against the front façade of the store. All choked-up, she fought back tears that were already starting to swell in her eyes. *She's just some stupid, crazy old lady,* Autumn tried hard to convince herself. *Don't let it get to you! It was just some sort of ploy to get you to spend more money. Yeah, that's all it was. It's nothing.*

Crouching, with her hands on her knees, Autumn slowly started to regain her composure. Her breathing became more normal. The dizziness started to fade. Trying to further clear her mind, Autumn casually looked around at the town. She watched as a car passed by; then at a man walking a dog down the block she was on; then at two men sitting on a bench in front of another store; then at a tall, bushy tree. They all helped to take her mind off of that damned palm reader. And Autumn felt calmer by the second. But then, while continuing to scan the area, she saw her. Standing across the street, to her utter shock, was April Glass. And for the first time, she was not wearing that ghastly, blood-covered nightgown. She was wearing brown, corduroy pants and a t-shirt. And she wasn't alone. She was holding hands with some woman. Then, with her other hand, she waved. She waved right at Autumn!

Almost getting run over in the process, Autumn darted across the street. She went to grab April Glass, but before she could get to her, a heavyset man walked between them, obscuring Autumn's view, if only for a second. But when he passed, April was no longer there. Instead, another little girl stood in her place. And she too was holding a woman's hand – Molly, from the motel. Molly, who had been looking in the other direction, turned around and caught Autumn like a deer in headlights. "Oh, hi Autumn," she said with a smile. But as soon as the words left her mouth, she realized that Autumn was in some kind of distress. "Are you all right?"

For a second – an extremely long second – Autumn just stood there frozen. There was no way she had mistaken this little girl for April Glass. And Molly was certainly not the woman standing next to her. Autumn knew what she had seen! Or did she? As unbelievable thoughts raced through her head at fractions of a second, Autumn finally realized that Molly had asked a question. "Oh yeah... I'm fine," she replied in a very unconvincing tone.

"Are you sure."

Autumn took a breath. "Yeah. Yeah, really. I just haven't been feeling very well lately."

"Oh, I'm sorry to hear that." Autumn just shook her head. "Oh, this is my daughter Mary. Mary, this is Autumn."

"You're pretty," Mary blurted out in the innocent voice of a child.

Even after what she had just been through, Autumn smiled. "Thank you. It's nice to meet you."

"Mary honey, why don't you go inside Ralph's and pick out what ice cream you want. I'll be in there in a second."

"But you know I always get..."

Molly gave her daughter a stern look. "Juts go inside. I'll be right in. I just want to talk to Autumn for a second."

"Oh-kay," Mary reluctantly replied before walking into the store in which they were standing right in front.

Molly then turned her full attention to Autumn. "Listen, if some one is after you, you can tell me. My uncle used to be the sheriff. He can help you... really."

Autumn was now finding herself in yet another quandary. "Oh no, no one is after me. It's not that. Really."

"Listen, I know what it's like to be in an abusive relationship. My asshole ex-husband tried to kill me. In fact he's in jail right now." Molly started to roll up her left sleeve. "He used to burn cigarettes on my arms," she went on, as Autumn looked at the numerous small, round scars that ran down her arm.

"I'm so sorry. But really, no one is after me."

Molly put her hand on Autumn's shoulder. "Ok, ok. But let me give you my number. I'm usually at the motel at nights, but..."

"No, really you don't have to."

"It's ok. You can call me any time." Molly then opened up her purse, scrounged around for a pen and piece of scrap paper and gave Autumn her home phone number. "It's just me and Mary."

For a moment, Autumn forgot that she had just hallucinated April Glass and some other woman. For a moment she forgot that some gypsy had just told her that she was dead. For a moment, Autumn was merely overcome by gratefulness for the concern that this stranger was showing her. Even if Molly misunderstood Autumn's situation, Autumn was glad that she had some one to which to turn. For the first time since stepping off that train, Autumn didn't feel so alone.

After walking through town for a while, Autumn found herself back at the Davison Motel. Not thirty seconds after getting into her room, there was a knock on the door. Autumn could see through the window that it was a woman and she opened the door. The woman introduced herself as Gayle – the person with whom Autumn had made the reservations over the phone – and explained that she had seen Autumn walking across the parking lot to her room. After exchanging brief pleasantries, Gayle informed Autumn that Kelly had called and left a message for her to call back.

As soon as Gayle left, Autumn retrieved the calling card that Kelly had given her, which up to that point, she had forgotten all about. Eagerly she punched in all the required numbers. Kelly! Oh Kelly! How Autumn longed to be hanging out by the pool with Kelly talking about boys and local gossip; how she longed for April Glass never to have appeared in her dreams. As the phone rang on the other end, Autumn anxiously awaited just to hear her best friend's voice. But after five rings the answering machine picked up (Kelly had her own phone line). "Hey Kell," Autumn started, with a tone of obvious disappointment. "It's me. I got your message. I was out having breakfast. Sorry I haven't called. Call me back. My room number is fifteen. If I'm out, you don't have to leave another message; I'll just try you back later."

Sitting on the bed, Autumn turned on the TV, but nothing could take her mind off feeling so forlorn. "What am I doing here?" she asked herself out loud. She wondered what Kelly and Dawn were doing back in Arizona – probably hanging out with Justin and Tom, having fun. She pictured them sitting around Dawn's pool, drinking beers and laughing. And that's where she belonged – not in some dingy motel in some backwards-ass town in Oregon. And why was she there, she asked herself again? What was she doing? She was just sitting on a bed, watching some small, antiquated TV. Maybe Kelly was right, she thought. Maybe she had seen or read something about the Pentagram Murders and for whatever reason it burrowed into her subconsciousness, lying dormant until it was awakened by some unknown event. Maybe she just needed some professional help, to talk to a shrink. Maybe she just needed some medication. Fighting feelings that no sixteen year-old should have, Autumn turned her head and looked at the phone sitting on the nightstand.

It was time, she told herself. It was time to stop the madness and go back to Arizona.

Autumn was reaching for the phone to make arrangements to go back home – she would have to get both a train and plane ticket – when a loud ring emanated from it. Taken completely off guard, Autumn jumped back in the bed, her heart given a quick jolt. Then, after the second ring, she picked up the receiver.

"Hey Autumn." Kelly! It was Kelly!

"Oh Kell, you don't know how glad I am to hear your voice."

"Why – are you ok?" It was a relative question.

Autumn paused for a second. "Yeah, I'm ok. You know, I mean nothing happened," she lied, deliberately not telling Kelly about the gypsy or her vision of April Glass. "It's just good to hear you."

"Listen… Autumn…. I think you should come home."

Kelly's words – and the thought of "home" – made Autumn smile. "Yeah, I was thinking the same thing."

"Really," Kelly replied in an elated voice.

"Yeah. Actually, it's funny. I was just going to call Amtrak and the airlines to see when the next train and flight I can get. In fact I was actually reaching for the phone when it rang. It scared the shit outta me." Autumn let out a laugh.

"Oh I hate when that happens."

"Me too." Autumn laughed some more. Merely hearing Kelly's voice made Autumn feel better. And the thought that she would soon be back with her best friend completely put her mind at ease.

After getting off the phone with Kelly, Autumn thumbed through the yellow pages that was in the nightstand draw (along with a bible). A half hour later, her travel arrangements were set. Autumn would catch the 11:15 am train, which would put her in Eugene at one o'clock. Her flight back to Phoenix was at 4:30 pm (she thanked God that there was still a seat left on the plane). By seven o'clock the next day, she would be back with Kelly – back home. Moreover, she only had to pay a $20 fee for changing her plane ticket.

After her travel plans were set, Autumn called Kelly to tell her the good news. Kelly, who said that she would pick her up from the airport, seemed as relieved as Autumn.

With nothing else to do, Autumn sat on the bed for a while, watching television. But there were only four channels – and none of them had anything worthwhile on – and after about an hour, Autumn started to go stir crazy. So she decided to go out and just walk around, explore the area some more.

Feeling like an overbearing weight had been lifted off her slender shoulders, Autumn casually strolled back into town. Every so often she could feel someone staring at her, but she no longer cared. In less than twenty four hours, she would be leaving Dewey – and never returning. Ahhh, just the mere thought brought a smile to her face. But it wasn't just Dewey. Autumn was also resolved to end her unnatural quest for April Glass. And whatever it took – counseling, medication – Autumn was willing to go through in order to banish April Glass forever from her head.

Under a partly cloudy sky, Autumn Grace took her time wandering through Dewey; not just the center of town, but also several side streets. Though the town itself was somewhat rundown, the surrounding landscape was actually quite breathtaking; deep, green woods with a backdrop of giant, carpeted mountains. Birds flew about, peacefully gliding under the afternoon sky. No one was honking their horns or even talking in loud voices. You could actually hear the slight breeze combing through the branches of the trees. Even the temperature was pleasing, warm, but not hot. Oddly enough, the more Autumn walked around, the more she found herself thinking *maybe Dewey isn't such a bad place after all.*

Stumbling upon a small pizzeria of all places, Autumn decided to go and have lunch. She was a little leery of how good the pizza was going to be, but the only other eateries she had passed was the ice cream parlor, the same diner she had breakfast in, a hamburger joint that had a group of local kids hanging out front and a bar/restaurant. And it seemed like she had been through the entire commercial area of the town. So she went in, ordered two slices and a coke and sat down. To her surprise, the pizza wasn't actually that bad.

Thick rain poured down from the black, night sky. If there were any stars, they were obscured by unseen clouds. Everything was drenched: the trees, the rocks, the turbid ground. And there was Autumn, standing listlessly, almost in a trance, sopping wet from her long, brown hair down to her open-toed sandals, which sunk into the mud. She had no idea where she was or how she had gotten there. There was no visible path or beckoning light, just dense woods. "Help!" she yelled. But her voice was drowned out by the roaring sound of the rain. Not that there was anyone around to hear her scream, anyway. As fear and helplessness pulsated through every molecule of her body, Autumn began to cry; her feeble tears mixing with the cold water that already covered her face.

Suddenly there was a flash of brilliant light, as the entire area illuminated, if only for a split second. Then, not two seconds later came the crashing roar of thunder. Autumn had thought that her fear had already reached its zenith – how could she possibly feel any more terrified – but when that deafening bang shook the night, somehow her fear found new depths. Her young heart raced uncontrollably and every nerve in her body pulsated. And unbelievably, it was about to get even worse. Another flash lit up the dense, foreboding woods. This time, its brightness lasted for a good two seconds. And as it illuminated the otherwise black night, through the barrage of rain, Autumn caught a glimpse of what appeared to be the silhouette of a child... being chased by a man. The shadowy figure running after the boy was holding something in his hand, maybe an axe or even rifle. Autumn could not make it out because almost as soon as the two figures appeared, they disappeared into the returning darkness. Then came another thunderous crash, so loud that Autumn could feel its deep sound passing in a wave through her body.

After the thunder faded, the sound of the rain continued to roar – as did the sound of wind whipping through the braches of the trees. But somehow, through all the noise, Autumn thought she heard a voice. Wiping the water from her face – both tears and rain – she listened intently. Was it just the wind? No, it was a voice! "Help us," it howled. Shaking uncontrollably, Autumn couldn't believe her ears. "Please…. Help us," it cried again.

"What do you want from me!" Autumn screamed defiantly, but at the same time, with overpowering fear. No sooner did her words fade into the night, came yet another flash of lightning. This time Autumn could actually see the splintering bolt hit the ground, in the nearby distance. As it lit up the woods and sky, the ghostly face of a demon, floating bodiless in the air, appeared in front of her. But even quicker than the grainy images of the man and child, it disappeared into oblivion. Then, right on cue, came another crash of thunder.

Suddenly, Autumn could feel something touching her hand, taking hold of it. Instinctively she looked down. Standing right beside her, holding her hand, was April Glass. And she was back wearing that white, blood-stained nightgown; back wearing that same look of despair and fear. As Autumn looked down at her, their eyes met; two tormented souls staring at each other. Then, April slowly opened her mouth and for the first time, spoke. "Please don't leave now." Suddenly, Autumn no longer heard the constant pounding of the rain or the wind howling through the trees. All she could hear was the soft, heartrending voice of April Glass. "You can't go now," she continued. "Please… you have to help us."

7

Molly was gazing out the window at the pouring rain when the phone rang, taking her by surprise. "Hello."

"Hey Molly, it's John." John Tucker, who had just checked into the motel several hours earlier, had a small firewood business. In the fall and winter he would come up to Dewey at least twice a month to bring back wood to Eugene, where he lived. But sometimes he would also come to Dewey in the summer, for a few days at a time, to fish.

"Hey John," Molly answered in a friendly voice. Molly always liked John. "How about this rain?"

"Yeah."

Molly then realized that John probably didn't call just to chit-chat. "So what can I do for you?"

"Listen, I was just coming back from The Crow's Nest (a local bar/restaurant) and when I parked my truck I noticed that the door to room fifteen was wide open. At first I didn't think too much about it – I figured that someone was just leaving – but by the time I got to my room, I saw that it was still open. If it was any other night, I still probably wouldn't have paid it much mind, but who would leave their door open in this rain? So I walked over there to see if everything was ok. I called into the room, but nobody answered. But the TV and lights were on. And the floor by the entrance way is soaked."

"Oh my god!" Molly instantly knew that number 15 was Autumn's room.

"I mean it still may be nothing. Maybe some knuckle head went out and forgot to close the door all the way and the wind blew it open."

Molly instantly discarded the possibility that Autumn had simply gone somewhere and didn't close the door all the way. No, Molly had a cold, sinking feeling that something was terribly wrong. "Did you see a young girl – about seventeen? Skinny with long dark hair, kinda wavy?"

"No. Why, is some young girl staying there?"

John's last sentence didn't even register; Molly was too unnerved. "Did it look like someone broke the door to get in?"

"No… why? Molly, what's going on?" John paused for a moment. "I'm commin' down to the office. I'll be there in a minute."

As Molly hung up the phone, her mind was spinning a thousand miles per second. What was she going to do? What could she do? Molly picked the phone back up and decided to call the police. But for whatever reason, after pressing the first number, she hung-up, deciding to first try and find Autumn herself. So she grabbed a flashlight that was behind the counter and headed out.

Without an umbrella or even a hat, Molly went outside in the pouring rain and was immediately met by John, who was wearing a poncho and also had a flashlight. "You sure she wasn't in the bathroom – in the shower or something?" Molly asked in a panic-stricken voice.

"I yelled in there several times. Besides," he pointed, "the door's still open. Do you know this girl?" he then asked, speaking loud enough to be heard over the pounding rain.

"No. She checked in yesterday. I've never seen her before." Molly paused to wipe a layer of water from her face.

"But I think she was in some sort of trouble. I think she was hiding from an abusive boyfriend or father. She just had this scared look about her."

The night lit up from a streak of lightning. And a few seconds later came the boom of thunder. "You think someone took her? Maybe we she call the police?"

Molly shook her head. "Yeah, I was thinking that too. But maybe we should go take another look inside the room first."

"All right. But why don't you put on a hood first. It's raining cats and dogs out here."

"Nah, I'm all right."

Under an angry, relentless sky, Molly and John started walking across the parking lot. Several thin lampposts lined where the lot met the guestrooms, but with the heavy rain and black sky, they provided barely any illumination. Still, out of the corner of his eye, John thought he saw something moving through the darkness, coming out of the woods. As he stopped, Molly instinctively also came to a halt. "What? What is it?" she asked. John didn't answer; he just pointed his flashlight towards the woods. As the beam of light cut through the rain, both John and Molly watched in astonishment as the shadowy figure of a girl slowly emerged from the dense tree line, about fifteen yards away.

"Oh my God!" Molly gasped as she ran over to her. Then, as if the two had been long-time friends, Molly hugged Autumn, squeezing her trembling body. "My god, you're shivering. How long have you been out here?" Letting go of her embrace, Molly put her hands on Autumn's soaked shoulders. "Are you ok?"

Autumn didn't reply. In fact she seemed in shock. She just stood there shaking, in her sopping wet shorts and t-shirt, staring right through Molly with glazed eyes.

"Come on," Molly yelled over the roar of thunder. "Lets get her back inside." With that, Molly put her arm around Autumn's shoulder and guided her back to her room. John followed, just wondering what the hell was going on.

Once inside the guest room – they finally closed the door – Molly wrapped a towel around Autumn and sat her down on a chair. Autumn still hadn't said anything. "What happened?" Molly asked, as she crouched over towards the still shivering teen. "Should I call the police?"

"I think she's on some kind of drugs." John bluntly suggested.

"I'm not on drugs!" Autumn defiantly replied, finally breaking her silence.

Molly looked back at John. "It's ok. I think I can handle it from here. Thank you John for all your help. Really."

John stood there for a few seconds before shaking his head. "Ok. Just let me know if you need me." He then went back to his own room.

Molly was concerned about Autumn, scared for her. She obviously wanted to know what the teen was doing out in the pouring rain, in the woods. Had she been running from someone? Molly wanted to help this girl that, despite only knowing for one day, felt a kinship towards. But before any questions could be answered, Molly figured that the first thing she should do was get Autumn into a hot shower. So after turning on the water, Molly went to help Autumn get undressed. Autumn thanked her, but was now feeling embarrassed and went into the bathroom and undressed herself.

As Autumn went into the shower, Molly, realizing that she had left the front office unattended, ran back, locked the door and put a sign in the window that read: *Will Be Back Shortly.* She then returned to Autumn's room. Molly was not worried about not tending the front office. It was after 9:00 pm and she wasn't expecting any guests. Hell, often days could go by without someone coming into the motel. There were only fifteen rooms and Molly never remembered when they were all occupied at the same time. In fact besides Autumn and John, there was only one other room occupied, by a hunter who sometimes passed through Dewey. Usually, most of the motel's guests consisted of local young lovers, looking for a place of their own for the night.

As Molly waited for Autumn to get out of the shower, she tried to dry the inner entranceway of the room with several towels she had brought up from the office.

The hot steam and water felt soothing on Autumn's skin. But the sixteen year-old's head was still fraught with fear, confusion and despair. She did not remember walking into the woods. She didn't even have any recollection of leaving her room. But, much to her dismay, she remembered everything she saw – and heard – in the woods: the grainy silhouettes of a man chasing a child; the voices; and of course April Glass. Bowing her head towards the ground, Autumn's tears mixed with water, which, like her sanity, flowed helplessly down the drain. What the hell was happening she frantically asked herself? The nightmares had been bad enough but now she was seeing things while she was wide awake. Were they hallucinations? Or was she really being visited by the ghost of April Glass? And in either instance, why?

As scared and confused as she was, Autumn felt that she owed Molly some kind of explanation. In an abyss of horror, this stranger that she had just met the day before seemed to be, at the moment, her only guiding light. Autumn felt guilty for letting Molly believe that she was this young, battered woman, even though she had told her that that was not the case. She also didn't want Molly to call the police. Autumn just wanted to stay in the shower all night. But suddenly, she heard the bathroom door creek open. "Are you ok in there Autumn?"

"Yeah, I'm ok. I'm going to be getting out," she shouted back.

After asking Molly to leave some clothes – underwear, sweatpants and a shirt – on the bathroom counter, Autumn dried off and got dressed. As soon as she walked out of the bathroom, she noticed the towels on the floor, by the front door. "I'm real sorry about that," she said sheepishly while pointing. "I thought I closed the door."

"It's ok sweetie, don't worry about it."

Autumn sat on the foot of the bed, across from Molly. Autumn was not really sure exactly what she was going to say. She just kind of figured that she would open her mouth and words would come out. She started by skirting the whole situation. "My God Molly, you're soaking wet. I have another pair of sweatpants and shirt you can borrow." Molly was almost as slender as Autumn, but about two inches taller.

"No that's ok. I used a towel to dry off a little." Next came a brief, uneasy pause; a set-up for the question that Autumn knew was coming. "What happened?"

Autumn looked down towards the ground, avoiding any contact. She was afraid that Molly would think she was crazy – or playing some prank – if she told her the truth – and who wouldn't. But the genuine concern in Molly's voice made Autumn feel too guilty to lie. "Listen Molly," she said in low, shaky tone. "I know that you think that someone – my boyfriend or father or someone – is after me; that I'm running away from some kind of abuse. But that's not the case. It's not that at all." Autumn looked up, but still found it hard, almost unbearable, to make eye contact with Molly. "It's just... I... I..."

Molly could hear the trembling in the teen's voice and see the shaking of her hands. "It's ok," she said placidly, while putting her hands on Autumn's quivering knees. "I don't mean to pry. But I just want to help you if you're in some sort of trouble. I mean you were out in the woods by yourself in the pouring rain, without any flashlight or gear. And this morning when I saw you, you looked like you had seen a ghost. And last night..."

Finally, Autumn could not take the charade any longer. "What do you know about April Glass?"

There was an overpowering silence. It was as if a bomb had fallen out of the clear blue sky and dropped on Molly's head – and theoretically speaking, it had. "What about April Glass?" Molly asked with a look of utter bewilderment still on her white face.

"I know this is going to sound completely crazy. It sounds crazy to me." Autumn stopped, finding the words too bizarre to even speak, especially to this woman she had just met.

"What? What is it," Molly asked in a now, almost frightened voice.

"Well… well…well, you see I first started having these nightmares about her."

Molly looked as if *she* had seen a ghost. "How do you know April Glass?"

Autumn stood up and began to pace about the small room. "Well that's the thing – I don't. In fact, at first I didn't even know that the girl in my dreams was April Glass." Autumn then continued to tell her whole bizarre story: the house in the woods; the blood and pentagram; the lifeless little boy; how she found out that the girl in her nightmares was April Glass; and the unexplainable force that told her to come to Dewey. The only thing she didn't describe was what she had seen – and heard – in the woods, right before Molly and John had found her. But it almost didn't matter. A quarter-way through Autumn's story, Molly had forgotten all about finding her coming out of the woods. It was as if Molly's whole life had been sucked into a vacuum; nothing existed but the unbelievable narrative that she was listening to.

"I can't believe it," Molly finally spoke in a slow, fading voice. "I always thought it was just urban legend, the talk of crazy people."

Autumn stopped pacing and fixated on Molly. "What are you talking about?"

Molly hesitated. "For years local folks have told stories about seeing April and Lilly – or at least their ghosts – walking through town or in the woods. Crazy Jim even swears that every fall, he sometimes sees all of them – April, her parents and brother and Lilly – walking through the woods by his cabin." Autumn's jaw dropped as she froze in place. Was the ghost of April Glass real after all?! "But that's Crazy Jim," Molly continued in a now skeptical voice, realizing what she – what they both – were saying. "They don't call him Crazy Jim for nothing. He also said that Jesus had visited him and told him that the apocalypse was upon us."

"What about the other people – that saw April walking around town?"

Molly looked towards the floor and shook her head. "I don't know. Most of it happened shortly after the murders, when everyone – the whole town – was still in some kind of shock. I think people saw what they wanted to see; not wanting to believe that April and Lilly were really dead. I mean nobody wanted to believe any of it. This is a small town. Certainly nothing like that had ever happened here." Molly paused as she stared at Autumn with mollifying eyes. "And I don't know if you realize this Autumn, but there are some strange people in this town. Don't get me wrong, most of them are perfectly normal, hardworking folks, but for whatever reason, we have our share of weirdoes." It was not Molly's intention to lump Autumn into that "weirdo" category, but a soon as the words left her mouth, she realized that's probably how Autumn had taken it. "I don't mean that you're…"

"No, it's ok," Autumn stopped her. "Believe me; I realize how crazy it sounds." With that, Autumn fell onto the bed, put her face in her hands and started crying. "Maybe I'm just losing my mind."

Molly did not know what to believe, but she felt terrible. Even though they had just met yesterday, Molly was a compassionate person and it troubled her to see this young girl in such dismay. And looking at Autumn's effusive emotions, Molly found it hard to believe that she was just making up some story. Whether it was just in her mind, a hallucination, or a real apparition, Molly was sure that Autumn had been seeing April Glass. And that made Molly think. What if – just what if – the ghost of April Glass was real? The mere question sent an unearthly chill down her spine. Kneeling beside Autumn, Molly put her hands on the teen's legs. "I don't know. I mean maybe April Glass has been coming to you. But I just don't get it. Why you? You never lived here or knew her. And what does she want… for you to find her?"

Autumn instantly lifted her head up from her hands. "What did you say?"

"Why you?"

"No, the other part." Suddenly Autumn had an epiphany, as Molly's words mixed with the remembrance of the dream she had about being buried alive. Was it that simple?! How could she have overlooked it?! "Yes," Autumn proclaimed almost triumphantly as she sprang up from the bed. "That's it! She wants me to find her! She's trying to show me where she is buried." Autumn then told Molly about her nightmare about being buried alive. She did not know where April was buried, Autumn explained, but was sure that April was trying to reveal the exact spot. That's why she had "brought" her to Dewey, Autumn went on.

When Autumn first starting telling her unworldly tale, Molly was completely taken off guard and completely spooked, especially that she had heard stories throughout the years of April and Lilly's ghosts wandering about the town. Then she gained her composure – snapped back to reality – and dismissed such talk as fairytale; urban legend. But then why was this girl, who had never stepped foot within Dewey until a day earlier, standing there saying she was having visions of April Glass? For a second, Molly thought that perhaps John was right – that she was on drugs. Or maybe it was even some crazy prank. Maybe, for whatever reason, she was simply obsessed with the Pentagram Murders. She wouldn't have been the first outsider to wander into Dewey asking questions about that fateful day nearly eight years ago. But then, Molly dismissed those notions as well. Seeing how effusively distraught Autumn was made Molly start thinking – at least a part of her start thinking – what if this girl was telling the truth? Just what if?

Despite the surrealism of the moment, the reality was that Molly was soaked and tired. Molly was supposed to stay at the motel until eleven, but it would not be a problem for her to leave forty minutes early. However, she was not about to leave Autumn alone. At first Autumn politely turned down Molly's generous offer to stay the night at her house. But in truth, Autumn didn't want to be alone any more than Molly wanted to leave her there. So when Molly refused to take no for an answer, Autumn was actually relieved and thanked her gracious host.

Though obviously Molly could not help but think of April Glass and the Pentagram Murders, she at least tried to take her mind off of them. On the ten minute ride to her house Molly tended to more practical matters. For the first time, she asked Autumn about where she was from and about her parents. Didn't they wonder where she was? Did she run away? Autumn explained that her parents were on a cruise and had no idea about her trip to Dewey. She explained that she had bought round trip tickets and would be back home before her parents. What Autumn didn't tell Molly, however, was that she had changed her tickets and was supposed to fly home the next day. That's because although just a few hours earlier Autumn was ready to *walk* back to Arizona if she had to, the pendulum in her mind had now swung back all the way in the other direction. After seeing what she did in the woods and now convinced that it was her mission to find April Glass' burial site, Autumn was more resolute than ever that she belonged in Dewey.

After introducing her to Autumn, Molly paid the babysitter, an eighteen year-old girl that, besides watching Mary, worked part-time during the day in Dewey's lone grocery store. The babysitter had her own car, so after she was paid, it was just Molly and Autumn (Mary was sleeping in her bedroom). The clock was already pushing eleven.

As Molly excused herself to change into some dry pajamas, Autumn stood in the living room and casually looked around the house. She wasn't trying to snoop; rather it was just instinct. It seemed like a cozy home. There was certainly nothing strange about it. In fact, besides maybe the structural layout, there was nothing to distinguish it from being in Dewey, Oregon, Long Island, New York, or Chandler, Arizona. It was well-kept and clean. There was a couch and mid-sized television set in the living room. There was a fireplace. On top of it was a long, wooden mantel, on which stood several framed photographs. Autumn walked over and nonchalantly started looking at them. One in particular caught her attention; it was a picture of Molly, what appeared to be Mary when she was a toddler and a man. As she held the picture in her hand, Molly came walking from downstairs, which was right by the living room. Startled, Autumn felt embarrassed to be caught poking around. "Oh I'm sorry," she said, putting the frame back down on the mantle.

Molly smiled. "That's ok." She then walked over to the picture and picked it up. "That's Mary's father, Marc," she said, looking right at him. "Mary was just three then. She's nine now." Molly put the picture back on the mantle. "I was just seventeen when we got married. Marc was a year older. A year later I got pregnant. We were both so happy. But in my third trimester I had a miscarriage."

Autumn, put her hand on Molly's shoulder. "I'm so sorry."

"I was devastated," Molly continued. "Marc was too, which was understandable. But he blamed me for the miscarriage. He beat me so bad." As she spoke, her voice crackled, but she did not cry. For unbeknown to Autumn, Molly had made a promise to herself some time ago, to never let Marc make her cry again. "Marc had hit me before, but I always told people that I fell or hit my head coming out of the car – you know the story. But this time was different. He actually broke my nose and my eye looked like it had been hit with a baseball…and that was just my face. Once I was on the ground, he kept kicking me in the stomach, saying I killed his son." Autumn cringed and felt sick to her stomach as Molly narrated her harrowing tale. An hour ago she would not have thought it humanly possible, but Autumn had, for the moment, forgotten all about April Glass.

"My father had died a year earlier from a heart attack," Molly continued, still not shedding a tear. "But his brother, my Uncle Henry, was the Sheriff at the time and as soon as he found out what happened he went over to the garage where Marc worked and beat the shit out of him." That memory made Molly crack a fleeting smile. "He said that if he ever touched me again he would kill him. Then he locked him up. We don't actually have our own jail in Dewey, but the police station has several cells. After I was released from the hospital, I heard what happened and begged my uncle to let him out. Of course he thought I was crazy and pleaded with me to leave Marc for good... before he killed me."

"But you stayed with him," Autumn replied in bewilderment.

Molly shook her head. "He said how sorry he was; how he had just been so upset over the miscarriage and not in his right mind."

"But you said he had also hit you before."

"I know, it's crazy. But things were actually good for a while. Then, three years later I got pregnant with Mary. And right after she was born, things were better than they ever were. But when Mary was two, Marc lost his job at the garage after he got into a fist fight with his boss. It was all downhill from there. He started drinking all the time and started to become abusive again. If Mary was crying, he wouldn't hit her, but he would hit me for not being able to make her stop." Molly paused as she remembered a not so distant memory that no woman should have to live through. "It was not too long after this picture was taken. I had finally had enough and one afternoon while he was at the bar – we were broke at the time, but he had sold his car to support his drinking habit – I packed up a suitcase and ran off to my friend Terri's house. But the complete idiot that I was, I left Marc a note telling him what I was doing and of course he went right over to Terri's house to get me. I wouldn't leave so he pulled out a gun – right in front of Terri and her kids – and said that if I didn't go back home with him, he would kill us all. So I left. But Terri called my uncle and he and his three deputies rushed over to our house. That's when the shit really hit the fan. When Marc heard them knocking, he yelled that if they came in he would shoot them. When they saw me running out the side door and realized that he didn't have me hostage, they kicked in the front door. Sure enough, Marc – he must have been drinking since the morning – pulled out his revolver and even got off a shot. But luckily, probably because he was so drunk, he missed. But one of the deputies didn't. He shot Marc in the stomach."

"Oh my God!"

Molly shook her head once more. "Yeah. He survived, but he was charged and convicted of kidnapping, aggravated assault and attempted murder. He's in Oregon State Penn, serving out a thirty-five year sentence."

As Molly turned to look at Autumn, she saw several tears streaking down her face. "Ah, it's ok honey," she said with a smile, wiping a tear from Autumn's cheek.

"I'm just so sorry."

"Really, it's ok. Me and Mary are doing well now. Mr. Adams, the man who owns the motel, pays me well. And when my mother died – she passed away of cancer three years ago – she left everything, which included a bank account with over fifty thousand dollars, to me and my sister, who lives in Kansas. Plus me and Helena – that's my sister's name – were the beneficiaries of her insurance policy." Molly smiled. "Helena and our uncle Henry pleaded with me to take the money and move to Kansas; to start a new life for me and Mary. I know my mother would have wanted it too," Molly continued before pausing to reflect upon her decision to stay. "But Dewey is my home. It's where I was born. So I bought this house and Mary and I live very comfortable. And with my job, I'm even able to put money away for Mary's future… And most importantly," Molly said with a smile, "I don't have to depend on a man."

"Well you have a very beautiful daughter."

"Thank you."

"And I want to thank you for everything you've done... really," Autumn said sincerely. "I mean I wouldn't have blamed you if you had thought I was some kind of nut," she followed, with an uneasy laugh.

Molly put her hand on the teenager's shoulder. "Well listen, tomorrow, if you're ok with it, I would like you to see my Uncle. As I said, he used to be the sheriff and he was the sheriff when the Pentagrams Murders happened. And nobody knows more about the case or about April Glass than he does."

Autumn had been so enthralled by Molly's life story that she had forgotten for a moment that she was in the middle of her own drama. But that name – April Glass – catapulted Autumn back into the unworldly reality of her own situation. Autumn's entire life had been kidnapped by her dreams and visions of this young girl that she had never met. A girl that by all accounts had died a horrible death, some time ago. And Autumn was now convinced that the only way she was going to free herself was by finding the remains of April Glass. But although April, or more appropriately her ghost, had been giving Autumn clues, they were just that – clues. For whatever reason Autumn was never allowed to see the whole picture. So how could she turn down an offer to meet with the sheriff who had led the local investigation into April Glass' disappearance? How could she turn down an opportunity to possibly receive the missing pieces to this haunting puzzle?

Before going to sleep, Molly fixed both her and Autumn a peanut butter and jelly sandwich. Neither of them had eaten in quite some time. It was after one in the morning when Molly finally showed Autumn to the upstairs guestroom. Molly was exhausted and wanted to go to sleep. Autumn wanted to wake up – and find that the past month was all nothing more than a bad dream.

8

The next morning, Autumn awoke to the tantalizing smell of sausage and bacon cooking on the stove. She should have been getting ready for her journey back to Arizona. But Autumn had no intention of making her flight; there was unfinished business left in Dewey, which she was now fully prepared to see through. So instead of panicking that she was going to miss her train, Autumn slowly wandered downstairs, following the welcoming aroma of homemade breakfast.

In the kitchen, Autumn was greeted by Molly and Mary. Molly asked if she had slept well, to which Autumn replied yes. Then, at Molly's request, the teenager, still dressed in her sweat pants and t-shirt, pulled out a chair and sat at the rectangular-shaped table. Not only had Molly prepared bacon and sausage, but also pancakes. The three ate and talked, keeping the conversation light, for Mary's sake. (Molly had told Mary that Autumn was a cousin, who was having some "troubles" at home and would be staying with them for a few days. She hated lying to her daughter, but could not possibly tell her the truth.) As the three conversed, Autumn couldn't help but keep looking at Mary. She always seemed to have this bright smile, which accentuated her big, blue eyes. She looked so vibrant and so innocent; such a contrast to the haunting images to which Autumn had become accustomed. To Autumn, Mary was a breath a fresh air, a reminder that a pure, ingenuous world still existed.

After a delicious breakfast, which Autumn so greatly appreciated, she took a shower and changed into the shorts and shirt that she had brought with her from the motel. Then it was off to see Molly's uncle. It was back to chasing the ghost of April Glass.

Henry Foster's house, where he lived with his wife Edith, was outside the center of town, on its own five acre lot. The house itself, which was actually rather small and rustic, was set off the road about thirty yards, perched atop a grassy knoll. Against its back were dense woods.

As Autumn approached the house, walking through the open, front yard, she did so with apprehension. What was she going to do – introduce herself and say "remember that big murder case you worked on seven years ago; well I've been seeing that little girl's ghost and she wants me to help you find her body"? Autumn didn't see how she was going to come off as anything besides a loon.

After one ring of the bell, the weathered front door swung open. In the entranceway stood a large man; about 6'2" and at least 270 pounds – none of which was muscle – with sparse, short gray hair on his almost bald head. His face was round with double chins and a big, coarse, red nose. Autumn was in a ball of nerves. However, at least for the moment, her appearance was deflected as Henry's attention was consumed by Mary. "There's my little girl," a husky voice rang out, as his bulky body crouched down to meet Mary, who enthusiastically jumped into his waiting arms.

"Uncle Henry," she gleefully replied as she tried to wrap her small arms around his girth.

Henry then moved on to Molly, who he also greeted with a hug and kiss in the cheek. Inevitably, however, the question came. "And who is this," he asked in a deep, but friendly voice.

"Oh, this is Autumn," Molly replied with a smile.

Henry, who looked to be in his sixties, was extremely affable as he introduced himself and led them into the house. Furthermore, Molly's introduction of Autumn appeared to quell any curiosity he may have had with the teen; figuring that she was a mere tag-along and Molly and Mary had stopped by for a routine visit.

As Henry asked Molly how she was doing, Autumn inconspicuously glanced around. The first thing she noticed was several empty beer cans on the coffee table. Then, through the open entranceway into the kitchen, she noticed a bottle of Jack Daniels on the counter. From that, as well as Henry's pock-marked, red nose, Autumn surmised that Molly's uncle was a heavy drinker.

After being in the house for not more than ten minutes, the front door opened again. It was Henry's wife, Edith; a short, round, gray-haired woman, who was carrying a bag of groceries. The family greetings and introduction of Autumn had to be done all over again

It seemed that Molly was as reluctant to talk about Autumn's problem as Autumn was – and for obvious reasons. But after Edith graciously poured each of her guests a glass of homemade lemonade, Molly decided to bite the bullet. "Uncle Henry, I was wondering if me and Autumn can talk to you about something out back?"

Henry sensed that something was up. "Sure," he replied in a deliberate tone.

"Mary honey, why don't you tell Aunt Edith all about Ellen's birthday party?"

"Sure," Mary replied with child-like enthusiasm.

With that, Autumn followed Molly and her uncle out the sliding glass door, to the backyard. As they did so, Edith watched with inquiring eyes. Who was this young girl named Autumn, she wondered.

Out by the back porch, under an overcast sky, Henry Foster, Molly and Autumn gathered, almost in a huddle. With Henry looking down on them, neither Molly nor Autumn wanted to start to explain – if it could be explained – the bizarre reason for their visit. But it was now beyond the point of no return and since Henry was Molly's uncle, she went first. "Autumn here is from Arizona," she started. "She... she has some interest in the Pentagram murders... well... actually it's a little more than that."

"What about the Glass case?" he huffed.

Autumn and Molly looked at each other and both took a deep breath. "Well I know this is going to sound crazy... but... well... Autumn... you see..."

Autumn saw Molly struggling to explain the situation to her uncle. And though she now found herself somewhat intimidated by Henry she felt that she had to bail Molly out. "I know this is going to sound crazy Mr. Foster," she managed to sputter out. "But... well... I have some strange connection. At least I think I do, to April Glass."

Suddenly Henry eyes lit up. "What is it?"

Inevitably, now came the "crazy" part. "Well... I guess there's no other way to say this, but for about a month now, April Glass has been coming to me in my dreams." Instantly, Henry's demeanor changed; his bushy eyebrows sunk low, his eyes turned cold and there was no escaping the obvious annoyance on his round face. "I told you... I know this sounds crazy, but..."

Henry shook his large head and then turned to his niece. "Molly, where did you find this girl?" he growled. "You know better than this. You should..."

"No, it's true," Autumn courageously interjected.

"Listen kid," Henry snarled as his eyes stared down at Autumn. "Over the years you know how many crackpots have contacted me about this case: psychics promising that they can help me, that they knew where April and Lilly are or that they know who did it; other people who just had some sick fascination with this case; even reporters or someone trying to write a book."

"Uncle Henry."

Henry paid his niece no mind. "Well I just want to tell you – to tell all you folks once and for all – that Dewey is a nice place with hard-working people. Despite what you may have heard, there's no devil worshipping in the woods, no animal or human sacrifices, no secret sects. What happened on October twenty-seventh, nineteen eighty five was the work of some sick bastard, nothing else. And those two poor little girls, though they've never been found, I'm certain they died that day or soon after. So please, just let us be."

The ex-Sheriff's lamentation would usually have been enough to make Autumn buckle and whimper away with an apology. But not today. She had been through too much, seen too much, to simply turn back now. "I know you've probably been hounded by dozens of crackpots over the years, but this is different. I've seen things – blood being splattered on the walls, the messages, the dead boy in the woods, visions of..."

"What did you say," Henry interrupted.

"I've seen things. I've..."

"No," he interrupted again. "About the dead boy in the woods?"

Autumn could sense Henry's demeanor changing once again; he now seemed more intrigued than angry. "In my dreams. I'm with April Glass and she's pointing to something by a tree stump. When I look, it's a boy – I guess her brother – and he's hunched over dead and his back has this big, terrible hole in it. Then other times I see him running out the front door of the house, being chased by this shadowy figure; a man, only I can't see his face."

Molly also noticed the change in her uncle's demeanor. "What is it Uncle Henry?"

Henry stood there for a few seconds, silent before answering. "John Junior's body was found in the house," he said in a slow, solemn voice. "We later ascertained that he was actually killed in the woods – by a cut-down tree – and then brought in the house by the killer. But that information was never released to the public. As far as everyone else knew, he was killed in the house. He had never left the house."

Autumn put her small hand on Henry's thick, bare forearm. "Listen Henry, I know this case has been very hard on you. I know you have nightmares about it every night. I know that not finding the killer or the rest of the bodies has haunted you, has destroyed your whole life. It's driven you to drink. It's changed the way you look at people. I know that you haven't been to church in six years, because you've lost your faith in God. But I also know that you've given this case everything you possibly could. And some nights, after Edith goes to sleep, you go into the basement and start looking through the boxes of notes and records you've kept; convinced that you've overlooked something; convinced that somewhere in those boxes are the answers."

As soon as the last word left Autumn's mouth, a cold chill overcame her. She was conscious of what she was saying, yet had no idea where the words had come from. Anyone could have surmised that being involved – being one of the main players – in such a gruesome and unsolved crime would have deeply affected the ex-Sheriff. But how could Autumn possibly have known about the boxes of notes and clippings that Henry kept in his basement – how did she even know he had a basement – or that he still spent nights going through them? And how the hell could she have known that Henry, who for 52 years had never missed Sunday mass, had not been to church in six years?

"Who are you?" Henry asked in an almost frightened voice. "Do you know someone that knows me? Did your father or uncle work on this case?"

"No," Autumn answered directly. "My name is Autumn Grace. And believe it or not, up until two weeks ago, I had never heard of the Pentagram Murders, never heard the name April Glass."

"Excuse me," Molly said in a shaking voice as she practically ran back in the house. Aghast, she simply could not listen to anymore.

As for Henry Foster, he too was shaken-up. Completely mystified, he walked away from Autumn and paced about the back porch, not saying anything. That left an uneasy Autumn, standing by herself, still pondering the words she had just spoken. She too, was spooked, but had become accustomed to that, or at least as accustomed to it as one could be.

After about a minute of just pacing around, saying nothing, Henry Foster went back to Autumn. He wanted to know more. He *needed* to know more. Henry invited Autumn to an old, round wooden table, about fifteen yards from the back entranceway to the house. There, in the backyard, the teenager from Chandler and the 63 year-old retired Sheriff from Dewey sat down for the most bizarre of meetings. At Henry's request, Autumn began to detail everything she had seen and been through since April Glass – that little girl in the woods – first appeared in her dreams. She told him about the blood-stained white nightgown that April always adorned (except the time Autumn saw her across the street from the palm reader). She told him about, in her dreams, being inside of the house, seeing the blood-drawn pentagrams and the words "He's Coming" on the walls. She told him about the dream where she was being buried alive. She told him about the green field and the church; about the flashes of two other, unknown, young girls, cowering in a darkened room; about her vision of April Glass on the train, with a severed human head in her lap. Autumn even told him about her encounter with April the night before; how she begged Autumn not to leave; how Molly had found her there, walking out of the woods in the pouring rain.

It took a while for Autumn to go through all her experiences, but not once did Henry interrupt. He just sat there across from her, not believing what he was hearing. Though he did not let Autumn know, exactly what April was wearing and the message "He's Coming", were other evidence of the case that were never made public. And although the fact that the bodies had been mutilated, the fact that Joanne Glass' head was completely severed was kept private.

After Autumn finished her fantastic tale, Henry spoke what were his first words in about twenty minutes. "Come on," he said bluntly, as he arose from the table. "There's somewhere I want to take you."

"Where?"

"To the Glass' old house."

It would seem that at this point, not much would shock Autumn Grace anymore. But she *was* shocked; not only that Henry would suggest it, but the mere thought of finally being face to face with that house that had so haunted her in her nightmares. For whatever reason, though the murders took place less than eight years ago, Autumn assumed that the house didn't exist anymore.

As Autumn and Henry went into the house, they ran into Molly, Mary and Edith. "Autumn and I are going for a little ride", Henry announced. "We'll be back in a while. Molly, wait here until we get back."

Not wanting to say anything in front of Mary, Molly and Edith left her in the living room and followed Autumn and Henry out the front door. "What's going on Henry?" his wife asked in a stern voice. "Molly came in the house before so upset she looked like she was going to cry. But she wouldn't tell me what happened."

Henry, almost to his pick-up truck, turned to his wife, who was standing by the front door. "Edith, don't worry about it. Everything's fine." Edith was taken aback by her husband's stern tone.

"Where are you going?" Molly asked, across the front yard.

"Just wait here. We shouldn't be longer than an hour." With that Henry climbed into his dusty, 1970's Ford pick-up truck. Autumn followed.

The "Old Glass house", as Henry called it, was about twenty minutes away isolated in the woods, outside of town, he explained. Henry took the opportunity of the drive to ask Autumn about her parents; did they have any idea where she was. She told him the truth, to which he replied that they should somehow try to get a hold of them. Henry was a parent – though all of his three children had grown and moved out of Dewey – and knew how he would feel if his teenage daughter had run off to a different state without telling them. Notwithstanding the extraordinary circumstances, as an adult and as a parent, Henry felt he had an obligation to notify her parents – somehow – about where she was. Autumn went along verbally, but it was more merely to placate Henry. She hoped that he was just saying what he was supposed to say and would not really follow through with it. In a way, Autumn now thought of her life as having a line running through it. On the one side was April Glass, The Pentagram Murders, Dewey. On the other side stood her parents; her lone bedrock of reality; the way things were supposed to be; the way things once were. If they knew about her whole ordeal and were drawn into it, she was afraid that line would disappear. Not to mention, they might have her committed.

After traveling about a half mile down a long, narrow, winding, dirt road that seemed like it led to nowhere, Henry stopped the truck. Without saying a word, he climbed out of the cab. Perfunctorily, Autumn also exited the cab. Henry still didn't say a word as he started walking, but somehow he sensed that Autumn was not following him. Turning to look back, he saw Autumn, still by the truck, standing almost frozen. She looked like a dog with a sixth sense, afraid to walk into danger that only it knew existed.

As they had driven down the dirt road, Autumn almost casually looked out the window, knowing that they had to be getting close to the house, but not feeling any more tense than when they started their journey. However, the second she stepped foot outside, she was paralyzed by a ghastly déjà vu. Autumn had never been there before – at least not in real life – but she knew those woods. She wished she didn't. But she did.

"Are you ok?" asked Henry.

What kind of a question was that, Autumn wondered. And as soon as the words left his mouth, Henry realized how stupid it sounded. But everything is relative and Autumn knew what Henry meant: was she able to carry on. "Yeah… I'll be all right."

Henry waited patiently and just like a scared dog, Autumn slowly and methodically walked towards him. Once they were practically side by side, Henry continued into the woods. Autumn followed, but kept looking around her as if someone – or something – was going to come out of the shadows and snatch her. And with each step she took, the terror only grew.

Though they had probably only walked twenty yards, the dense, towering trees had already completely swallowed-up where they had parked the truck; had completely obscured the dirt road or any visible path to it. Suddenly, Henry came to a halt. "That's where they found John Junior's body," he said in an understandably, dreary tone, as he pointed towards a general area.

Without saying a word, Autumn scurried over to the vicinity where Henry had pointed before stopping at a small bare patch of dirt. "This is it," she stuttered. "This is where he died." Henry was in cold shock. For he knew that that was the exact spot where the tree stump, which the authorities had surmised because of the amount of blood, was where John Jr. had met his fate. The entire dead stump had been unearthed and shipped off to an F.B.I forensics lab for analysis, leaving only a barren patch of dirt. How could this girl possibly have known that this was exactly where the stump had been; that this was where April's brother had died?

Henry was still speechless, frozen in place, when Autumn ran over to nearby tree and vomited. In some strange way, Henry was glad that she did, because it – at least for the moment – snapped him out of his ghostly trance and back into the practicality of reality. He waddled over to tend to her. "Are you ok?" Again, that absurd question. What the hell did "ok" really mean?

"Yeah, I'll be fine," she answered, still holding her long, straight brown hair away from her face.

Autumn hadn't thrown-up much, but she still needed to rinse her mouth out. But with what? There wasn't exactly a water fountain around – or a store. And despite becoming physically ill, Autumn did not want to leave, even for just a short drive into town. Henry did not want to leave either. Though for different reasons, they were both under the spell of a case that had long ago gone cold. "Wait here. I'll be right back. I'm just going to go to the truck to see if I have any water."

Henry was almost positive that there was no drinking water in the truck, but he went to look anyway. Out of a feeling of obligation, he rummaged through the cab, looking for something that he knew wasn't there. But under the driver's seat he did find a more than a half empty pint bottle of Wild Turkey Whiskey. After thinking about for a few seconds, Henry took it and hurried back to Autumn. "It's not water," he said in his regular deep voice, holding the bottle towards Autumn. "But it's all I can find. You can just use it to rinse your mouth out." Henry paused. "Or we can go back to town and get some water."

Autumn grabbed the bottle. "No, that's ok." The teen then took a big gulp, swished it around in her mouth and spit it out.

As a slight drizzle started to fall from the gray sky, Autumn and Henry Foster looked at each other in eldritch awkwardness. "Well," Henry said slowly. "Are you ready to go see the house?"

Autumn took a deep breath. Then, in a moment of improvisation, she once again took the cap off of the whiskey and put the bottle to her mouth. Only this time, instead of spitting it out, she took a healthy shot. "Now I'm ready."

Without any hesitation, Henry, the 63 year-old retired sheriff, took the bottle from the teen and finished off what was left in one large gulp. "Now I'm ready too."

About thirty yards from where they had been, the fragments of a house started to reveal themselves through the obscuring trees. Autumn could feel her stomach tightening even more. After passing a few more trees, they hit a clearing and there it was – the house that she had seen over and over again in her darkest nightmares. Only, although its structure looked the same, its condition was quite different. All of its windows – on both the first and second floor – were boarded up. Some of the boards and parts of the siding of the house had been spray-painted, obviously by kids. One of the boarded-up windows had the words – in red of course – *The Devil Lives Here* painted on it. The house's wooden façade was faded and in a few place, splintering. The front and side yard was overgrown with weeds and ferns. It was evident that it had been nearly a decade since someone last inhabited the house. Appropriately perhaps, it looked like… a haunted house.

In a trance-like state, Autumn slowly walked up to the front door, which had two, rotting 2x4s nailed in front of it, forming an "X". Henry followed two steps behind. At first, she just stood there, inches away from it, staring at its weathered surface. Though Henry stood in back of her, he could feel the fear exuding from Autumn's body.

Without saying a word, Autumn reached passed the intersecting 2x4s and grabbed the faded, metal doorknob. As soon as she touched it there was a flash. The next thing Autumn knew, she was in a bed, under the covers. As she looked at the bedroom door, the knob turned slowly. But then the door burst open and in the entrance way was a shadowy figure of a man – the face was a blur, but Autumn knew it was a man – and he was holding a large handgun, pointing it right at her. Then, in an instant, Autumn was no longer in the bed, but somewhere else in the room. She could not see her body, but could see everything that was happening, as if looking at a movie. The bed was now occupied by a woman and a man, the latter of which had been awakened by the intruder. But before he could do anything, before he could even alert the woman, the faceless man, who was dressed in black, fired his gun. A simultaneous roar and flash came from the gun's long barrel. As soon as it did, Autumn's view was transported once again; now she was looking straight at the couple, as if she was looking through the eyes of the killer. And he was a killer, because, in slow motion, Autumn could see the back of the man's head exploding from the blast, spraying blood, flesh and brain matter all over the headboard and wall. The woman sprang up in shocked horror. Another shot rang out. This one hit the woman in the center of her body. Then another shot. And another. Autumn watched helplessly as terror webbed through her like a bolt of electricity. But then, without a flash or warning, Autumn found herself standing on an open field, by a rivulet.

Henry Foster watched as Autumn reached passed the intersecting boards and grabbed the doorknob. For the next ten seconds or so, she said nothing; she just stood there frozen, still holding onto the knob. Then, without warning, Autumn simply collapsed. Henry grabbed her and broke her fall before she hit the ground, but she was out cold for almost a minute. Scared, Henry lightly smacked her small face with his oversized hands, wishing that he had some water. "Autumn! Autumn!" he bellowed. In a daze, she opened her eyes. "Are you ok?! What happened?"

It took a couple of seconds for Autumn, who was still in Henry's thick arms, to regain her senses. But once she did, she remembered everything. Releasing herself from Henry's loose embrace, she kneeled on the hard ground and told him what she had seen. Her words wrapped around the old, hardened cop like a constricting snake. "What's happening?" Autumn moaned, before burying her head in her hands and started to cry uncontrollably.

What's happening? It was a question Henry Foster wanted to answer just as badly. The ex-sheriff had thought he had seen it all, heard it all. Even though Dewey was a small town, throughout his years, he had come face to face with conmen who could sell a crucifix to a Jew. And he had always seen them for what they were. But he could tell that this was no con, no parlor trick. But could it be... could it possibly be that April Glass was really coming to this girl from beyond the grave? *Get a hold of yourself, Henry,* he ordered his mind. There had to be – had to be! – a logical explanation. But this girl, who called herself Autumn Grace, knew too much about the case; inside information. And whatever her real story was, if she could help him solve this case – she was right; not finding April, Lilly or their killer had tormented him through the years – Henry was going to use her. But he also had a sense of compassion and seeing Autumn in a ball of tears made him realize that enough was enough... at least for that afternoon. "Come on," he said softly while putting his hand on her shoulder. "Let's go back to my place."

9

Autumn and Henry Foster arrived at his house to an eagerly awaiting Molly and Edith. Before even saying anything, Henry walked right passed his wife and niece and went straight into the kitchen, where he poured himself a quarter glass of Jack Daniels. He then proceeded to gulp it down. "Molly," Edith said in an agitated voice, "why don't you take Mary outside for a little bit."

Mary, only nine years old, knew something was going on, but could not figure out what. And her curiosity was killing her. Though she didn't want to see her great uncle and aunt argue – which she sensed was coming – she wanted to stay to see what all the tension and secrets were about. But grudgingly, she went with her mother out back. Autumn also followed.

As soon as Edith heard the sliding glass door close, she laid into her husband. "Henry Foster, what the hell is going on?! And don't you lie to me! Molly already told me that this has something to do with the Glass Case." Neither Edith nor Henry ever referred to it as The Pentagram Murders.

Henry put the now empty glass on the kitchen counter and turned to his wife, who although was old fashion and could appear meek, also had a strong-willed side to her. About a year after the murders and abductions the overbearing frustration of the unsolved status of the case drove Henry to start drinking heavily. And one day, in an irate, drunken stupor, he hit Edith for the first time ever. Excusing her husband because of the tremendous amount of emotional strain he was under, Edith stayed by his side. But when it happened again a few weeks later, Edith packed her bags and moved in with a friend. Henry might have been a drunk, but he was not about to do to Edith what Molly's husband did to her. Instead, he quit his job as sheriff, stayed home like a hermit and drank himself into oblivion every day. Some nights, he would put his loaded revolver to his head, but as drunk as he was, never pulled the trigger.

After not having any contact with her husband for over three weeks, Edith went back to the house early one afternoon to find Henry, passed out on the living room floor, with an empty bottle of whiskey still in his hand. At first, the way he was sprawled out, Edith feared the worse: that her husband had drank himself to death. But Edith was able to revive him and when he came to, Henry clutched his wife and cried unabashedly in her arms, saying how sorry he was and how much he loved her. After guiding him upstairs and making him take a long, cold shower, Edith made her one and only love some coffee and something to eat. Edith – who in reality missed Henry as much as he had missed her – then gave her husband an ultimatum: she would come back home, but if he ever hit her again, she would leave and never come back. She also wanted him to get help with his drinking. For a while, Henry cut down his drinking considerably on his own. But inevitably, the ex-sheriff could not help personally re-examining the Glass case and because of it, started drinking more. And he never stopped. But although they had their shares of arguments – some even heated – he never raised his hands to Edith again.

Now, Henry Foster was looking at his wife, standing there in the kitchen seething with both aggravation and disappointment. He preferred not to talk to her about what

Autumn had told him. But Henry loved Edith and appreciated – in a way, even felt guilty for – her standing by his side all these years. "What did she tell you?" he asked, referring to Molly.

"Not much. Mary was always around wanting to know what was going on, so we couldn't talk much. She just said that this girl knows something about the case, in particular, April Glass. Who is she Henry? What does she know?"

As much as Henry didn't want to lie to his wife, he couldn't really tell her the whole truth. It would just sound too crazy. "I'm not really sure yet."

"There's something you're not telling me. There's something neither of you are telling me." Edith paused to take a deep breath. "You went to the old Glass house, didn't you? That's where you took her."

"Yes."

Edith had been mad at Henry for not telling her what was going on. But suddenly, she asked herself a question: what if this girl really did know something about the case? "Do you think she really knows something?" (Molly hadn't told Edith that the reason Autumn knew about the case was because of dreams.)

Henry stood silently for a second, pondering the question. "I think she does," he replied matter-of-factly. "I don't think she's like the others – just some crackpot with an obsession about the case. I think she really might know something."

"But what? How old is she?"

Henry put his hand on his wife's shoulder. "Listen Edith, you're gonna have to trust me on this one. I can't really get into everything."

"Well if she really knows something than shouldn't you notify Don?" Don Harrelson was the current sheriff of Dewey. "We talked about this before – you're a civilian now, Henry."

Henry and Edith went around in a circle a few more times before Henry was able to, if not placate his wife, at least keep her at bay for the moment. Edith was still extremely leery of this girl Autumn and worried about what her obsessed husband was going to put himself through. But she had stated her case and objections; what more could she do? In the end, Henry was going to do what he was going to do.

As Edith and Henry were having their talk in the kitchen, Autumn and Molly were out back with Mary. And because Mary was there, Molly didn't ask any question about Autumn and her uncle's trip and Autumn did not volunteer any information. Instead, they both tried to put up a façade of normalcy.

After Molly, Mary and Autumn went back into the house, Edith tried to persuade them into staying for dinner, saying that it would be no problem to "whip something up". But it was already 3:00pm and Molly reminded her aunt that she had to be at work at the motel at six. "Don't worry, it won't take that long for me to fix something," Edith persisted. But Molly again turned down her generous offer.

Henry asked Autumn if she would stay; what else did she have to do anyway. Autumn thanked him – and Edith – but explained that she needed to get back to the motel, where all her stuff was. "Well I'll call the motel for you later. We still have some things we have to talk about," he said in a matter-of-fact tone. Autumn acknowledged with a simple nod of her head.

Though Molly and Autumn left, Molly asked if Mary could stay the night. Things were getting strange, to say the least, and Molly, understandably was spooked about this whole April Glass matter. Beth, Mary's regular babysitter, had always been responsible and Molly didn't think anything was really going to happen. What could happen; what did Mary have to do with anything? But Molly just felt more comfortable having Mary stay with her aunt and uncle. Besides, Mary, who was always thoroughly spoiled by Edith and Henry, was more than happy to stay.

Before going back to the motel, Autumn and Molly went to Steve's, a local burger joint. Although they sat in a booth, some guy who knew Molly came by and asked who her friend was. Molly introduced Autumn as her cousin and after a few words, the curious patron left – but not before looking Autumn over.

Molly wanted to know how Autumn could know so much about her uncle; the things she had said in the backyard. She also wanted to know about the short trip Autumn and her uncle had taken. But her curiosity was trumped only by her trepidation. Molly was sure that she would eventually ask Autumn those questions. But for the time being, she had heard enough about April Glass and the Pentagram Murders. So over their meal, she mundanely asked Autumn about Chandler and Arizona. For her part, Autumn was equally content to talk about something besides April Glass for a change.

At the end of the meal, Molly tried to pay the bill, but Autumn wouldn't let her. Autumn also took the opportunity to once again thank Molly for taking care of her.

By 6:00pm, Molly was back to tending the motel office and Autumn was back in her room. Not knowing what else to do, Autumn plopped herself on the bed and flipped on the TV. Somehow, Autumn had learned to keep herself from thinking she was going insane, from being mentally obliterated by her situation. But obvious, she could not completely stave off the thoughts of April Glass; of what happened in *that* house almost eight years ago; of what she was doing in Dewey; and if things would ever return to "normal" again.

Autumn figured that she would eventually, maybe even later that night, meet back with Henry Foster and yes, even return to that godforsaken house. But for the moment, all she wanted to do was zone-out in front of the television. She needed at least a partial reprieve from April Glass.

Sometimes you can see evil. Sometimes you can even smell it. But more often than not, it is just a feeling. And that feeling of evil permeated through the darkened night. Its unseen tentacles reached down from every branch; rose up from every grain of dirt and blade of grass; whipped through every passing wind; rained down from the black sky. It overwhelmed Autumn, who had her back to the woods and was facing the front of the Glass' house. But she was not alone. Right along side of her, holding her trembling hand was little April Glass. Though Autumn knew April was there, for a while, she just stared straight ahead, across the clearing to the house. Gone were the boards over its windows; the vandalism on its siding; the planks over its front door. And a lone, tired lamp hung by the side of the door, illuminating a small circle around the entranceway. By the side of the house was the faint image of a swing set, blowing helplessly in the wind.

Peeling her eye off the house, Autumn looked down at April, who was dressed in her usual, blood-stained nightgown. Autumn wanted to speak; wanted to ask the girl where she was buried. But although Autumn could feel her mouth open, no words came out. However, April turned her head and looked straight into Autumn's eyes. Her face wore such sorrow, such torment. It was the face of a soul that knew no rest.

Without saying a word, April raised her small hand and pointed towards a dark and narrow, dirt road that led to the house. Suddenly, the faint image of a figure appeared, walking down the road, out of the darkness towards the house. Autumn could feel her heart beating faster, pulsating throughout her entire body. As the figure crept closer to the house, she could see it was that of a man. From the side, Autumn could not see his face; but perhaps even if she was standing in front of him it would have been too dark. Almost casually – he never bothered to look around or stop – he walked up to a large side window on the first floor.

Autumn could feel April squeezing her hand tighter. She took her eyes off the intruder to comfort the little girl. But as Autumn looked down, she was stunned to see, not April Glass, but another young girl. She was wearing long pajamas and looked to be about the same age as April, maybe a little younger. Her pale face, which was un-obscured by her short, bang-less hair, was stricken with terror. Suddenly, her lips began to move. "Why?"

In utter panic, Autumn jumped-up in bed. Her heart was racing and sweat covered every inch of her body. And that haunting word – "Why" – still rang through her head. Trying to catch her breath, Autumn looked around the room, only to find out that she was not in the motel. It was a bedroom, but not one that she had ever before been in or seen. Upon further inspection, Autumn quickly noticed there was another bed to her left. And there was a girl sleeping in it. Suddenly, the tell-tale sound of a gunshot roared through the air. No more than a second later came another one. The girl in the other bed sprung up from her slumber. Autumn realized that it was not the same girl as she had just seen by the woods, but she looked familiar. "What was that?!" The girl asked in a quivering voice. "April, I'm scared." It was Lilly. It was Lilly Flowers! And she thought that Autumn was April Glass.

Without warning the bedroom transmuted into what could only be a cellar. But still by Autumn's side was Lilly Flowers. Only now she had duct tape bound around her ankles and wrists, as well as a strip across her mouth. But nothing was covering her eyes and the unadulterated terror that lied within them.

Autumn lunged up in bed. Looking around, she instantly found the familiar surroundings of her motel room. But there was still that dam ringing. Finally, Autumn realized that it was the telephone and picked-up the receiver. "Hello."

"I told you there's no escape," answered a slow, sinister voice.

"Who is this," Autumn cried into the phone.

"This is The Demon."

Covered in a thick layer of cold sweat, Autumn was awaken by the sound of someone pounding on the door to her room. Breaking into tears, the teen sat there on the bed as the banging continued. "Autumn, are you in there?! Are you ok?!" It was Molly.

Her entire body shaking, Autumn made her way to the door and opened it. She then fell into Molly arms, bawling uncontrollably. "Oh my God, are you all right! What happened?"

Autumn just continued to cry. "Did you have another nightmare?" Molly could feel Autumn shaking her head in acknowledgement. "It's ok honey," she said as she closed the door and then sat Autumn down on the foot of the bed. "I was so worried about you. I tried calling you, but no one answered, so I came over here and started banging on your door. I was just ready to call my uncle before you finally opened it."

Autumn wiped some of the tears from her face. "I'm sorry," she then said in a nasally voice.

"Oh honey, don't be sorry."

"It was just so horrible." Autumn then told Molly about her nightmare.

Everyone has had nightmares. Molly was no exception. But she knew that these were not mere bad dreams. Molly now knew they were something much, much more and so Autumn's most recent tale of horror made the 32 year-old mother shiver with fear.

"What were you calling me for?" Molly, who was still pondering Autumn's harrowing account, didn't answer. "Molly."

"Oh… I'm sorry… what?"

"You said you were trying to get a hold of me."

Autumn was expecting Molly to say that her uncle had called, or that she was just checking up, but that was not the case. "Oh yeah. Your friend Kelly called. She was extremely upset when I told her you were still here. She said that you were supposed to have flown back to Phoenix today. I tried patching her through to your room, but…"

"Oh my God! Kelly! What time is it?" Autumn answered her own question by looking at the clock. It was already 8:25pm!

After assuring Molly that she would be ok, Molly left and Autumn called Kelly with the calling card. No one answered and Autumn didn't leave a message. However, not more than ten minutes later, the phone in the room rang. Somewhat cautiously, Autumn picked up the receiver. "Hello."

"Autumn, oh my God, what are you doing?!" It was Kelly and she was in a frenzy. "I was waiting at the airport for you! What happened?!"

"Kell, I'm so sorry. I... I... know I should have called, but..."

"Why didn't you get on the flight?"

Autumn swallowed a lump in her throat. "I just have to stay here a little longer."

"What are you talikn' about?"

Without going into every detail, Autumn explained about Molly, Henry Foster and needing to find out what happened to April Glass. Her explanation nearly brought Kelly to tears. Kelly who had been drifting away from the possibility that all this ghost business was real, was afraid that Autumn was actually loosing her mind. And worse, she now seemed to have found enablers in this hotel clerk and retired sheriff.

Autumn tried to assure Kelly that she was ok (whatever that meant); that "this" would soon be over – which was more wishful thinking than anything else – and she would be back home. Kelly asked what the latter meant and reminded Autumn that she *had to* be back home before her parents. Autumn then revamped her statement and assured Kelly that she would be; that she would change her tickets back to the original return date. After much cajoling, Autumn was finally able to end the call. But Kelly was still distressed and worried... and so was Autumn. By pushing Kelly away, Autumn felt that she was pushing away the life preserver to her "old" life. Every day, every hour, it seemed like Chandler, Arizona and her life before April Glass was drifting farther and farther away. And that terrified Autumn. But she was now convinced that the only way to fully return to her old life was to solve the mystery of April Glass and quite possibly the entire Pentagram Murders. And though Kelly had always been there for Autumn, through thick and thin, this was a journey that she had to travel without her.

In a whirlpool of emotions – fear, anguish, anger – Autumn sat on the bed and started crying again (she had cried more over the past three days than the entire rest of her life combined). But only ten minutes after hanging up the phone with Kelly, there was s knock on the door. Figuring it was Molly, Autumn didn't even look to see who it was before opening the door. Standing in the entranceway was Henry Foster. Concerned about Autumn, as soon as Molly returned to the office she called her uncle, who came right over. Henry was there to take the girl from Arizona back to his place for the night. It was for two reasons: so she wouldn't be alone; and also so they could further discuss the case. At first Autumn tried to turn down Henry's offer, saying that she was "ok" (there was that word again). In truth, she felt uncomfortable and even embarrassed about staying with this man and his wife, both of whom she had just met – especially under the circumstances. But she then realized that she was way past the point of worrying about feeling uncomfortable or embarrassed. Besides, Henry wasn't going to take a simple no for an answer. So Autumn grabbed her entire suitcase – she had never unpacked – and left with him.

On the way out, Henry went into the office to let Molly know that he was taking Autumn. Molly advised her uncle that he had to get in contact with Autumn's parents and tell them what was going on (though she realized how crazy the truth was going to sound). Henry said that he would, but was lying. For selfish reasons, Henry, going back on his initial instincts, had no intention of tracking down Autumn's parents. He knew that if her parents found out what was going on, they would be on the next plane to Oregon to take their daughter home. And Henry could not afford that. He had too much invested in the Glass case – basically his whole life – to let what could be a chance of finding out what really happened slip away. And though like Autumn, Henry wanted to find April Glass and Lilly Flowers, he wanted even more to find their abductor – and most likely also their killer. Not only to finally make him pay for what he did, but also because no one in law enforcement, himself included, believed that the Glass family and Lilly were this psycho's only victims. Henry's greatest fear had always been that this guy –it was always assumed it was a man – was still out there, killing and/or abducting other children. Some one doesn't simply wake up one morning from a life of normalcy and say "I think I'll go kill a family and steal their child today." Nor does someone who kills three people and kidnaps two girls simply stop after that and never kill or kidnap again. The only way a monster like that was going to stop was either die or be caught. And though Autumn's entire story seemed unbelievable, especially to a conservative like Henry Foster, she knew too much about the case to simply be dismissed as a whacko or con-artist. Was she really going to be able to lead Henry to April's and Lilly's bodies? Could she really help Henry finally, after all these years, track down the perpetrator? Perhaps it was a stretch. But Henry could not afford not to find out. And if Autumn went back to Arizona with her parents, perhaps he would never find out what she could have told him, where she could have lead him. That was a chance he could not take.

Henry could tell that Autumn was extremely upset. On the ride back to Henry's, she told him about her latest dream.

When they arrived at Henry's house, Edith fixed Autumn a small meal. After Autumn was finished eating, Henry could tell how tired she was and although he had hoped to discuss the case with her that night, figured it could wait until the next day. Without asking about April Glass or the Pentagram Murders, Edith showed the weary teenager to the guestroom. It had been a long day.

10

Autumn slowly rose from the bed, stretched her arms and yawned. The clock in the dresser read 10:00 am. She had slept well, which meant that there were no nightmares. And she thanked God for that. But her real-life nightmare was not over yet. It would be Autumn's third full day in Dewey. Though she had found an unlikely friend in Molly and Henry and Edith had taken her in, Autumn hoped that she would not have too many more days left in the small, Oregon town. She wanted nothing more than for the whole business of April Glass to come to some kind of closure. And she wanted that closure to come as soon as possible; not only for the sake of her sanity, but Autumn was also very cognizant of the fact that her parents would be returning home in eight days.

Like the morning before, Autumn was greeted by the tantalizing smell of bacon and sausage, rising from downstairs. After a few more stretches and yawns, she followed the alluring aroma to the kitchen. Henry and Mary were already sitting at the kitchen table, eating. In fact it looked like they were both about done. "I'm sorry dear," said Edith, who was standing by the stove. "We were going to wait for you, but I didn't want to wake you."

"Oh no, it's ok. Really. I should have woken-up earlier."

"Good Morning Autumn," Mary said with a bright smile.

"Hi Mary."

Without any talk of April Glass or the Pentagram Murders, Autumn sat down for a home-cooked, country breakfast. It was even bigger than the one that Molly had made. There was bacon, sausage, eggs, homemade hash browns and toast. "Boy, you guys sure do know how to cook around here," Autumn commented. "Do you guys eat like this every morning?"

Edith laughed as she dished some links of sausage onto Autumn's plate. "Well we certainly can eat here in Dewey. But if we ate like this every morning we'd all be three hundred pounds." Edith didn't say it, but Autumn assumed that the extra food was on the account of her and Mary.

Autumn took a bite of the ham and cheese omelet that Edith had just whipped up for her. "Mmmmm. This just might be the best omelet I've ever had Mrs. Foster."

"Well I'm glad you like it dear."

Although Henry and Edith had already eaten – though Henry continued to pick – they stayed at the table with Autumn. It was the hospitable thing to do. Mary also stayed at the table. It was evident that the nine year-old had become fond of Autumn – and Autumn had grown fond of her. Mary asked her about Arizona and Autumn was more than happy to discuss something besides April Glass.

After breakfast Autumn tried to help Edith clean-up, but Edith wouldn't let her. "You're a guest," she said, referring to some unwritten rule of hospitality. So Autumn went upstairs and took a shower. After that, she went back downstairs to talk to Henry Foster, who had become her de facto guide into the macabre world of the Pentagram Murders.

Autumn found Henry out in the backyard, having a second – or maybe third – cup of coffee, by the porch railing. Without saying anything, she took up a place beside him. It was a beautiful day. The sun was shining across a clear, azure sky. It was warm, but not hot and any humidity seemed broken by the rain of the last two days. Standing alongside Mr. Foster, Autumn leaned her forearms on the white, wood railing of the back porch and gazed out at the ring of majestic mountains. They looked so peaceful. The entire landscape looked so peaceful. But Autumn knew better.

Autumn assumed that Henry would say something as soon as she approached, but he seemed almost in a trance, staring out into wilderness. Autumn didn't know if it was part of his daily routine or if he was just consumed with thoughts of April Glass and the Pentagram Murders. If it was the latter, she certainly could not blame him. Henry took a sip of his still smoldering coffee as he continued to look straight ahead. Autumn decided to break the silence. "Mr. Foster," she said in a meek voice, "I want to apologize for yesterday."

Henry looked down at her with a look of puzzlement. "What for?"

"For all that stuff I said to you yesterday; about knowing that this case has ruined your life and how I know you still spend time in your basement going over boxes of records." Autumn paused as she looked towards the ground. "I don't know where I got all that stuff from. I really don't. I just…"

Henry put his over-sized hand on Autumn's shoulder. "It's ok Autumn, really. Don't worry about that."

With that, the two went back to staring at the landscape. Then, after almost a minute, Autumn again broke the silence. "So I guess we'll be going back to the Glass house today, huh?"

"Actually, I would first like you to look over some papers I keep in the basement. Of course, all the official files are at the police station, but I kept notebooks of personal notes and newspaper clippings." Henry paused. "I also made copies of some of the official records – photographs and police reports – before I left," he said in a low voice, as if someone else was listening. "Of course they don't know about that. So that'll just be our little secret."

"Sure," Autumn replied without hesitation.

Before their eerie conversation could continue, the sliding glass door to the house slid open. It was Molly. She said hello to Autumn and her uncle and then all three of them went back into the house. There, everyone conjured in the living room and conversed mundanely. "I don't know what you and my uncle have planned, but I was going to take Mary to the flea market. They have it every Saturday." That was the first time Autumn realized it was Saturday. "If you wanted to come…"

"Oh, please Autumn," Mary pleaded. "You'll love it. They've got all kinds of cool stuff there."

Autumn smiled at her new little friend. "I would love to Mary, but I think me and your uncle have some things to take care of."

"That's ok," said Henry. "Why don't you go along with them. It'll give me some time to look through some things anyway. The when you get back, I'll have everything ready."

"We won't be more than two hours," Molly added.

Molly had been hoping to get her uncle by himself, but the opportunity never arose. So after getting into the car, Molly said that she had forgotten her keys in the house. But it was just a ploy. She ran back into the house and finally cornered her uncle. The purpose was to make sure he had contacted Autumn's parents. Henry said that Autumn had told him what ship they were on and he called the cruise line, but could not actually get in touch with them. However, he left a message for them to call him. Henry didn't like lying to his niece – she was more like a daughter to him – but felt he had to.

Molly never asked Autumn if she told Henry what ship her parents were on. There was no reason. Molly simply took her uncle at his word, just as she had always done. To her knowledge, he had never lied to her before.

The flea market was on the same lot as Dewey's only high school. Like any flea market, there were rows of booths and tables with people selling different odds and ends. There were also a few food vendors. When Autumn, Mary and Molly arrived, the grounds were already bustling with locals – though it was not too crowded. Everything seemed civilized. If someone did happen to bump into someone else the person would say "I'm sorry" and the other one would reply "no problem". There were a few men, who all seemed to be dragged there by their wives, but it was mostly women. However, there were also quite a few kids; some running around freely, some attached to their mothers.

Autumn was glad that she had gone to the market with Molly and Mary. Though she wanted to solve the mystery of April Glass as quickly as possible, she needed some time away – a distraction – from the nightmare that had become her life.

Under the bright, blue sky, the girls sauntered through the spread-out flea market. Sometimes, when Mary was out of earshot looking at trinkets on one of the tables, Molly would whisper gossip to Autumn. "You see that woman over there. That's Judith Hudson, a teacher at the elementary school. Last year, two kids caught her having sex with the gym teacher. They were doing it one night in her car, right in the school parking lot."

"You're kidding," Autumn replied with a smile.

"No. One of the kids went home and told his parents. Soon everyone in the town found out and there was a big uproar."

Autumn laughed. "What happened?"

"Both she and the gym teacher – Marc Poller – were suspended from school for two weeks. But that's not the worst of it. Marc's wife wound up divorcing him over it."

"Oh my God."

"Yeah," Molly replied before her and Autumn started giggling like two mischievous schoolgirls.

Mary would come back and Molly and Autumn would return to child-safe conversation. But then, once Mary was again out of earshot, Molly would feed her new friend with juicy stories about other locals. It was definitely the most relaxed Autumn had been since she boarded that plane to Dewey. Hell, she was actually enjoying herself. And Molly, who with her job and being a single parent didn't have much time for friends, enjoyed Autumn's company.

At one point Autumn, who still had plenty of money left, bought Mary an ice cream cone. It was hard to tell who was getting more enjoyment out of it; Mary, licking the cone with a big smile as she walked around or Autumn, seeing how much pleasure Mary got out of it.

After taking another look at Mary lapping her now melting cone, Autumn lifted her head right before she nearly walked right into someone. Autumn stopped cold in her tracks. Standing face to face with her was the young man who had given her a ride to the motel that first night. Neatly groomed, as he was that night, he smiled. "Oh hey, it's you," he said with a smile.

Autumn just stood there frozen, trying to hide her fear. Noticing that Autumn wasn't responding, Molly jumped in. "Hello Ritchie," she said in a overtly dry tone.

"Hello Molly," he nonchalantly replied.

"Do you two know each other?"

"I gave her a ride to your motel the other night."

Molly looked at Autumn, who was still standing there silent. Molly could tell that something was not right; then she remembered how upset and shaken Autumn had been when she walked into the motel office that first night. At first Molly thought it was because she was running from an abusive boyfriend or family member. Then, once she learned of Autumn's situation, she figured that it was something to do with April Glass. But now, Molly surmised that it had something to do with Ritchie. "Did he do something to you?" Molly asked in a heated tone, right in front of him.

"No," Autumn unconvincingly replied. "It's ok. It's nothing."

"You see," Ritchie added with a smirk.

"If you did something to her…"

Ritchie inched his shaven face closer to Molly. "What? You'll call your uncle? He's not the sheriff anymore, remember."

"Mommy," Mary whined in a scared voice as she tugged on Molly's arm. "What's going on?"

In the heat of the moment, Molly forgot that Mary was right by her side. Molly was about to tell her to wait by one of tables, that she would be right there, but before she could, Ritchie kneeled down so that he was face-to-face with Mary. "Hello Mary," he said in a slow, devious voice.

As merry and gracious as Molly could be, she became a completely different person when she felt that Mary was threatened. Seeing Ritchie kneeling in front of her with his cunning little smile made her snap. "You get away from her," Molly yelled, right before pushing Ritchie over.

Instantly Ritchie sprang up. "What the hell's wrong with you?!"

"Don't you touch her!" Autumn hollered, afraid that he was going to strike Molly.

Just as Autumn's words left her mouth, a husky, thirty-something year-old man burst on the scene. "What the hell's going on here?!" He barked at Ritchie.

As he did, another, younger man also ran over. "Are you all right Molly? What did this asshole do to you?"

"Hey fuck you," Ritchie snapped back.

"Mommy!"

The first, older, more muscular man grabbed Ritchie by the shirt. It was official: it had become a full fledged scene. As the melee now became the focal point of the small-town flea market, Autumn felt as if a spotlight was shining on her and she did not know what to do. Then, through the growing crowd of people, Autumn thought she saw something – April Glass. The entire clamor surrounding her suddenly fell silent as she tried to get a better point of view. Through the slim, empty spaces between spectators, Autumn followed the little girl with her eyes. Fractions of a second felt like minutes. Then finally, in a clear line of sight, about ten yards away, the blonde, long-haired girl stopped and turned to look right at Autumn. It *was* April Glass! She was wearing normal clothes, not her usual blood-stained nightgown and she looked as real as anyone else at the market. Someone passed in front of Autumn's line of sight for just a second, but as soon as he was gone, so was April Glass. Oblivious to the fracas still going on right beside her, Autumn frantically scanned the area. In less than a second, she found April, now walking father away. But as soon as Autumn found her, she was again obscured by bodies and tables of merchandise. Not saying a word, Autumn gave chase.

No more than twelve seconds had passed from the time Autumn first spotted April Glass to when she ran after her. So when she jolted off, Molly naturally thought it was because of Ritchie and the tensing commotion. "Autumn, where are you going?!" Autumn didn't answer. In fact she didn't even hear Molly – or Ritchie and the two men arguing. She was too consumed with finding April Glass. Pushing her way through the crowd, not paying any mind to the people staring, and even talking to her, Autumn ran over to the area where she had last seen April Glass. Frantically, she looked behind people, down isles of vendors, even under tables. But April was nowhere to be found.

The first man who had come to Molly and Autumn's aide was still grabbing onto Ritchie's shirt, looking like he was about to deck him. "It's all right. It's ok," Molly pleaded. Things had gotten out of hand and she had Mary with her. She also naturally wanted to track down Autumn, who was now out of sight. Finally, at Molly's pleading, things started to cool down. The two men were still warning Ritchie, but Molly felt she could now leave the scene. Grabbing on to Mary, she went to find Autumn. She found her by a group of several people who were all standing around staring at the teenage stranger. "Autumn, are you ok?" Autumn looked dazed. "Are you all right?" Molly asked again.

Giving up on her search for April Glass, Autumn responded. "Yeah... Yeah, I'm ok."

"Let's get outta here."

With the burning eyes of spectators still on them, Molly, Autumn and Mary scurried through the flea market back to the car. On the way, several different people that knew Molly asked if she was ok. She would reply with a quick "yes" and keep on moving. Once in the car, the pressure lifted somewhat, but the carefree atmosphere that they enjoyed only twelve minutes earlier was long gone.

On the ride back to her uncle's, Molly filled Autumn in on Ritchie Clarke – though she tried to be careful with her words, because Mary was in the car. Despite his clean-cut appearance, Ritchie, who at 24 was seven years younger than Molly, was known all around town as a troublemaker. He had been arrested several times – for possession of cocaine; disorderly conduct; and even for stealing a car – and had spent some time in jail. However, Molly insisted that Autumn shouldn't worry about him. "He tries to come off as all tough and scary, but he's actually pretty harmless – that is to everyone but himself. Besides, he knows that some of the guys around town – like the two that came over to us – are just waiting for a reason to kick his butt." Molly paused. "Ritchie is really just a coward." Molly didn't press Autumn about what really happened the night he drove her to the motel. And Autumn never volunteered.

Autumn also didn't tell Molly about seeing April Glass.

Molly dropped Autumn off at her uncle's. But before leaving, she made Autumn a generous offer. "Since I don't work on the weekends, if you want, I can pick you up and you can spend the night with me and Mary."

"Oh please Autumn," Mary added from the backseat.

"My aunt and uncle are real nice people, but, well you know… you just might feel more comfortable with us. And I mean we'd love to have you."

Autumn looked at Molly and smiled. Where would she be without her, Autumn wondered. "Thank you. That sounds great."

"All right, I'll just call later to see how things are doing."

"See you later," little Mary yelled out the window as they drove away.

Edith, who opened the front door, told Autumn that Henry was in the basement, waiting for her. Edith then showed her the way. Autumn walked apprehensively down the long, narrow staircase, wondering what awaited her at the bottom. The first thing she noticed was that there were no windows; the cellar was completely underground. The contrast between the dimly lit basement and the bright, sunny day from which Autumn had just come from was overwhelming.

Henry surely heard Autumn coming – or at least someone coming – from the creak that every stair made. But he said nothing. Alone in his thoughts, the hefty ex-sheriff sat by a desk with his back to the staircase. As Autumn walked over she noticed that he was holding a picture in his hands. "She was only nine years old," he finally spoke. "The same age as April." Standing right over Henry's shoulder, Autumn leaned in to get a better look at the photo: a portrait of a smiling young girl with dimples and long brown hair.

Henry swiveled around in his chair so he was now face-to-face with Autumn. "By all accounts Lilly was April's only friend." As he spoke, Autumn could now smell the telltale odor of alcohol on his hot breath. She then noticed three opened cans of Old Milwaukee on the cluttered desk. "The entire family – the Glasses – were very private people. I mean, Dewey being a small town and the Glasses living here their whole life, people knew who they were. But they always kept to themselves. In fact, although John Jr. went to school in town, April was home-schooled. But Peggy Glass and Lilly's mother, Gillian, were friends since they were little and stayed close. "

"It must have been so hard on Lilly's parents."

Henry let out a deep sigh as he looked towards the ground. "It's something that no parent should ever have to go through," he replied in a slow, solemn voice. Then he paused for a few seconds before continuing. "Two years after Lilly was born, Gillian gave birth to a baby boy. The doctor said he was healthy, but after only six months, he started getting really sick. It turned out he had Leukemia. You believe that," Henry said shaking his head, as the look of pain and grief drained down his face. "Anyway, the doctors tried everything – drugs, chemotherapy – but it spread too fast. At only sixteen months old, he finally died."

"That's horrible," Autumn said in a shaky voice as she fought back tears.

"Yeah. And Gillian never got pregnant again so Lilly was basically an only child. Then after she disappeared... well, as any parents would, despite what happened at that house, Gillian and Steve – that was Lilly's father's name – held out hope that she would be found alive. But after six months went by I think they finally realized the inevitable. One afternoon, Steve took a walk in the woods and never returned. He shot himself in the head with a forty-five." Autumn put her hand to her face and let out a loud gasp. "After that," Henry continued in a grave voice, "Gillian just completely shut down. She wouldn't eat or talk... or do anything. She would just sit there, crying. All day, all night. Just crying. Gillian's brother took her to Redmond where he and his family lived. But Gillian still refused to eat or bathe. He said she would just sit there in the corner. So he had no choice... he had her committed. Oregon State Hospital, up in Salem. I believe that's where she still is today."

Suddenly, Autumn felt a sense of guilt. She had wanted to find the bodies of April Glass and Lilly Flowers – and maybe even their killer – but mostly for her own self-interest; she believed that it would stop the nightmares, the apparitions of April and she could return to a "normal" life. But now the sixteen year-old thought long and hard about Lilly's mother and the insurmountable pain, anger and grief she must have endured. And whether Gillian Flowers was cognizant of reality or not, Autumn realized that she owed it to her to find out exactly what happened to her daughter. At that moment, Autumn told herself that no matter what, she would give Gillian Glass the closure that had eluded her for nearly ten years.

"Autumn, would you be so kind as to get me another beer," Henry asked in his usual husky voice as he pointed to a refrigerator not far away.

"Sure."

After bringing Henry a cold can of Old Milwaukee, Autumn grabbed a nearby chair and sat next to him. It was time to get to business. Henry started by showing Autumn several photocopies of different men's pictures. "Do any of these men look familiar to you?"

Autumn looked long and hard even though in all of her nightmares, she had never seen the killer's – or any man's – face. "No," she answered disappointingly to each picture. "So you guys did have suspects?"

Henry placed the last picture on the cluttered desk. "We actually had quite a few suspects, but none of them panned out. Some were cleared after they volunteered for and passed a lie detector test. Others had iron-clad alibis." With a visible look of frustration on his face, the old sheriff cracked-open his new beer and took a chug.

Autumn looked at one of the photos, now on the desk, and gently glided her fingers along it. "What made you consider them suspects?" she asked in a serene voice.

"We looked at everybody: anyone with any kind of sex crime on their rap sheet that lived in the area; anyone that might have done work at the Glass' house at one time or another; John Glass' co-workers; anyone that might have been passing through Dewey at the time of the murders. Then, by process of elimination – most people completely cooperated with the investigation – we ruled each person out. Some individuals, for one reason or another, it took longer to rule out." Henry paused as if he wanted to add another sentence, but didn't.

"But you still have your suspicions about some of suspects?" It was a statement as much as it was a question.

Henry took another chug of his beer. "There are a few that we couldn't rule out one hundred percent. But we couldn't prove anything either... and believe me, we tried – the local and state police force, the FBI. And like I said, early on, there were a lot of suspects." Henry paused again as he stared straight ahead at the blank wall of the basement. "Even Molly's ex-husband was considered a suspect at one time?"

A chill ran down Autumn's spine as she recalled the harrowing tale of abuse Molly had told her. "Molly told me what happened," she said in a somber voice, "about him hitting her; about the miscarriage; and how he kidnapped her at gunpoint."

Henry looked at Autumn. "She told you all that?" He was surprised.

"Yeah." Autumn's words were followed by an eerie silence. "Do you really think he could've done it?"

"Well he tried to kill a police officer and threatened to kill Molly's friend and children," he answered without hesitation. Then, in a more disappointed tone, Henry countered, "but he was cleared." Henry didn't say why he was ruled out as a suspect and Autumn didn't ask.

"What do you know about Ritchie Clarke?" Autumn asked.

Henry looked at Autumn with puzzlement. "What about Ritchie? How do you know him?"

Autumn paused before answering. "Well, the first evening I arrived in Dewey," she said, avoiding eye contact with Henry, "I got off my train and I figured that I would take a cab to the motel, but there weren't any there. And the only payphone there wasn't working, so I started walking. I wasn't even sure if I was walking in the same direction, but after about five minutes, this car pulled up next to me. It was Ritchie. Of course, I had no idea who he was at the time, but he asked if I needed a ride and he seemed clean-cut and I was afraid of getting lost in the dark. So I took him up on his offer." Glancing at Henry, Autumn could see that his face was turning red. "Anyway, he took me to the motel, but when I tried to get out he..."

"That son-of-a-bitch!" He shouted as he rose from his seat.

"No. It's all right. He didn't really do anything. He just grabbed my arm and tried to offer me money to… well…"

"I'll break that little bastard's neck!"

"No, it's ok. I told him that he had the wrong idea and he finally let me go. He didn't hurt me." Henry slowly sat back down, but still looked like he was ready to find Ritchie and squash him like a bug. "Anyway, when we were at the flea market today, we ran into him." Autumn didn't get into the whole melee that happened, figuring there was no point. "And right after we ran into him, I could've swore I saw April Glass."

"What? Where?" Henry asked excitedly.

"I mean not actually her, but her…" Autumn was going to say ghost, but realized how crazy it would sound (as if it was stranger than anything else she had told Henry). "I mean… well… I don't know… well, like… like a vision or something," she finally spit out, realizing there was no *sane* way of saying it. "She was just walking through the flea market. I don't know… I guess what I'm trying to say is that do you think that Ritchie could have done… well, you know."

Henry leaned back in his chair, absorbing what Autumn had just said. After rubbing his thick, double chin, he answered. "I don't know. I mean Ritchie's a bad apple, no doubt about it. He's been in trouble with the law, but nothing violent. And he would have been only fourteen or something."

After asking Autumn to get him another beer, Henry asked about her dreams. He was hoping that she had previously left something out – or that he had missed something – that could help at least point a finger in the right direction. As Autumn once again narrated her nightmares, Henry listened intently to every detail, trying to decipher its meaning. Every so often he would nod, scratch his head or take a gulp of beer. He didn't interrupt Autumn; that is until she started explaining the open field by a church, which appeared briefly in several of her dreams. Autumn had told Henry about it the previous afternoon, but at the time it was overshadowed by all the other, more spellbinding details. But now Henry realized that Autumn's depiction of the field was out of place. He explained to her that there was no place like the one she was describing – an open field by a church and ravine – in or around Dewey.

Autumn also asked Henry questions about the case. For one, she wanted to know why the police had been so certain that there was only one killer. Henry explained that though the possibility there was a getaway driver or that someone else helped the killer at a later time was never completely ruled out, all the forensic evidence pointed to one killer.

Autumn and Henry had been down in the basement for nearly three hours. Autumn had gone over all of her dreams – in great detail. Henry told Autumn about inside aspects of the case. The two bounced questions off of each other. But in the end they had gotten nowhere; they were no closer to finding April or Lilly's body; no closer to finding out the identity of the killer. No new pieces had been added to the puzzle.

"Well, maybe we should go upstairs," Henry suggested in a frustrated voice. "I think we've been down here for a while." Henry could have stayed in the basement all night – some nights, he did – but thought that Autumn probably needed a break. Besides, they weren't getting anywhere anyway.

Autumn shook her head. "I guess," she said in an equally frustrated voice. She was convinced that her nightmares held a trove of clues but, even with the help of Henry Foster, she could not make sense of them. What was the point, she wondered? What was the point of April letting her see all of these things if they couldn't solve where she was buried or who killed her? Why did she have to be so damn cryptic?!

Autumn was about to get up, when her eyes caught a photograph, half-underneath a piece of paper, on the large cluttered desk. Almost instinctively, she gently retrieved it. It was a picture of April Glass, wearing a big, puffy winter coat, standing next to a snowman. Autumn stared at the Polaroid, mesmerized by how happy April looked, how carefree.

"That was taken the winter before…." Henry's voice crackled. He could not finish the sentence – that it was taken a mere seven moths before April was abducted. "She looks just like any other happy little kid playing in the snow, doesn't she?"

"It's not fair," Autumn replied, choking on her own words as her eyes began to swell with tears.

"She would have been seventeen next week."

An ice-cold sensation shot through Autumn's entire body, from head-to-toe. "Next week?" she asked in slow, cautious voice.

"Yeah, the tenth." Henry watched as Autumn put her trembling hand over her mouth. "What, what is it?"

At first, Autumn didn't reply; she just stood there with her hand over her mouth. Then finally: "That's my birthday! I was born June tenth, nineteen seventy-six."

Speechless and numb Henry sat back in his chair. Like Autumn, he didn't know what to make of the fact that Autumn and April were born on the same day. *Where is this all going*, he asked himself. *Who is this girl that calls herself Autumn Grace?*

Just then, the cellar door creaked open. "Henry," Edith's voice carried down the stairs. "Molly's here."

Autumn looked at Henry, her hands shaking uncontrollably. "I'm sorry. I'll be all right."

"It's ok, you don't have to be sorry," Henry replied as he put his hand on Autumn's shoulder.

"Henry... did you hear me? Molly and Mary are here."

"I heard you," Henry yelled back. "We're commin'"

Henry waited while Autumn further composed herself. Then, the both of them slowly made the journey upstairs into the house. As nonchalantly as possible Autumn then went into the bathroom and splashed some cold water on her face. But as she looked at herself in the mirror she couldn't help but start crying. "What the hell is going on?" Autumn asked aloud, but in a low enough voice so no one else could hear. Autumn was starting to freak out (again) – and who could blame her – but summoning every last fiber of strength, she tried to pull herself together. *It'll be ok*, she told herself. *You're gonna get through this. Somehow, it'll all be over soon.* The teen splashed some more water on her face, before patting it dry with a towel and then taking a few, deep breaths. Then, after one last look in the mirror, it was time to join Molly and the Fosters.

Molly had come to take Autumn back to her house. "But if you and my uncle still have some things to talk about I understand," Molly said. "Or if you want, I can even come back for you later."

Autumn looked at Henry as if to ask for permission. Though Autumn wanted nothing more that to bring this whole living nightmare to an end, she had had enough of April Glass for the day. And Henry realized that. "It's ok," he said in a reassuring tone. "I think we've done enough for today. We can pick-up tomorrow morning."

Autumn smiled as if to say thanks.

It was 5:00pm and Edith tried to persuade Molly, Autumn and Mary into staying for dinner. "Thanks Aunt Edith. But I told Mary that we would rent a movie and pick up a pizza tonight."

The thought of sitting around a couch, eating pizza and watching a movie sounded so normal to Autumn. It sounded so appealing. Could she really put April Glass aside and live an "ordinary" life, if just for the night? Autumn prayed that the answer was yes.

Before they left, Henry was able to pull his niece aside for a moment. "Listen," he said in a sly voice, as his warm beer breath blew on Molly. "When Autumn checked into the motel, did you see her ID?"

Molly thought about it for a second. "No."

"Well tonight, when Autumn's sleeping, I want you to go through her purse and see if she has some identification."

Molly gave her uncle a look of disbelief. "What are you talking about?" Henry repeated himself – while making sure that Autumn was not in earshot. "I can't do that," Molly replied in a low, but defiant voice. "I *won't* do that."

"Listen… think about it… how do we really know that this girl is who she says she is?"

"Well why don't you just ask her for some ID?"

Just then, Mary and Autumn walked over. "Are you ready mommy?" Mary whined.

"Yes honey, I'm ready." With that, Molly, Autumn and Mary said their goodbyes and went on their way.

11

A fter getting a movie – *Better Off Dead* – at the only video-rental store in town and picking up a pizza, Molly, Mary and Autumn found themselves back at Molly's house. It was around 6:00pm.

At Mary's pleading, Molly brought the pizza to the coffee table in the living room, so they could eat as they watched the movie. Mary happily retrieved plastic plates, napkins and glasses and placed them neatly on the table. "I'll put in the movie," she then cheerfully volunteered.

"She really likes you," Molly whispered to Autumn as she poured soda into awaiting glasses.

After putting the tape in the VCR, Mary eagerly returned to the table for her slice of pizza. "It's really good pizza. You're going to like it."

As the previews started, Autumn instead watched Mary; watched her sitting on the couch, gleefully eating her pizza, wanting nothing more in the world than to just watch her movie. She was your average, happy-go-lucky nine year-old – without a worry in the world. As Autumn watched Mary sitting there, she found herself caught in a paradox of emotions. Mary was proof to

Autumn that there was still good and innocence in the world; that there was still hope left in Pandora's Box. At the same time however, she could not help but think about April Glass. April couldn't enjoy the simple pleasures of watching a movie with her mother or enjoy the taste of pizza. She never was afforded the chance of growing up. What happened to April Glass was proof that unfathomable evil and tragedy existed in the world. What happened to April Glass was proof that sometimes even hope abandons us.

Autumn realized that as much as she owed some sense of closure to Gillian Flowers, she also owed closure to April Glass (and to Lilly). April may have been dead, but her soul was trapped on Earth, unable to free itself. And Autumn promised herself to do everything possible to see that April was released into heaven – where she now belonged.

Autumn tried to watch the movie, but understandably, her head was somewhere else. There were so many questions going through her mind: what did it mean that she had the same birthday as April Glass; when was April going to visit her again; why was she only being teased with snippets of cryptic clues; what was the next step?

About half-way through the movie, the phone rang. Not wanting to be interrupted, Mary pleaded with her mother not to answer it. But Molly paused the movie and went into the kitchen to see who it was. "Hello." In the otherwise silence of the house, Molly's voice easily carried. But before any further of her conversation could be overheard, Mary started talking to Autumn about the movie.

About two minutes later Molly walked back into the living room with the cordless phone in her hand, her face ashen. "It's for you," she said to Autumn in a sober voice. "Maybe you should take it in the kitchen or out back."

Autumn's body went cold. "Who is it?" she asked fretfully as she slowly walked over to Molly.

Molly waited until Autumn was right by her, before whispering in her ear. "It's your mother."

It was as if all the blood had been flushed from Autumn's body. One might think that after all she had been through she would be prepared for anything. But she was not prepared for this. No way. Fighting not to fall as her knees buckled, Autumn coldly took the cordless receiver from Molly. Before putting it up to her ear, however, she walked through the kitchen and out the sliding glass door to the back porch.

"Mmm...m...mom."

"Autumn, what the hell are you doing?!" Her mother sounded more angry than concerned – though she was both.

"H...how did you get this number? How did you know where I was?"

"Kelly got a hold of us. She's worried about you. We're worried about you."

Autumn cursed Kelly underneath her breath and wondered exactly how much information was divulged by her best friend. "What did she tell you?" Autumn asked, afraid of the answer.

"Listen to me Autumn, it's going to be ok. Your father and I are in Aruba now and we're going to get the next plane back to the states. Then we're getting the next plane to Oregon and coming to get you."

"Mom no, please... you don't understand!"

"Autumn Grace, we are going to get you the hell outta that place. I want you to listen to me very carefully – I want you to stay with Molly and don't leave. We'll try to get to you as soon as possible."

"Mom no..."

"Autumn, you cannot stay there!" Her mother barked. Then, in a more calm voice, "listen sweetheart, it's going to be ok. Everything's going to be ok. We'll all go back home and take care of this."

Autumn, now starting to cry, pleaded with her mother some more not to come to Dewey. But her mother was not listening. After finally hanging up, Autumn fell onto a wooden patio chair and cried uncontrollably. It now seemed that all was lost. Her parents probably thought she was crazy – God only knew how much Kelly had told them – and possibly might have her committed. The thin line that separated the safe reality of home she used to know from the nightmare that she was now living had finally washed away. And worse, her parents were on their way to bring her back to Arizona. If Autumn left Dewey she may never solve where April and Lilly were buried or who killed them; she may never be free from the ghost of April Glass.

After about ten minutes, Molly finally came out back to check on Autumn, who was still crouched over in the chair, sobbing into her hands. Not really sure what to do, the 32 year-old bent down and put her arms around Autumn. "It's gonna be ok. Your parents love you very much."

Autumn lifted her heavy head and wiped away the tears from her eyes. "You don't understand. I can't leave now. I just can't."

Molly had spent the past three days going back and forth in her mind over just what to believe. Autumn's story was understandably just so otherworldly to accept as fact. Yet at the same time, there seemed to be no reasonable explanation for the things Autumn had known. Hell, Molly's own uncle – a hardnosed ex-sheriff that was skeptical of everyone and everything – seemed to believe her. And Molly was torn on what to do. She wanted to help Autumn, but was not sure exactly what that meant. Her instincts told her it was best for Autumn's parents to come get her. But another, deep-seeded part of Molly wondered what if Autumn was right; what if she was meant to come to Dewey to solve the Pentagram Murders? One thing was for certain though: Molly had become more than a mere bystander helping a stranger. For better or for worse, she had become entwined in Autumn's macabre journey.

Eventually, Mary wandered out back, wondering what her mother and Autumn were doing. She just wanted everyone to sit back on the couch, have another slice of pizza and watch the rest of the movie. Molly told her daughter that Autumn wasn't feeling well. Though only nine years old, Mary knew that there was something more to it – some kind of grown-up stuff. Somewhat reluctantly, she scampered back inside. Not long afterwards, Molly and Autumn also went inside. But not wanting Mary to see her so distressed, Autumn went straight upstairs to the guest bedroom, under the guise of still feeling ill.

With no television or radio, Autumn laid on the bed, in the overwhelming silence of the room. So many thoughts were running through the teenager's mind, none of them good. After about an hour, Molly came to check on her, but Autumn pretended that she was sleeping. She appreciated everything that Molly had done for her – God only knows where she would have been without Molly – but Autumn was too worn, distressed and embarrassed to talk to anyone. She just wanted it to be over. She wanted it all to be over.

On her way out, Molly turned off the lamp that was on the dresser. Now, the only light in the room was from the faint illumination of a starry night that filtered through the translucent curtains. Once again, Autumn was all alone. She was exhausted, yet could not go to sleep. A part of her didn't want to go to sleep. After all, she feared what waited in her dreams. At the same time however, another part of her wanted, albeit with great trepidation, to visit that nightmarish world; for she needed more clues, more pieces to the puzzle. It was as if Autumn was trapped in a capsized ship and the only escape was for her to dive further into the dark, cold water and find a way out... if she didn't drown first.

While everyone else was surely sleeping, Autumn lifted herself off of the mattress and walked over to the room's lone window, if for nothing else, to merely break up the monotony of laying awake in bed. In surreal silence, she looked down at the woods from her second-floor view. As Autumn stood there, she could not help but think of that first nightmare that started it all: a bizarre dream about a little girl in the woods. How could Autumn ever have fathomed that here she would be, a month later, chasing that little girl's ghost, staring at those very woods with her own eyes. Perhaps, she allowed herself to think, that it was all just one big bad dream. Perhaps she was yet to awake from that first nightmare.

As Autumn let out a long, audible yawn, her eyes closed, though just for a second. But when they reopened, it was if someone had stolen the breath from her lungs. For standing outside, in front of the tree-line of the woods, was April Glass. In fright, Autumn looked away, but when she turned back, April was still there – dressed in that godforsaken, bloodstained nightgown. As a tear trickled down Autumn's face, she stared out the window at the pallid image. April was just standing there, looking up at Autumn. Was it a dream? Was it a hallucination? Not even thinking about waking Molly and Mary up, Autumn was about to open the window and scream down "What do you want from me?!" But before she could, just like that, as instantly as she had appeared, April Glass was gone.

Her heart palpitating and out of breath, Autumn slowly backed away from the window. After two cautious steps, she though she felt something on her hand. Instinctively she turned to look. There was April Glass, standing right next to her in the room, holding her hand. She looked not like a ghost, but rather as real as flesh and bones. Autumn opened her mouth to scream, but nothing came out. Paralyzed with fear, all she could do was stand there in disbelieving shock. But though April Glass' eyes were still filled with the sorrow and anguish perhaps only a lost soul can know, she looked up at Autumn and smiled. Then, for only the second time, April spoke: "You can't leave now Autumn," she said in a sad, yet almost strangely soothing voice. Autumn! She actually called Autumn by her name! "Please… it has to be you." How real April Glass looked and felt – the look in her eyes; that bloodstained nightgown so close she could touch it; that surreal voice and its haunting message; the way she said Autumn's name – it was all too much for Autumn to take. After a vertiginous, hot flash she collapsed helplessly to the ground.

"Autumn." There was no response. "Autumn."

Slowly, Autumn opened her eyes to find Molly kneeling next to her on the ground.

"Autumn, are you ok," Molly asked in a low, but panic-stricken voice.

After clearing a lump in her throat, Autumn finally answered. "Yeah… yeah," she replied in a weak voice.

Just then, Mary appeared in the open doorway. "Mommy," she said, rubbing her eyes, "what's going on?"

"Nothing sweetie. Autumn still isn't feeling well. Just go back to your room and I'll come by in a little bit to tuck you in again."

"Autumn, are you ok," Mary asked in a squeaky voice.

"Yeah, I'm ok honey. I'm ok. I just feel a little sick – that's all."

"Why don't you go back to my room," Molly added. "You can sleep there tonight.

After Mary left, Molly explained that she was lying awake in bed when she heard a loud thud, apparently Autumn hitting the ground. When she checked on Autumn, she found her lying on the ground, out cold. "I was calling your name and shaking you for nearly a minute before you finally opened your eyes. I got real scared. I thought I was going to have to call nine one one."

Autumn finally, slowly started getting up. "I'm sorry. I don't know what happened. I was just going to open the window to get some fresh air and all of a sudden I got real dizzy and must've passed out.' Of course, Autumn remembered everything: seeing April out the window and then in the room next to her. The fact was, however, that she lied not for her own sake, but for Molly's. She knew Molly had heard enough about ghosts and visions. There was no need to suck her even deeper into this bizarre, living nightmare.

Around 8:30 the next morning – Sunday – Henry Foster showed up at Molly's house. "Where's Autumn?" he asked in his usual husky voice.

"She's still sleeping."

"Well can you get her up? I have to take her somewhere."

"Where you plan on taking her?"

"I can't tell you – just that we'll be back later this evening."

Molly, still in her robe, turned away from her uncle. "Well it doesn't matter anyway." She then told Henry about Autumn's parents calling and that they were on their way to get her. Molly also told him about Autumn fainting and that she was in no shape to go anywhere. But although Henry was visibly taken aback by the news that Autumn's parents were on their way to Dewey, he was persistent about Autumn going with him. Now Molly and her uncle found themselves in a heated debate about the girl from Arizona – in a human tug-of-war. As they were arguing – which they hardly ever did – a sleepy-eyed Mary came slumbering down the stairs, wanting to know what the commotion was about. Taking a pause, Molly assured her daughter that everything was fine.

At the same time that Mary was wandering downstairs, Autumn was awakened by Henry's and Molly's animated voices carrying through the otherwise quite house. Though still exhausted, she flung off the covers of the bed and instinctively went to see what they were arguing about – although she was already sure it was about her. Autumn's intuition was proven correct: "I promised her parents that I would keep her here till they got here," Molly's voice carried.

Feeling like a walking, breathing burden, Autumn timidly crept down the hall. By the time she reached the stairs, Mary had already scampered off into the kitchen and Molly and Henry were standing silently in the living room – though their faces spoke many words. "I'm sorry," Autumn said in a shaky voice. Not realizing that she had been on the stairs, Molly and Henry, startled, looked up. "The last thing I want is to burden you more than I already have."

Molly took a step towards Autumn. "Oh no honey, you're not a burden. I'm just worried about you, that's all." Molly meant every word of it.

Cognizant that Mary was in the other room, the three adults – if at nearly 17, you could call Autumn an adult – congregated on the living room couch. Henry explained that he wanted Autumn to go with him. Molly made the case why she could not. But before Autumn even knew their destination, her mind was made-up: she was going with Henry. She felt awful about putting Molly in the predicament of worrying about her and having to deal with her parents. But no matter what it took, Autumn had to solve this macabre mystery and Henry was the key. "Why can't you tell me where you're taking her? Why?"

Fed up with going around in circles and wanting to get the show on the road, Henry finally relented. "We're driving up to Salem to see Gillian Flowers."

Molly's and Autumn's jaws collectively dropped. Molly was thinking that her uncle was crazy. Autumn was ready to jump into Henry's truck. Though the thought of coming face to face with Lilly Flowers' mother sent a chill down Autumn's spine, she felt in her heart that somehow Mrs. Flowers was – or could provide – an integral piece to this haunting puzzle. Molly tried again, even harder now that she knew their destination, to keep them from going. But it was to no avail. Autumn was now even more intransigent than Henry about the trip. She apologized to Molly over and over again, but she had to go. "Don't worry, we'll be back before my parents get here. They were still in Aruba when they called. Who knows when they'll be able to get a flight. And even if by some chance, they beat us back, I'll tell them that you tried to stop me, but I snuck out." With that, Autumn went upstairs to change. She didn't even take a shower.

The ride up to Salem would take about three hours. Realizing that Autumn had not yet eaten anything that morning, but not wanting to waste anymore time, Henry stopped at a local deli and ordered her an egg and ham sandwich that she ate in the truck. After about fifteen minutes, in which Henry described the passing landscape like a tour guide, the cab of the pick-up fell eerily silent. In the mundaneness of the moment, it seemed too deviant to be talking about ghosts and murders and evil. It, at least for the time, felt too unnatural to discuss what they were doing. But what else were they going to talk about? Neither of them could pretend that it was just an ordinary Sunday trip up north. Trying to escape, or at least diminish, the uneasiness of the moment, Henry turned on the radio, fidgeting with the knob until finally settling on a news broadcast.

So many thoughts were swirling through Autumn Grace's mind. But the somniferous motion of the truck on the open road and the hypnotic rolling of the landscape eventually put her to sleep. There were no nightmares, no visions of April Glass. When Autumn opened her eyes again, they were 20 minutes out of Salem.

As Autumn followed Henry Foster into the hospital her legs felt weak and the air seemed thin. For a few seconds, she thought she might pass out, but was able to hold it together. It had been a strange journey, to say the least – born from a single nightmare. But Gillian Flowers was no dream. She was real and what happened to her – or more importantly, what happened to her daughter – was real. As Henry talked to a woman behind the front counter, Autumn paid no attention to what they were saying. Instead, she only heard the silent, yet resounding questions in her mind: *what would Gillian Flowers look like; would she even be cognizant enough to talk to; how in the world was Autumn – or Henry – going to explain what they were doing there; would Gillian scream at them to get out; would they be awakening long-sleeping demons?* Autumn felt guilty – and understandably, extremely apprehensive – about being there, but it had to be done.

As Henry led the way to the elevator and then down the hall of the eleventh floor, neither he nor Autumn said anything. Surely, Autumn surmised, he must have been asking himself the same questions, must have had that same apprehensive feeling in his gut.

The hospital itself looked clean and well-kept; nothing like the dark, decaying, chaotic insane asylums depicted in movies. Still, as Autumn looked around, she thought *this is no place to live*. Thinking about the heartrending travail that Mrs. Flowers had had to endure, nearly brought Autumn to tears. But her mind-wandering was cut short as they came to two, closed metal doors with a guard post in front. "We're here to see Gillian Flowers," Henry said in a clear tone.

The young, burly, black guard picked up his phone and intercom-ed the main visitor desk in the lobby. "Yes... Ok. I'll let them in." With that, the guard punched in several numbers on a keypad, near the entranceway. "Just check at the nurses' station and someone will take you to her," he said as the two, tall doors slowly, opened. "They're expecting you." This was it.

"Just let me do all the talking at first," Henry quietly said to Autumn as they walked the fifteen or so feet to the small nurses' station.

Trying to quell the frenzied butterflies in her stomach, Autumn nodded in agreement. "Ok," she then added in a crackling voice.

At the nurses' station Henry once again explained who they were there to see. Like the guard had said, the nurse was expecting them. "I'll show you to her room," she said in an amicable voice as she came out from behind the counter. "After lunch, some of the patients sit around in the rec room," she went on as they walked down the hall. "But Gilly likes to stay by herself. We try to get her to interact with other patients, but she loves to just gaze out her window."

The helpless feeling of fainting once again overcame Autumn as the nurse stopped in front of a door. She was utterly unprepared for what awaited her in the room. But nevertheless, she was going inside.

It was a clean, but small room; a little larger than an average hospital room. It seemed devoid of living touch; there were no framed photographs or other personal trinkets lying about. The bed was neatly made and the television, which hung from the ceiling, was off. It was hard to believe that anyone stayed there, let alone lived in it. Yet there she was – sitting in a chair, facing the window, staring at God knows what. She didn't even turn around to acknowledge the trio's existence when they walked into the room. Autumn feared that they had made a wasted trip.

As Henry and Autumn stayed by the entranceway, the nurse walked over to the white-haired figure staring out the window. "Gilly," she said in her ear, though loud enough for Henry and Autumn to hear. "You have visitors."

Gillian Flowers looked up at the nurse, revealing the portrait of a lined, weathered face. "Paul?"

The nurse slowly shook her head. "No Gilly, it's not your brother." Again, Autumn found herself wanting to cry. "It's Henry Foster… and he's got his niece Autumn with him."

There was a pause, which they all took as Gillian rummaging through her fractured mind, trying to remember the name. "Henry?" Finally she twisted around in the chair to look at her two guests. She was in her fifties, but looked even older. Her skin was wrinkled and dry. Her eyes looked black and distant, almost as if she was blind. "Oh yes, Sheriff Foster," she said with a cracked, smile.

Autumn felt a release of tension from her body. *She remembered! She knew who Henry was! She wasn't incoherent after all.* But then, perhaps naturally, Autumn found herself asking: *Then what is she doing here?*

After a few brief words to Henry, the nurse left the room, closing the door behind her. Autumn still stayed by the doorway as Henry slowly walked over to Gillian Flowers, who was still sitting in her chair. Autumn was beginning to think that Gillian was crippled, but she was not in a wheelchair, nor was there one in the room. "Hello Gillian," Henry said in a soft, almost guilty voice.

"It's been a long time Henry."

"Yes, I know. I'm sorry I haven't come to visit you more, but..." Not having an excuse, and not wanting to lie, Henry didn't finish his sentence.

"And who is this?" Gillian asked, pointing to Autumn.

"This is someone I'd like you to meet," he replied as he motioned Autumn to come over.

Ever so cautiously, Autumn gravitated towards the slender, white-haired woman. With each step she took, her stomach churned harder, her heart beat faster, her legs became weaker. That one and a half second walk felt like five minutes. But alas, Autumn was standing right in front of Lilly Flowers' mother. Then Autumn kneeled down so that she was face-to-face with her. As Gillian took hold of the teen's hands, Autumn was about to introduce herself. But before she could, Gillian gasped in shock. Her jaw dropped, eyes opened wide and grip squeezed tight Autumn's hands. "April? April... is that you?"

Not knowing what else to do, Autumn looked up at Henry for help. "No Gillian," he said in a noticeably shaken-up voice as he kneeled over. "It's not April. This is Autumn. You never met her before."

For another second or two, Gillian continued to stare at Autumn as if she didn't believe Henry. But then, gradually, she loosened her grip on Autumn's hands and reluctantly accepted the fact that it was not April Glass. Henry explained that he might have a new lead in the case, though he did not elaborate what it was. Oddly enough, Gillian did not ask. Henry introduced Autumn by name, but did go into who she was – though the nurse had introduced her as his niece – or why she was there. Again, Gillian did not ask, though she continued to look over the teenager. At first, it seemed that Mrs. Flowers was just glad to have visitors and who could blame her. But soon, at Henry Foster's wheedling, she started talking about that the Glasses and inevitably, that fateful October night, nearly eight years ago. Though Henry may have gently prodded Gillian to open up about the past, once she did, it was like an unstoppable waterfall of memories – painful memories. As she spoke, her eyes once again stared out the window, as if she was watching a movie of the past playing on a screen in the sky. Depending on what she was saying, her words intermittently drifted between melancholy, anger and anguish. Even the shifting lines on her face, the periodic clinching of her lips and hands told the story. And sometimes a pause told more than the words that preceded it. At times tears swelled in her eyes, which was certainly understandable, but whether by her sheer will or not, none ever escaped down he face.

For nearly forty minutes straight Gillian Flowers talked about her daughter; Lilly's relationship with April; her own relationship with Peggy Glass; dropping her daughter off at the house that fateful night; discovering the unspeakable scene the next day; and dealing with the aftermath. To say her tale was heartrending would be an understatement. But though they were both undoubtedly moved by her narrative, Henry and Autumn had not come to Salem merely to hear Gillian Flowers' jeremiad. In the end, they learned nothing new. The missing pieces to the puzzle that was the Pentagram Murders appeared to remain elusive. Then it happened. As Henry and Autumn were getting ready to say their goodbyes, Gillian asked a simple, seemingly innocuous question that would turn the investigation – and even more so, Autumn's life – upside down: "How old are you dear?"

Autumn paused before answering. "Well I'm going to be seventeen next week," she then replied in a solemn voice. "Oddly enough, I was born on the same day as April Glass."

Without warning Gillian Flowers' face grew white and her jaw dropped open, as if she had just seen a ghost. The reaction sent a chill down Autumn's spine. "It's you," she then said in a startled, but drawn-out voice.

"N...nn...no... I'm not April."

Still in her seat – she had stayed there the entire time – Gillian stared right through Autumn. "No, I know. Don't you understand? You're her twin sister."

"What are you talking about?" Henry asked as Autumn just stood there frozen. "April didn't have any sisters – only a brother." Henry asked the question more for Autumn's sake; he didn't want her to get even more spooked-out than she was already. He figured that Gillian was just confusing reality, undoubtedly one of the reasons she was still in Oregon State Hospital.

For the first time, the frail woman slowly stood up from her seat, leaning her hand on the indented window ledge. "You don't understand Henry," she said while looking straight at him. "You never knew about it. No one did." She then went on to explain, in an almost ghostly tone, that when Peggy Flowers had a sonogram, the doctor informed her that she was going to have twins. This might have been good news – even great news – for some people, but at the time, money was extremely tight in the Glass household. John had recently lost his job and already with a young son, the family was struggling to stay afloat. Selling one of the babies was John's idea. At first Peggy berated him for even mentioning such a thought. But reality has a way of overcoming ideals and eventually Peggy realized that selling one of her infants would not only lessen the family's burden, it would actually provide them with cash that they so desperately needed – especially with a newborn on the way.

According to Gillian, she, John, Peggy and her doctor were the only ones that ever knew April had a fraternal twin. Peggy had a home delivery and Gillian believed the one girl was taken that same day. So the Glasses were able to hide the fact about there being twins from even their son. Peggy told Gillian, her closest friend – her only real friend – about April having a twin a year later, in a moment of guilt. It was a well-kept secret, because up until that point, Gillian had no idea. In fact, when Peggy first told her, she didn't believe her, but then quickly realized she was telling the truth. Gillian had made her friend promise to never tell another soul. And she didn't – not even her husband – until today.

Gillian said she did not know the recipient of April's sister. However, Peggy did tell her that it was not a wealthy couple, like she and John had hoped.

"But you don't understand," Autumn barked. "I'm not April's sister. I've lived in Arizona my whole life. I wasn't adopted!"

Gillian looked at Autumn with dejected eyes. "I'm sorry dear. But it has to be you."

In visible frustration, Autumn turned to Henry, who was just standing there digesting everything he had just heard. "I was born in a hospital in Phoenix," she said, sounding as if she was trying to convince herself more than anyone else.

"Your mother would have gotten you when you were just born."

Finally Henry decided to step in. He did not believe that Autumn was April Glass' twin sister. He wasn't even sure if he believed any of Gillian's fantastic story. And he was afraid that this could finally be the piece that brought Autumn to the breaking point – which would not be good for anybody. "Listen, thank you for your time Gillian." He then turned to Autumn. "I think we should go."

Henry was literally pushing Autumn towards the door, but Gillian Flowers was not yet finished. "Have you seen any pictures of when you were born?" Autumn pushed Henry's large hand away and stared back at Gillian. "Have you ever seen pictures – in a photo album – of your mother or father holding you in the hospital?"

"Gillian!" Henry barked.

"Every parent has pictures of their child right after birth."

An unsettling silence befell the room. Both Henry and Gillian watched as Autumn stood there, almost in a trance. It was evident that she was deep in thought. Then, after nearly half a minute, she answered Gillian's question. "When I was only four, we had a fire in our old house. I was too young to even remember it – my parents told me about it – but supposedly it destroyed everything we owned... including the family albums."

12

For Autumn, the car ride back to Dewey seemed to take twice as long as the drive up to Salem. She perpetually gazed out the window, but all she kept seeing was Gillian Flowers' wrinkled face. And her words kept echoing in Autumn's weary head like the amplified sound of a marble spiraling down an empty sink. "You're her twin sister. It has to be you." Autumn would tell herself that it was just the ramblings of a crazy woman. *She's not in a mental hospital for nothing. You were born in Arizona. How can I even entertain the idea?* But then the pendulum in Autumn's mind would start swinging in the other direction. *But what if it is true? It would all make sense – why April had come to me. And I never have seen any proof of where I was born.* Then the pendulum would swing once again. *But why would April be coming to me now – after all these years? Besides, it can't be true. It just can't be!*

Henry told Autumn that she shouldn't put any stock into what Gillian Flowers said. "She went through a lot – more than anyone ever should – with what happened to Lilly and then her husband killing himself. It took a toll on her mind. You have to understand, she may sound coherent, and there's a lot she does remember, but sometimes her memory cannot differentiate reality from fantasy."

Henry's right. I should listen to him. But then Autumn would be back to letting Gillian's story play tricks on her mind. Autumn had been through a mental and emotional rollercoaster ride the past month – especially the past several days – and even if she knew she wasn't April Glass' long, lost sister, the mere assertion by Gillian had stretched her already strained nerves to the breaking point. There were so many questions: did April actually have a twin; where do she and Henry go from here; what did happened to April Glass – and Lilly Flowers; was she going to be given more clues; were they going to find the "killer"? But there seemed to be no answers. Her head pressed against the window, Autumn stared outside as her body was overcome by intervals of fever and cold. At one point, about an hour and a half into the journey, feeling an extreme case of nausea, she had Henry pull over. As soon as Autumn opened the door of the truck, she threw-up on the side of the road.

Henry felt guilty, knowing that he was exacerbating Autumn's situation by facilitating her search for April Glass. And he was beginning to have second – or third – thoughts about his role. *Ghosts? Visions? Chasing a dream? Come on Henry, get a hold of yourself! What are you doing?!*

It was around 7:00pm by the time Henry and Autumn arrived back in Dewey. As they approached Molly's house, they both noticed a police car parked out front. Henry wondered about it more than Autumn; Autumn already had enough on her mind. However, the soon-to-be-seventeen year-old was in store for yet another shock to her system.

As Autumn walked by Henry's side to the house, the front door swung open. In the doorway stood a thirty-something year-old, uniformed police officer. And right behind him stood Joanne and Bill Grace! Autumn stopped right in her tracks. She was completely frozen, not believing that her parents were actually there – in Dewey.

For a second, Joanne and Bill also stood there frozen, but only for a second. As Autumn remained paralyzed by the entranceway, Joanne darted out the door and gave her daughter a bear hug. "Oh honey, I'm so glad you're safe," she practically yelled, squeezing a still motionless Autumn. "It's ok, we're gonna get you outta here."

Now Bill came over. "It's gonna be all right Autumn."

It was not all love and kisses. "What the hell were you thinking Henry?" the policeman – who happened to be the sheriff – barked at his elder.

"What the hell are you doin' here Donnie?"

Don Harrelson, who was elected sheriff after Henry "retired", used to be Henry's deputy and protégé. They worked closely on the Pentagram Murders and were both understandably personally affected by the grizzly crime. Even when the strain of the case caused Henry to turn to the bottle – he started showing up for work drunk and sauntered around town completely inebriated – Don originally stuck-up for his mentor. However, their relationship started to fray after Henry was forced to retire, but still acted as though he was on the job, specifically when it came to the Pentagram Murders investigation. Don knew that Henry had kept confidential information – copies of police reports, photographs and copies of tapes of interviews – about the case. At first, because of their close relationship, Don reluctantly – and against his better judgment – let it slide. But when Henry continued to interview, and in some cases even harass people around town, Don confronted him on it. Besides having a duty to protect the town's folk's privacy and civil liberties, he felt that Henry was undermining his authority as the new sheriff. Henry was drunk when Donnie came to his house – which was the norm – and the confrontation ended with them nearly coming to blows. A few weeks later Henry, drunk once again, showed up at an award ceremony for Don – he had pulled a local boy from a burning car after an accident – and started shouting things like "If he's so great, ask him why he refuses to follow-up on leads about the Glass Murder?!" "Ask him why he refuses to look at new evidence?!" The statements were more drunken rants than assertions of reality. Needless to say, Don Harrelson did not take too kindly to the show. Months later, when things cooled down, Henry sought him out and apologized. Donnie perfunctorily accepted, but although there were no more confrontations – until now – their relationship remained strained, at best.

Unlike most people, Don Harrelson, although smaller than Henry, was not intimidated by him. In fact, he got right up into his one-time mentor's mug. "What am I doing here?" he repeated Henry's question. "These poor folks have been worried sick about their daughter. Then I find out that you've taken her to see Gillian Flowers, filling her head up with who knows what kind of crazy ideas." Henry looked at Molly, who just stood there, looking towards the ground. He wondered exactly how much his niece had told Donnie – and Autumn's parents.

"No, please, it's ok," pleaded a visibly shaken Joanne. "We just want to take our daughter home."

"You shouldn't talk about things you don't know anything about," Henry barked back at Don, not paying Mrs. Grace any mind.

Now Mr. Grace chimed in. "No, it's not ok honey."

"Please Bill," she quickly shot back.

As everyone was jockeying to be heard, it was apparent that things were reaching a boiling point. Molly thanked God that she had had the insight to take Mary to a friend's house.

Still standing by the doorway, everyone was now talking – or in some cases shouting – at once. "I'm sorry Mr. Grace. If there's anything we can..." "We'd just like to ask you a few questions," Henry interrupted. "Maybe you should go home and sober up." "You forget who you talking to Donnie. I knew you when you..." "All right, maybe we should all just calm down a little," pleaded Molly. "Bill, let's just take Autumn back to the hotel," Joanne practically begged. "Well wait, I think we should know a little more about what's going on. Autumn?" "Mr. and

Mrs. Grace, your daughter might have information…" "Henry!" "Bill let's just go!" "Mrs. Grace, have you ever been to Dewey before?" "Of course not!" "Henry!" "Joanne?!"

"Are you my real mother?!" Suddenly, all the adults went silent as Autumn's question – the first words she had spoken – hung in the air like a piano about to be dropped on their heads.

Joanne Grace put her hand over her heart as if she was having a heart attack. After a few long, long seconds – seconds never felt so long – her lips moved, but at first, no words came out. Then, finally: "O…Of… course I am. Wh…what are you… I mean…"

Autumn could tell by the stuttering response – and the scared look in her mother's eyes – that she was lying. An icy rush surged through the teenager's body and for a second or two she thought she was going to collapse. But then came the rage. "It was all a lie, wasn't it: the fire destroying all the old pictures?! Me being born at Saint Luke's?! You bought me, didn't you?!" Autumn yelled with tears in her eyes.

Henry, Don and Molly stood there stunned, staring at Joanne for an answer. "Autumn, how can you say that?"

"Joanne." The expression on Bill's face finished the sentence: *tell her the truth.*

Autumn looked at the only person she had ever called father. "And who are you?!"

Now Joanne was beginning to cry unabashedly. "Autumn, I never wanted you to find out."

There was now absolutely no doubt. The revelation that Joanne was not Autumn's biological mother – and Bill not her biological father – was out there for all to know. But obviously, no one was more affected than Autumn. And the certainty of the truth stabbed through her heart like a rusted dagger. Too much for her to bear, she just turned around and ran away. As she did, Joanne, now crying hysterically, fell to her knees. "Autumn!"

For a few seconds, no one gave chase. Joanne was too beside herself. So was Bill. And Henry, Don and Molly were still frozen in shock.

Finally, when Autumn was already about half way down the block, Molly gave chase. "I'll get her," she yelled as she ran off. But it was to no avail. Autumn ran faster than she had ever run before in her life.

As Molly ran down the block after Autumn, Don Harrelson came out of his stun. "Somebody wanna tell me what the hell is going on here?" When neither Bill nor Joanne answered, he turned to his old boss and tutor. "Henry?" Gone was the exasperation in his voice. He was past that point. For the first time in a long, long time, Donnie turned to Henry as a friend.

"Mrs. Grace here," he said in an even-keeled tone as he pointed to Joanne, "bought her daughter from the Glass' when she was just born. Autumn is April Glass' fraternal twin."

"Joanne, what the hell is he talking about?!" Bill Grace demanded an answer. Apparently Joanne had kept the whole truth even from her husband.

Joanne looked like she was going to literally fall apart. And who could blame her. Her, long dark secret – a secret that she had vowed to take to the grave – was out. Her deepest fear had been realized. "Please, let me explain," she replied in a quivering voice.

Right at that point Molly returned. "I couldn't catch-up to her," she said with bated breath as she bent-over, putting her hand on her knees. "Don't worry, we'll find her. She couldn't have gone far."

"What does that mean – 'let me explain'?" Bill Grace's voice had a mixture of anger and trepidation. "What are you saying?"

Molly looked at Bill in puzzlement. What the hell was he talking about? Had she missed something in the minute or two she was gone?

Though Molly had a spacious front yard, by now, neighbors were coming out to see what all the commotion was about. They knew it was something juicy – the Sheriff, the ex-sheriff and out-of-towners. And all that yelling before. Oh yeah, it had to be something good, and people were eagerly waiting for the next act of the show. However, Molly somehow managed to move the show inside the house. Disappointed, the neighbors were left to mere speculation – and they were already coming up with all kinds of theories – about what was going on at Molly Foster's house.

In the living room, to an utterly captivated audience – none more so than her husband – Joanne Grace divulged a secret that until a day earlier, she was certain would die with her. Bill Grace had met Joanne when Autumn was already a year and a half old. She had told him that Autumn was adopted and her fiancée had died in a car accident six months earlier. Neither was true. Her long-time boyfriend, Carl, had simply left one day, when Autumn was only eight months old. Joanne went on to explain that after four months of trying to track him down, she finally gave up on trying to find him – for good. In fact she had never heard from him – or about him – since.

As for Autumn, Joanne now had to tell Bill, sixteen years later, the truth. "I wanted so bad to have a baby and Carl did too – at least that's what he said." As Joanne spoke, Bill stared at her in disbelief. He had looked into those eyes everyday for well over a decade, but now he found himself staring into the eyes of a stranger. "I had known for some time that I could not have children of my own; I was infertile because of problems with my uterus. Of course we thought about adopting. We even went to an adoption agency. But we were naive. Carl had a record. He was caught stealing a car when he was nineteen and had a couple other misdemeanors. We were in our early twenties and neither of us had a job at the time. But both his parents died in a car accident and he got about seventy thousand dollars from their life insurance. So we were kind of living off that for a while. But the adoption agencies don't care if you have cash; they want some record of stability. Of course, I can understand that now." Joanne paused to wipe away a stream of tears that were rolling down her face. "Anyway, we actually tried two adoption agencies, but they both basically said no way. But then, almost like an angel from heaven, I meet Peggy Glass. Actually, her doctor – Doctor Weiss – introduced us."

"How did you know her doctor?" Henry asked.

"It was a chance encounter. We had this Black Lab that had a litter of puppies – five of them. We were able to give two of them away to people we knew and kept one. The other two, we put an ad in The Bulletin [an Oregon newspaper]. Doctor Weiss was one of the people that answered the ad. He came to our house – we were living in Eugene at the time – and we started talking. We found out he was a doctor and we told him about our troubles about trying to adopt a child – that I couldn't have any children of my own. Then, he says that he may be able to help us. We exchanged numbers and a few days later he called back and arranged for us to me the Glasses."

Henry and Donnie looked at each other. They both knew Dr. Weiss – he had delivered nearly all the babies born in Dewey for thirty years – and would loved to have interrogated him (as well as give him a piece of their mind). But they could not. The good doctor had died in an automobile accident a year and a half ago.

Joanne went on with her tale. She and Carl took Autumn – they had already come up with the name – home to Eugene. The two mothers figured it would be best to never let their respective daughters know the truth about being twins. To ensure that secret was kept, Peggy and Joanne made a pact to never have contact with each other again. And they never did.

Joanne explained that she didn't work and neither she nor Carl had close family. The few friends they did have were told that they had adopted the baby girl. So no suspicions were really aroused.

At first, baby Autumn seemed like a Godsend. Joanne was able to have the child that she could never conceive. Carl seemed happy. In fact, a week after brining home Autumn, Carl proposed. Joanne explained that she would have been satisfied with just getting married at the county courthouse. But Carl insisted, even though they hardly had anyone to invite, that he would give her a "worthy" wedding. However, after a couple of months, it was becoming apparent to Joanne that her fiancée was having second thoughts – not only about the wedding, but about their entire relationship. While Joanne stayed home with Autumn, Carl would often spend hours at the bar. Sometimes he would disappear for days, supposedly to go hunting. Soon, he started complaining that they were spending too much money; that they were using up all if his inheritance (though he didn't try and find a job). Then, one day, when Autumn was only eight months old, Carl left for a hunting trip and never came back. At first she feared that something had happened to him; perhaps a hunting accident. Joanne called the local hospitals. She called the police and reported him missing. Then, five days after Carl left, Joanne found an unmarked envelope in the mailbox. In it were a letter and a cashier's check for $3,000. The letter was short and cold:

> Dear Jo, Please forgive me, but this is not my life. I just cannot go on any longer pretending to be this man that you want me to be. Please know that it's not you. In fact I don't deserve someone as good as you. Trust me, you and Autumn will be better without me. It's better I leave now than a year or two down the road.
>
> I know it's not much, but here is $3,000. You can also keep everything I've left behind.
>
> Please do not try to find me… It's for the best…
>
> Love,
> Carl

Joanne explained that despite Carl's request, she did try to find him. But it was to no avail.

Two months after Carl disappeared, Joanne sold basically everything she owned and moved in with her estranged sister in Gilbert Arizona. Since her sister only worked during the day – as a dental assistant – she was able to watch little Autumn at night. This allowed Joanne to get a part-time job as a waitress at a nearby diner. That is where she met Bill. It was love at first sight and after only seeing each other for six months, they got married. Now, fifteen years later, here they were, standing in a living room in Dewey Oregon; Joanne talking about a past that Bill never knew she had.

Bill had let his wife speak without interruption. He just stood there, helplessly trapped in a whirlpool of shock, anger and disgust. But as soon as she finished her tangled tale, Bill could stand there no more. He could not even bare to look at her face anymore. Part of him wanted to slap – maybe even punch – Joanne – but he restrained himself (Bill had never raised a hand to her in all their years together). Instead, he simply shook his head in repulsion. "You make me sick," he snarled before turning around and storming out of the house. Joanne did not follow; she just fell onto the couch and started crying profusely, her head in her hands.

A part of Molly wanted to put her arm around Joanne and console her, but for whatever reason, she did not. Naturally, Molly was still trying to digest everything she had just heard. It all sounded like something out of either a movie or bad episode of Jerry Springer. But it was neither. It was all real. Of course Molly was most concerned about Autumn. Where was she? Was she going to do something stupid? If Molly's head was spinning and stomach churning, she could only imagine how Autumn felt.

Henry, too, was concerned about Autumn – for both selfish and unselfish reasons. But unlike Molly, he had little sympathy towards Joanne.

As for Sheriff Harrelson, he just stood there, trying to figure out what it all meant. It was definitely a revelation – no doubt about that. But what bearing did it have on The Pentagram Murders? Probably not any, Don told himself.

Though a slight breeze combed its way through the evening, the temperature was still in the mid-to-upper seventies. However, Autumn felt so cold inside, as if ice pumped through her veins. What was to become of her? Where did she go from here? As a crushing avalanche of uncertainty roared in her soon-to-be seventeen year-old head, only one thing did seem certain: things could never go back to the way they were before. Regardless of if she ever found out what happened to April Glass – who Autumn now knew to be her sister – or who took her, regardless if April never came to her again, things could never be the same. The life that Autumn knew – thought she knew – before April ever came into her life no longer existed. The truth had been discovered; the secret – a secret she was never supposed to know – revealed.

Autumn had no idea to where she was walking. She just wanted to get away. But where could she go? Autumn was trapped: trapped in some macabre mystery; trapped in a bad dream; trapped in a life she suddenly felt she didn't know; trapped in some small Oregon town, in the middle of nowhere. As her weary legs sauntered down the sidewalk, a weak street lamp cast an ominous shadow on a brick building she was passing. Lifting her head – it had been pointed towards the ground for some time – Autumn looked at her own shadow, as if to say: *at least I know I'm real.* As Autumn walked along the side of what was obviously a school, she kept watching her fallaciously tall outline until she reached the end of the wall and it vanished into oblivion. Once again, Autumn Grace was all alone.

At the edge of the school's track field was a path into the woods. It was not paved, but obviously well traveled; its dirt trail hardened and cleared by the repeated trotting of passersby. After pausing for a second at its entranceway Autumn, almost subconsciously, slowly ventured down the path. She really didn't know why; it was almost as if her legs had a mind of their own. Though it was nearly eight, the dying day still emitted a fading mist of light. And the moon, which already adorned the clear sky, was three-quarters full. As she gingerly walked further into the jaws of the woods and farther away from the school and the road, she told herself that it was still light enough to find her way back down the trail. But after another thirty or so yards Autumn wondered what the hell she was doing and decided she had gone far enough. But rather than turning back, she noticed a large rock and figured that this was as good as place as any – away from everyone else – to sit down and cry for a while. So that's exactly what she did. Under a swiftly darkening sky, Autumn Grace sat on the rock, put her head in her hands and cried. She only wished that the pain and the fear and the anger could escape like the tears that poured from her eyes.

Sobbing loudly and uncontrollably, Autumn must have sat on that rock for twenty minutes. Despite her overwhelming predicament, *she* was even surprised by how long and hard she could cry. But eventually, she simply had no more tears left. Noticing that, even with the nearly full moon and plethora of appearing stars, the woods had become threateningly dark so she decided to head back the way she had come (though she still had no particular destination). But just as Autumn was about to head back, she thought she heard music. Instinctively scanning the horizon, she noticed the faint telltale glow of a small fire, coming through the trees, about thirty yards away, though it was hard for her to grasp the distance.

Impulsively, she walked towards the radiating glow and in doing so, left the path she had been on. As she crept closer, the music became clearer – it was Black Sabbath. She could also hear the faint inaudible voices of several people. Cautiously, she kept going, following the ever-growing orange light.

By a small, manmade drainage ditch were three teenagers: one girl and two boys. One of the boys and the girl were sitting on an old, beaten-up couch that someone had discarded. The other guy was sitting across from them on a large tree stump, which was uprooted and lying on its side. In between the couch and the stump was a shallow, round pit, which had a small fire in it. Rocks of various size and shape formed a border around the pit. Right next to the embankment of the cracked-cement drainage ditch, the other three sides were cleared of trees and brush for about ten yards, so if tended to properly, the fire would not ignite the surrounding woods.

The long-haired teen sitting on the tree stump suddenly sprung up and turned down the boom-box that was right next to him. "Hey, who's there?" The other two instinctively looked in the same direction as their friend. Immediately, they saw the same thing: the shadowy figure of what appeared to be a teenage girl standing by a tree on the other side of ditch. Still holding his beer, the boy sitting on the couch stood up and asked his friend who it was, as if he knew. "I dunno," he practically whispered. Then again, to the figure: "Hey, what are you doing?"

"I'm sorry," Autumn yelled back. "I just happened to notice the fire and kinda just walked over to check it out."

The guy who had been sitting on the couch gave his friend a dirty look. "I told you the fire was too big," he growled.

"You fuckin worry too much," the long-haired teen nonchalantly replied. "Hey, it's all right," he then yelled back across the narrow, dry ditch. "Why don't you come over?! You wanna beer?!"

Actually, I could use a fucking drink, Autumn thought. Besides, what else did she have to do? Where else did she have to be? Carefully, Autumn, who was dressed in shorts and a short-sleeve shirt, made her way down and across the u-shaped trench. One of the guys extended his hand and helped her up to the other side. Dewey was a small town and naturally they were all curious who Autumn was – and why she was out in the woods by herself. Rather than freak them out by telling them the truth, Autumn mundanely said she was visiting her aunt – Molly. She also told them her name and that she was from Arizona. Why was she out in the woods? She was just bored and wandering around. They all shook their heads as if to say *yeah, it's pretty boring here in Dewey.*

The three teens then introduced themselves: Mike, Dave and Lisa. Mike, who had been sitting on the log and was the first to spot Autumn, was lanky with long, wavy, black hair and a spotty complexion. Dave was shorter by about a foot, but stockier

– though not fat – and had short, straight blonde hair. Both were wearing jeans and a concert t-shirt; Mike, *Rush* and Dave, *Iron Maiden*. Lisa, who had long, flowing brown hair halfway down her back, was Autumn's height, but a few pounds heavier – though she was certainly not overweight. She was an attractive girl, even with her boyish wardrobe of ripped, faded blue jeans and wife-beater tank top. All three were affable and nothing really stood out on them. In fact Autumn made a mental note that they looked – and acted – just like kids who might have gone to her high school.

Mike offered Autumn a barely-cold can of Budweiser, which she appreciatively accepted. Then, sitting around the fire, the three teens from Dewey asked what it was like back in Arizona. Autumn replied candidly. While listening to Autumn talk, Dave picked-up a half-empty fifth of vodka that was laying on the arm of the couch and took a swig, before casually passing it around. When the bottle came to Autumn, she took a shot without even really thinking about it. "Hey," Mike said as he went into his pants' pocket and retrieved a crumpled-up Ziploc baggie, "you get high?"

"Yeah sure," Autumn replied without hesitation. For the first time since she had stepped foot off that plane, Autumn felt like she was in her element. And for the first time in a long time, she was not consumed with April Glass. Somehow, she wasn't even thinking about just learning that her parents weren't her "real" parents. All Autumn was thinking about – all she cared about – was getting wasted with her new friends.

After about forty minutes of laughing and drinking and getting high, Dave and Lisa started making out on the couch, oblivious to their company, mere feet away. Now it was time for Mike to put the moves on Autumn. Being a seventeen year-old male, he had started thinking about it the second he saw her. But he waited until he thought the time was right; until Autumn was buzzed and high and Dave and Lisa set the stage. "Those guys are always going at it," he said as he moved himself closer to Autumn on the log. Autumn looked down on their now touching legs. Obviously knowing what Mike had on his mind, there were only two questions: was she going to put on the brakes; and if not, how far was she going to let him go? She was still contemplating the answer when Mike put his arm around her shoulder. "So, do you have a boyfriend back in Arizona?" he asked, not knowing what else to say. Autumn turned her head and knew what she would find: Mike's face mere inches away from hers. She said nothing and Mike took that hesitation to mean he had the green light. Without saying another word, he went to kiss her. Deciding to throw all caution to the wind, Autumn reciprocated.

Like a dog getting a taste of steak, Mike could not contain himself. While they continued to kiss, his hand went from her shoulder, to the back of her head, to her breast. Still, Autumn went with the moment – even when his hand inevitably found its way beneath her shirt and unlatched her bra. Just happy to be doing anything but thinking of April Glass or her predicament – and also because it felt good – Autumn let him fondle her bare breasts. But when he went to unbutton her shorts, she stopped him. "What are you doing?" she panted, as she gently brushed his rough hand away from her crotch.

Undeterred, Mike drew his hand back and grabbed her crotch, over her shorts. "Come on, you know you want it."

Autumn pushed herself away, though she remained sitting on the stump. "No, I can't... especially not here," she said looking around at Dave and Lisa – who were still making out – sitting no more than five feet away and their less than ideal surroundings. Then, buzzed as she was, Autumn gathered her senses and thought about what she was doing. "Besides, we don't even know each other."

"So, that's what makes it perfect. In a week or whenever, you'll go back home, we'll never see each other again and they'll be no strings attached... no head games or emotions."

Unbeknownst to Mike, he had said the worst word he could have said: "home". The word instantly snapped Autumn out of the moment and made her think about her inescapable predicament. Suddenly, Autumn's entire demeanor changed. However, Mike was too young, drunk, stoned and horny to read the sign – or to care. He pulled her back towards him. "Come on."

Autumn pushed him away and stood up. "I said no!" Dave and Lisa finally stopped what they were doing and looked up to see what was going on. Mike was embarrassed. "What the hell's your problem?!" Now it was Mike's demeanor that had completely changed.

Autumn was suddenly feeling extremely uncomfortable and vulnerable; out in the middle of the woods with three complete strangers, no one else knew of her whereabouts. Now all she was thinking about was a safe – and if possible, graceful – exit. "Nothin', nothin'. Listen, I just think I should go."

"What are you talkin' about? Don't be like that. I'm sorry." Mike was still angry, but was now trying to bite his tongue so he could wheedle Autumn into staying and finish what they had started. After all, his goal of getting laid overrode everything else. Slowly, he walked over to Autumn, who was now standing by the fire. "Come on," he said in a cajoling voice, as he gently touched her long brown hair. "I'll behave."

Without warning, Autumn pushed the lanky teenager with both hands, with all of her might. Taken completely off guard, Mike collapsed to the ground, his hand landing in the fire. "You're a liar!" Autumn yelled in a strangely, high pitched voice. "And a murderer! You killed my parents – and my brother – and now you're going to kill me!" Still on the ground and clutching his slightly burned hand – he had pulled it out of the fire instantly – Mike looked almost scared at first. Dave and Lisa, still on the couch, just sat there in shock. "They'll find you!" Autumn yelled, but at the same time, now began to cry. "You'll see! I'll lead them to you!"

In an almost defensive manner, Mike pushed himself up and took a few steps back from Autumn. "What are you, some crazy fuckin' bitch?! What the hell are you talkin' about?!"

Her entire body shivering – though it was anything but cold out, especially with the fire – Autumn stood there for a second, terrified. She no longer was afraid of the three teenagers; she was afraid of herself, of what was happening to her. She was conscious of every word she had said, but it was as if it was somebody else saying them. And she knew by now that that somebody was April Glass – her twin sister.

Without saying another word, Autumn turned her back to the three teens and ran off. With tears flowing down her face, Autumn fled into the darkened woods, not paying attention to where she was going. It didn't take long before she slipped on the embankment of the drainage ditch and tumbled six feet down to the bottom. Instantly, her left arm, thigh and ankle shot with pain. But she painfully picked herself up and kept going, hobbling down the length of the ditch.

13

The clock was pushing midnight and the few people in Dewey that knew Autumn Grace even existed were extremely worried about her. It had been over four hours since she ran off from Molly's house. Splitting-up, all parties searched the town and surrounding area for her. Sheriff Harrelson took Joanne with her in his car; they combed the streets, back roads, parking lots and stopped in the few stores that were still open to ask if anyone had seen a girl fitting Autumn's description. The Sheriff also had his two deputies that were on duty out looking for the teen, each in a separate car. Mr. Grace, who still didn't want to even look at his wife, walked through town, checking alleyways, nooks and enlisting the help of anyone he might have run into. Henry Foster and Molly combed the nearby woods with flashlights, though each in different areas. It was night, but neither was worried about getting lost, knowing the woods like the backs of their hands.

"Autumn! Autumn!" A week ago, Molly did not even known Autumn – or anything about her. Yet here she was, frantically searching the woods, sick to her stomach in worry about the teenager's safe being. The whole story – Autumn being

April Glass' separated twin sister; her bizarre tale about being visited by April; the assertion that she could (finally) help solve the Pentagram Murders – was too surreal to completely digest. But the 32 year-old mother of one had bonded with Autumn and knew that beyond all of that ghostly freakishness was just a girl that needed help.

"Autumn!" Molly yelled out again, her voice reverberating through the otherwise quite woods. Then, suddenly, the subtle sound of something brushing along branches caught her attention. Thinking that it was an animal – maybe a bear – she quickly pointed her long, black flashlight in the direction in which she had thought it had come. Seeing nothing, she slowly started moving the light as it hazily illuminated a nearby, diminutive fraction of the woods. There it was again – a faint rustling. Having grown-up in the woods her entire life told Molly that if it was an animal, she would have heard it scurrying away into the distance, spooked by the light. "Hello! Is somebody out there!"

"Help!" Cried out a familiar voice. Simultaneously, Molly could see a visibly distressed Autumn waddle towards her from behind a tree. Immediately Molly ran to her. Autumn almost couldn't believe her eyes. She was overjoyed to find anyone – but running into Molly was like a godsend.

"Autumn, are you ok?!"

"Oh Molly!" Autumn wailed as she collapsed in her arms. Autumn had been lost in the woods for nearly an hour, but somehow, miraculously managed to wind-up less than a quarter mile from Molly's house. She could have just as easily wandered deeper into the vast wilderness of the woods and have been lost for God knows how long. She had neither a flashlight nor any idea of where she was going. It was almost as if someone was looking after her, divinely guiding her.

Unable to hold back her own tears, Molly seemed as thankful of finding Autumn as Autumn was of being found. Molly explained how worried everyone was about her, especially her parents. Autumn did not even want to think about her parents

– or who she had believed all her life to be her parents. The embattled teenager just wanted to get indoors and lay down. As they slowly began to walk back, Molly noticed Autumn limping. She also noticed an abrasion on her arm and one on her leg. Autumn, in a nasally, post-crying voice, explained that she had fallen into a ditch – but that she was ok. She did not tell Molly about the three teens she had met; there was no reason.

As Autumn followed Molly through the woods, the joy of being found was beginning to subside enough to let her once again start thinking about the quandary that she was running from in the first place. Holding onto Molly's arm as a human crutch, Autumn stopped. "Are my parents still at your house?"

"I don't know… they might be. Everyone was out looking for you, but they might be back there now."

Autumn looked up – Molly was about three inches taller – and stared Molly right in the eyes. "Please, I just can't face them." As soon as the last word left her lips, she started crying again. "I just don't want to see them right now. I don't wanna see them ever again!"

Molly looked back at Autumn and could see the torment in her teary eyes. What could she do? She couldn't keep Autumn from her parents. "I tell you what; I have to let them know you're ok. They're very worried about you. But I'll *try* and convince them to let you stay with me tonight." Molly didn't know what else to say.

"Oh please Molly. Thank you."

When the pair arrived back at the house Henry was there waiting. "Oh my God, Autumn, are you ok?!"

"Yeah," she sheepishly replied. Henry had been nothing but nice to Autumn. But unlike Molly, who was still fifteen years her senior, Autumn viewed Henry more as an uncle or grandfather and felt humble in his presence.

Together, Henry and Molly went out front to Henry's truck and used the CB Radio to let Harrelson and Joanne – and the deputies – know that they had found Autumn and she was safe. After some trying, Molly was able to convince Mrs. Grace –

and Sheriff Harrelson – that it would be best if Autumn sleep at her house for the night. She explained that she was afraid that if Autumn saw Joanne or Bill now, in the state she was in, she would probably run away again. And certainly no one wanted that. Maybe after sleeping it off, clearer heads would prevail. Obviously, Joanne's first inclination was to come and get her daughter. But then she realized that Molly was probably right. And though she had only met her that afternoon, Joanne felt that she could trust Molly.

Henry Foster left. He was not finished with Autumn – or Joanne Grace. Autumn had already persuaded him she might be able to help solve the Pentagram Murders. But now with the revelation that Autumn was actually April Glass' sister, separated at birth – and that Joanne knew the Glasses – the ex-lawman was convinced that Joanne and Autumn somehow held the key to unraveling this macabre mystery that had haunted him – and the entire community – for years. But he knew that Autumn had had enough for the day. He knew she was already past her breaking point. Whatever had to be done, whatever had to be said or asked, could wait until tomorrow.

Molly fixed Autumn some food; she hadn't eaten since the morning. Then the pair went upstairs; Molly to her room and Autumn to the guestroom. It was one thirty in the morning and it had been a long day, especially for Autumn. However, she could not fall asleep. In her night clothes – sweat pants and a loose, long-sleeve shirt – she laid on the bed, trying to stave-off her demonizing thoughts. But they were too overpowering and there was too many of them. Most disturbing off all, she knew that in the morning, all her troubles would still be there. Though everything she was now going through started off with a simple vision in a dream, this was no nightmare that she could wake-up from.

Though Molly had been dead-tired, she was by nature a light-sleeper, and was awoken by what sounded like the sliding glass door to the backyard being open. Her first instinct was to look at the clock on the nightstand: it was 2:46 am.

Then apprehensively, Molly crept out of her bedroom and into the hall, turning on the light. "Hello." No one answered. As her mind further transformed from sleep-mode to consciousness, she remembered Autumn. Almost simultaneously, Molly noticed that the guestroom door in which Autumn had been staying was ajar. Dressed in long, dog-pattern pajamas, she walked over and gingerly pushed the door open. The lights were off in the room, but the starlight and moon let in enough illumination for her to instantly see that Autumn was not in the bed. *Oh my god, she ran off again,* Molly frantically told herself. *No wait, maybe she just couldn't sleep and went downstairs to watch some TV.* But Molly didn't hear the television – and the downstairs seemed dark.

Molly went downstairs to investigate. A small light in the kitchen was on, but no Autumn. Standing at the foot of the stairs, Molly called out for her, but there was no answer. Her heart now beating – not only did she care about Autumn, but she was also responsible for her – Molly scurried into the kitchen and towards the back door to investigate further. However, before she even opened the sliding glass door, she saw Autumn sitting on the back porch. She breathed a sigh of relief.

Alone, deep in her thoughts, Autumn was completely startled by the door opening. Reflexively, she jerked around – she had been facing the woods – and saw Molly.

"Autumn, what are you doing out here? It's three o'clock in the morning. And aren't you cold?"

Still sitting on the wooden, porch chair, Autumn looked at Molly with disconsolate eyes. "I'm sorry Molly. I just couldn't sleep."

Molly pushed another chair with her foot so it was right next to Autumn. She then sat down and put her arm around the teen. "It's ok honey. I was just worried about you." Molly then paused as the quietness of night encased them. "I just wish there was something I could do for you."

"Oh Molly, you've done so much for me already. I mean if it wasn't for you…" Autumn didn't finish the sentence. She just stared back towards the dark, silent woods – the same woods that had haunted her so – as a tear trickled down her pale cheek. "It's just that my whole life has been a lie. It's all been one big lie." After a stabbing pause, she angrily added: "I never want to see those people again!"

Molly had to stop herself from crying. "Oh Autumn, your parents love you very much."

"Please don't call them that Molly. They're not my parents."

"They raised you didn't they? They took care of you; were there for you all these years – since you were a baby. If that doesn't make them your parents, what does?" As Molly's words drifted into the night, Autumn used her sleeve to wipe away the now flowing tears. "They just didn't want to hurt you. That's why they didn't tell you."

Autumn looked back at Molly, smeared tears covering her white face. "Well look how that turned out." Molly couldn't help but silently agree. "But I mean it's one thing if I was adopted. But my mother," Autumn didn't want to use that word, but didn't know what else to call her, "buying me?! And how could my real mother sell her own child?! I mean I had a twin sister that I never even knew about… and a brother. And now they're dead," she wailed as she buried her head in Molly's shoulder.

Molly had not told Autumn that her mother had lied to her father about Autumn being adopted. She felt it was not her place. But now, she felt she had to. So she told Autumn everything that Joanne had told her, Bill, Don and Henry, earlier that evening. Under a starry sky, Autumn listened, not in disbelief – how could she find anything impossible to believe after all she had been through – but in appalling astonishment. Unfortunately, it had the opposite effect that Molly was hoping. *How could Autumn's mother not only have lied to her all these years, but also her husband. What kind of sociopath was she? And who was this Carl character?*

Now standing, leaning forward with her hands on the porch railing, Autumn shook her head in disgust. "I just can't believe it. I mean my father… or maybe I should just call him Bill… still knew I wasn't his biological daughter. And he still kept if from me. But my mo…," she stopped herself from saying mother; "…I mean I don't even know who she is."

Molly stood up beside Autumn. "She's your mother Autumn. She took you in when your biological mother couldn't support you. She nurtured and loved you from the time you were born. And when Carl left her – and you – high and dry, she could have said it was too much… but she didn't. She never abandoned you. She worked hard, not so she could buy nice things for herself, but so you could have a better life. Everything she did, she did for you."

Autumn was so confused. She knew Molly was right. Yet she was still so mad for being lied to – her whole life – even if that lie was only meant to shelter her.

"And fate has a very strange way of unfolding," Molly said in a more tranquil voice. "I mean if you had stayed with your biological parents – the Glasses – you would have been there that night. You would have suffered the same fate as April." Molly surprised herself by her words. They were completely improvised. She just kind of opened her mouth and they came out. Nonetheless, they were true.

Autumn looked at Molly with a speechless face as a chilly breeze blew in from the woods. Molly was right. And that thought drove through her soul like a spike.

It was probably 4:00am. The sun would be rising soon. It was time to go back to bed.

Autumn wearily opened her eyes. The room was bright from the morning sun piercing through the translucent curtains. Still in a daze, Autumn was surprised to find Mary standing over her, by the side of the bed. She was wearing her usual radiating smile and holding a letter-size notepad. While stretching, Autumn smiled back. "Hey Mary," she said drowsily as she gently propped herself up.

"Good morning Autumn," Mary answered in her usual, upbeat, all-is-well-with-the-world voice. "I'm sorry to wake you."

"Oh that's ok sweetie. Come here," Autumn said, patting a space on the bed next to her. "Sit down." Molly sat down, her feet dangling over the edge of the bed. "Whadaya got there?"

"I drew something for you."

Especially after all she had been through, Autumn immensely enjoyed Mary's company. She was the one thing that still made sense in the world; the one thing that could still make her smile. "For me. Oh thank you. Can I see?"

Shyly, Mary released the pad she was clutching and handed it to Autumn. Eager to see what Mary had drawn, Autumn looked down at the white piece of paper. It was a large, inverted pentagram, drawn in red crayon. In horror, Autumn dropped the pad on the bed.

"What's the matter Autumn? Don't you like it?"

"Why did you draw this?!" Autumn barked. "What would make you draw something like this?!"

Mary was visibly shaken. "I'm sorry," she whined, as she stood up from the bed. Tears were swelling in her eyes. "I thought you'd like it." Mary then turned around and with her head towards the ground, started slowly walking out of the room.

"No wait Mary. I didn't mean to yell."

Mary stopped, a few feet from the doorway. Then, after a few long seconds, she slowly turned around and lifted her head. Autumn's heart abruptly stopped. Mary had transformed into – not April Glass – but Lilly Flowers! It couldn't be! But it was! Autumn tried to breathe, to no avail, as she now stared straight at Lilly Flowers – flesh, bones, hair, pajamas and all. In fact she looked so real that Autumn could plainly see the tears trickling down her face. "Please help me April."

Her entire body now trembling, Autumn extended both arms towards Lilly. But before she could do anything else, a thin, red line magically appeared across Lilly's throat. Almost immediately, the line grew thicker – and then streaks of bright, red blood started to ooze from it. It was as if some unseen knife had just slashed the young girl's neck. Overcome with indescribable angst, Autumn cried out. "Lilly! No!"

Bill and Joanne Grace arrived at Molly's at 9:30am, Monday morning to take their daughter back. Molly invited them and explained that Autumn was still sleeping. (Mary was still at her friend's house, where she had spent the night.) As they stood in the living room, Bill stayed at a noticeable distance from his wife. His disgruntled face and body language told Molly that he was still angry; that had it not been for Autumn, Bill would not be there with Joanne. And Molly certainly could not blame the man for feeling that way after what he had learned the previous day.

Molly explained that Autumn had been up until four in the morning, but she would wake her if they wanted. After all, they were Autumn's parents. Molly then offered her guests a cup of coffee and some breakfast. Suddenly, a bellowing, scream pierced the uneasy air. It had come from upstairs and sounded like "Lilly, no!" After a second of looking at each other in alarm, Molly, Joanne and Bill ran upstairs. Molly burst into the guestroom – with the Graces behind her – to find Autumn still in bed, apparently in the throes of a nightmare. She was tossing and turning violently and just kept repeating the word "no" in a long, drawn-out, painful cry. Molly immediately rushed to the bed to wake Autumn. Joanne, overcome with anguish over what she was seeing, just stayed in the doorway and started crying, holding her hand over her open mouth in disbelief. Bill stood in between Joanne and Molly, not really knowing how to react.

"Autumn, Autumn," Molly said loudly and she shook the sweat-drenched teenager. Slowly, Autumn opened her eyes. "It's ok, we're here. You were just having a nightmare." *Just a nightmare* – Molly knew that in Autumn's case, there was no such thing, but she did not know what else to say.

It took Autumn a few seconds to realize that she was now in fact awake. As soon as she did, she sat-up and fell into Molly's awaiting arms. "It was so awful," she cried into Molly's shoulder.

Joanne came over and sat on the opposite side of the bed. "Are you ok honey," she asked in a shaky voice as she put her fingers through Autumn's hair.

Autumn lifted her head and turned around to face Joanne. "What are you doing here? Please – just go away."

"Autumn!" Molly said sternly.

"How could you have lied to me all those years?! Just go away! Please – both of you – just leave me alone!"

In between shirting gears, Henry Foster sipped steaming-hot coffee from his mug. He knew time was running out; that there was little he could do to stop Autumn's parents from taking her back to Arizona. And he already knew that they were hell-bent on taking her back. Processing all the information he had learned the past few days, especially the previous day, he had devised a plan. There was a hypnotist in Eugene that sometimes worked for the FBI. In fact she had worked on the Glass Case. She had hypnotized Gillian Flowers in an attempt to see if she could remember someone nearby her or the Glass' house the days before the murder/abduction; to see if she could unearth anything in her memory that the police could use. Unfortunately, it was all for naught. Obviously, Autumn's case was much different. She wasn't even in the state of Oregon when the crimes took place – or the preceding eight years. But Henry didn't know what else to do. Time was not on his side. He could not just sit back and wait for Autumn to have another dream or vision in hopes of acquiring more clues.

When Henry walked into the Dewey Police Station, Sheriff Harrelson, who was standing by a file cabinet, looked almost as if he had been expecting his old boss. "Henry."

"Donnie."

"I came to run something by you," Henry said matter-of-factly.

Don closed the file draw he had been rummaging through and turned his full attention to Henry. "What is it?"

Henry looked around to see if there was anyone else around; there wasn't. He then walked towards Don and in a low, calm voice explained his desire to have Autumn hypnotized – by Dr. Michelle Pallance.

Don Harrelson sat on the edge of a desk and ran his fingers through his thick, black hair. "Listen Henry – I know how much you care about this case; how you would give anything to find out who did this and what happened to April and Lilly. But you've got to let this go... for your own good." Don spoke to his former mentor in a much different tone than the previous evening. Gone was the animosity and frustration. Now he sounded more like an old friend – which he was.

"Let it go? How can you say that after what you learned yesterday?"

Don looked at the ground and then back-up at Henry. "I admit it, the whole story is bizarre: that girl being April Glass' twin sister, separated at birth; no one ever even knowing about her. But I still just don't see how that has anything to do with what happened that night in nineteen eighty-five." The Sheriff paused. "And I'm not just saying that because of what happened between us." He paused again – this time longer. "As a matter-of-fact... well, I'm sorry what I said to you yesterday and... well, if it's all the same to you, I think it's time for both of us to put all this stupid shit...all this tension over the years, behind us."

Henry accepted Don's apology and apologized himself – for how he had treated Don over the years. Henry, too, was ready to burry the hatchet on their childish riff, which he knew he started. Even in the most heated days of their rivalry, deep inside, Henry knew that Don – the person he mentored for over a decade – was a good person. And he knew that Don would give anything to solve and finally give closure to the Glass Case. So that's why he politely tried to push the acting Sheriff on the idea of hypnosis. Without going into all the details of what Autumn had told him the past several days – that would have just made Don think he was crazy – Henry tried to convince Don that she *somehow* knew *something* about what happened to April Glass and Lilly Flowers.

Besides, he argued, what was the harm of having her hypnotized? At worst, she wouldn't be able to give them anything and they would go home.

Don still balked at the idea. "Henry, it's not up to me anyway – you know that. It's not a police matter. I mean you would need her parents' consent… and I doubt they're gonna go along." (Of course, there was now the issue that Bill and Joanne did not technically have legal custody of Autumn. After all, Joanne had purchased her from the Glasses, almost certainly without any paperwork. But the Glasses were dead now and it was not Sheriff Harrelson position to determine Autumn's fate. The most he could do was notify some other agency, but what was the point; Autumn would be eighteen in a year and Joanne and Bill had raised her since she was an infant.)

Don was right – there were no legal grounds to compel Autumn to go under hypnosis, and Henry knew it. Henry didn't come to the station to get Don's approval; there was no approval he could give. But he knew if he went to Autumn's parents with the request, it would appear more legitimate if the Sheriff was on board with the idea. "What if I get their consent?"

Don looked like what he was: a man that had been put in an uncomfortable position. "I don't know Henry," he said as he rubbed the back of his neck. I just…"

"We have nothing to loose and everything to gain."

"What about the girl's mental wellbeing? Have you thought about that?"

"Donnie, if the Autumn balks at the idea at all it's a dead issue." Henry knew well that Autumn would go along with the idea.

"And what about Doctor Pallance? She's not some psychic; she's a highly, respectable psychiatrist. You think she's gonna go along with this? When was the last time you even spoke to her?"

Henry was undeterred. "Don't worry about her. First things first. Let's talk to the parents. But we gotta work quick."

Don Harrelson finally relented, figuring that Bill and Joanne Grace would never go along with the idea and Henry would have to drop it. So piling in a squad car – it was the first time in a long time that Henry had been inside a police cruiser; he missed it – they headed off to the Davison motel, where the Graces were staying. When they found out that Bill and Joanne were not there, they went to Molly's house.

Molly let her uncle and Don in and told them that Mr. and Mrs. Grace were in the kitchen. Autumn was still upstairs sleeping, Molly explained; she had awoken about a half hour earlier from a nightmare. In the kitchen, the greetings went around. Both Henry and Don silently noted that Bill Grace was standing on the other side of the room from his wife, refusing to even acknowledge her. It was certainly understandable, they respectively thought, considering what he had learned. They, like Molly, knew he was only there with Joanne because of Autumn.

Now that the uneasy pleasantries were finished, it was time to get down to business. It was time for Henry to explain why he and the Sheriff had come. There was really no easy way to say it. "I'm not sure exactly what's happening with your daughter Autumn…but…well…she seems to know certain details about the murders of Peggy and John Glass and their son and the abductions of…"

Bill Grace interjected. "What details? What are you talking about?" Henry had told him the evening before about the murders and about April and her friend Lilly being abducted – and that they were never able to find the girls or who committed the crime. After Henry had originally told him about the crimes, Bill vaguely remembered seeing something about it on the news, some years back, as the grizzly nature of the murders and the girls' disappearance made national headlines. Joanne also learned of the infamous Pentagram Murders from the news when it took place. But obviously, it affected her on a much more personal level. She actually knew the Glasses. And she knew that Autumn was April's fraternal twin sister. But keeping the promise she made to herself – to never let Autumn know her true origin – Joanne painfully mourned in solitude. The secret was kept – but not a week went by that Joanne did not think about what happened.

"She knows certain facts about what happened that were never made public. Now we're not sure how she knows this information," Henry deliberately used the word "we" to imply that Sheriff Harrelson agreed with him all the way, "but we would like her to see hypnotist."

Bill waved his hands in the air. "Hypnotist! What the hell are you talking about?!"

"She's not some psychic. Dr. Pallance is a certified psychiatrist... she has testified in many high-profile criminal cases." Don just stood there and let Henry do all the talking.

"I don't understand! What is she supposed to remember? She was with us in Arizona when all this took place. I mean..."

"I think we should ask Autumn," Joanne sternly interrupted. "If she's willing to do it, then I give my consent." Joanne knew that's what Henry was looking for.

Don Harrelson was surprised by Mrs. Grace's stamp of approval. So was her husband. "Joanne, what are you talking about?!"

"Bill, what harm can it do? If she knows something..."

"How can she know anything about this?!"

Bill had a point. But Joanne was unwavering. Wondering what happened to April Glass ate at Joanne over the years – like some kind of cancer. And though she was not convinced that Autumn could help solve this nightmarish mystery (how could she?), if Autumn was willing – and what would she have come to Dewey for if she wasn't – and if it meant putting her under hypnosis – Joanne could not say no. Joanne owed that much to

Autumn… and the sister she never knew. "Please Bill. Just think of those two poor little girls. Think of what happened to that family. I don't know how… I don't know… you've heard stories of twins being able to speak to each other telepathically. You've heard Mister Foster: Autumn knows details about what happened that no one but the police should know. What if…"

Bill threw his hands up in the air. "This is lunacy."

"I have to do it." The adults turned around. Standing in the living room, by the entranceway to the kitchen, was Autumn. "I don't care what he says" referring to Bill." This is something I have to do."

Though Autumn was hell-bent on being hypnotized with or without her father's consent, she tried to convince him. Finally, reluctantly, Bill gave what was as close to his approval as he was going to give. "I just don't understand. I don't like it Autumn, but I guess I'm not going to be able to stop you". With that, Mr. Grace, feeling like he was caught in a bad dream for the past two days, frustratingly went out into the backyard by himself.

Once again, Joanne gave Henry and Don her explicit consent. As Henry explained that they were going to call Dr. Pallance, Sheriff Harrelson was wondering what happened; Autumn's parents were supposed to shoot down the idea. *Are we really going to go through with this,* he wondered? *How did I let Henry get me in the middle of this, anyway?*

Less than a half hour later, Henry and Don found themselves back at the police station, sitting in Don's office. As Henry dialed Michelle Pallance's number, Donnie assured himself that even if they were able to get a hold of her, she wouldn't be able to schedule Autumn in. And even if she could, once she heard Autumn's story, she would laugh at the idea. The Sheriff was still convinced that the hypnosis was never going to come to fruition.

The receptionist explained that Dr. Pallance was with a patient; Henry left a massage for her please to call as soon as possible. Ten minutes later, she called back. "Hi Henry," she said over the speakerphone in a pleasant, professional voice. "It's been a while. How are you?"

"Ok," he perfunctorily replied. "I have Sheriff Don Harrelson with me." There was silence on the other end. Michelle knew Don as Henry's deputy. Henry quickly explained that he had "retired" from the force and Don was now the Sheriff of Dewey. Don then re-introduced himself over the speaker phone.

"Listen Doctor Pallance," Henry continued. "I know you're very busy, so I'll cut right to the chase. We have a girl – a teenager – that has inside knowledge of the Glass Case."

Michelle was intrigued – the case had troubled her, especially that it remained unsolved, as it had everyone that worked on it – but wondered what this all had to do with her. "What kind of information?"

Henry paused before answering. "Well let's just say that she has knowledge about what happened that night that she shouldn't have. But she only recalls bits and pieces. It seems a lot of her memory is suppressed. That's why we're calling you. We would like for you to put her under."

"Are you saying she might have been a witness?" Dr. Pallance asked in an audibly excited voice.

Afraid that Henry was going to continue to sidestep the truth, Don stepped in to tell Dr. Pallance the real story. "No. In fact, by all accounts, she was thousands of miles away in Arizona when the crimes took place."

"You think she had some association to the perpetrator," she asked, still trying to find the connection.

"Not exactly," replied the Sheriff. He then explained that Autumn was April Glass' fraternal twin sister, separated at birth.

Henry then, somewhat hesitantly, explained that Autumn had been having dreams about what happened the night her sister was taken; and in those dreams she learned details about the case that by all accounts, she should not have known (It was the first time that Sheriff Harrelson heard the whole story – that this was all because of dreams.) "I realize that it sounds crazy." Don was surprised that Henry had admitted it.

There was an uneasy pause as Dr. Pallance processed the information she had just learned. "There have been plenty of purported cases of mental telepathy between twins. I'm sure you've heard stories: a man had a dream that his brother is in a car accident, only to find out the next day that at the same time he had the dream, his brother *was* in a car accident; a woman has a feeling that her sister is in some kind of trouble and gets a call two hours later that her sister was murdered. But almost always, it's between identical – not fraternal – twins. But there is no scientific proof of telepathy, even between identical twins. And in most purported cases, one sibling is having a dream – or feeling – at the same precise time that something is happening to the other sibling." Dr. Pallance paused again. "Although, there have been rare cases where a period of time has elapsed between the actual event and the other sibling's perception. But I've never heard a case where one sibling has communicated from beyond the grave," she went on rather matter-of-factly.

"What has this girl told you? You know better than anybody the amount of press this case received. There are people out there who are obsessed with high-profile – especially violent – crimes. Are you sure she couldn't have picked-up all these details by studying the case?"

"Yes," Henry quickly answered before Don had a chance. Without going into detail, Henry reiterated that Autumn knew things that were never made public.

"Well look, though it hasn't been fully accepted by the scientific community, I have to admit that some cases of extrasensory perception between twin siblings is pretty convincing. But the only way this Autumn is receiving messages from April Glass – telepathically or otherwise – is if April is still alive."

Henry and Don looked at each other. Could it be? Could April still be alive – being held captive somewhere? No, it couldn't be. It just couldn't. But what if?

Henry was now more resolute than ever to have Autumn put under hypnosis. Dr. Pallance, not believing that April Glass had telepathically communicated with Autumn, politely declined, blaming it on her full schedule. But Henry would not take no for an answer. He begged and pleaded, reminding Dr. Pallance that not only were there two girls still out there – dead or alive – that they needed to find, but also a psychopathic killer, quite possibly still looming in the streets. He and Don would come to her, he volunteered. All they needed was a few hours of her time.

Henry was right to play on Dr. Pallance's conscious. She strongly believed that hypnotizing this girl would be nothing but a waste of time. But the question "what if?" would not let her take the chance of never finding out. Dr. Pallance remembered conducting hypnosis on Mr. and Mrs. Flowers. She remembered the crime scene photographs. She remembered the smiling faces of April Glass and Lilly Flowers on the missing persons' posters. She remembered it all like it was yesterday. What if she was wrong? What if being under hypnosis, Autumn *could* provide useful information? No, Michelle Pallance could not take the chance of being wrong – of not finding out.

14

They arrived at Dr. Michelle Pallance's Eugene office at 2:00pm on Tuesday afternoon. Accompanying Autumn was her mother, Henry Foster and Sheriff Harrelson. The sheriff originally had no intention of going. Even if he had wanted to, which he didn't, Don Harrelson couldn't just skip town for a day or two. After all, he was the Sheriff. But Henry had talked him into it. "I'm just a civilian now Donnie. What if Autumn provides something useful during her session? Who knows what she's liable to tell us. You have to be there." Don reluctantly caved in.

Bill Grace did not make the trip. In fact, not able to handle what was going on – learning that Joanne had lied to him all those years about Autumn's true origin; his daughter's insistence that she was being visited by the ghost of the twin sister she never knew; and the implication that this was all somehow connected to a notorious (and unsolved) murder and abduction – Bill flew back to Phoenix that morning.

Though the first time she had heard of Autumn was the previous day, Dr. Pallance had been anxious to finally meet her. When she did, the board-certified psychiatrist made a mental note that Autumn looked like "your average teenager".

Dr. Pallance was a slender woman with a soft, welcoming face and warm smile. Though her shoulder-length, black hair was starting to gray, she looked in fine fettle for her 52 years of age. One of the reasons she was good at her job, she had a calm and affable presence.

Dr. Pallance spent the first twenty minutes or so getting acquainted with Autumn – and to a lesser extent, Joanne – and explained exactly what she was going to do. She then asked if Autumn was comfortable with "Mr. Foster" and "Mr. Harrelson" being in the room while she was "under". Autumn assured her that it was important they be there to hear what she had to say – if anything. The truth was, the one person Autumn didn't want in the room was her mother. But Autumn rightfully figured that Joanne was not going to leave; and this was no time for an argument.

It was time. Dr. Pallance ordered the room quiet. Sheriff Harrelson and Henry each had a pad in their hand, ready to take notes. As Autumn reclined back in the over-sized chair, she was not afraid. Quite to the contrary, she was eager to try and find the missing pieces to this macabre, improbable puzzle. Whatever awaited it was necessary to go through in order to put this all behind her. Autumn now knew in her heart that she would never be free of the nightmares until she found out exactly what happened to April and Lilly – and most likely, the identity of their abductor.

Within two minutes, Autumn was under. "Can you hear me Autumn?"

"Yes," responded a slow voice.

"Autumn, I want you to go back to the night of October seventeenth, nineteen eighty-five." Dr. Pallance spoke in a soft, but deliberate voice. She was conducting the hypnosis just as she always did – with complete professionalism – even though she still thought that it would prove useless. After all, Autumn was not even in Dewey on the night of the murders and abductions. "Where do you see yourself," she continued.

Everyone in the room was surprised when a beaming smile appeared on Autumn's face. Then, she actually let out a fleeting giggle. "Lilly's imitating her father."

Joanne put her hand over her mouth as tears began to swell in her eyes. Henry too, found himself fighting back tears. Sheriff Harrelson simply could not believe what he was hearing. Was this for real?

At the sound of Joanne gasping, Dr. Pallance motioned the three to remain silent. "Lilly Flowers? You're with Lilly?"

"Yes," Autumn replied matter-of-factly. "She's playing with April. But April's mother is making them go to sleep – it's getting late."

Dr. Pallance had hypnotized hundreds of people and many times had gotten "real" results. But in every case, the person being hypnotized recalled his/her own memories. Autumn was speaking in third person, as if she was narrating a movie or dream. This Dr. Pallance never encountered. She was starting to think that Autumn was not really under hypnosis – hypnosis didn't work on everyone – but rather, was pretending. But if Autumn was pretending, she was good. Dr. Pallance had been doing hypnosis for decades and was not easily fooled. "Autumn...I want you to tell me what else you see. Can you describe the room?"

"Wait," Autumn snapped. "It's dark now," she continued in a somber tone. "The lights are off... except for a small Wonder Woman nightlight." A cold sensation shot through Henry Foster's veins. How could she have known about the Wonder Woman nightlight? Don Harrelson did not remember the nightlight – no one remembered more details about the case than Henry – but one glance at Henry's pale face and he knew it was for real. "Everyone's asleep. They look so peaceful there... April and Lilly."

"Autumn, I want you..."

"What's that," Autumn interrupted.

"What?" Dr. Pallance asked.

"I think I hear someone walking down the hall." There was an eerie pause. "Oh my God!" Autumn screamed – though she remained reclined in the chair. "What was that!?"

"What was what Autumn?" Dr. Pallance asked in a stern voice.

"April and Lilly – they're so scared. April's calling for her mommy."

"Oh my God," Joanne howled as tears streamed down her face.

"April's telling Lilly to hide inside the closet. They're both going in and closing the door." There was a painfully suspenseful pause. "Shhh. Someone's coming. I hear the doorknob to the room turning. Someone's at the door!"

Dr. Pallance was no stranger to dramatic – and often tragic – testimony. But she was still feeling that the teenager from Arizona might be putting on a show. She had no idea about the Wonder Woman nightlight.

"He's inside the room. He's turned on the lights. I'm so scared. So cold." Autumn let out a loud, demonstrative gasp.

"What is it Autumn?"

"He found them."

"Who found them Autumn? Can you see his face?"

"Wait! There's a boy. He just ran past the bedroom door. The man is running after him. He's chasing him down the hall with a gun in his hand. They're running downstairs and out the front door. He's trying to get away. They're running through the woods. No!" Autumn paused; her face was tense with fear. "He tripped over something. The man's pointing his gun...a pistol... right at the boy. Oh god, no!! Don't!!"

"Oh my god, I can't take this," Joanne cried hysterically.

"Do you want me to stop?" Dr. Pallance asked.

"No," Henry quickly answered for Mrs. Grace. Though his normally iron stomach was churning in knots and his legs shaking, after all those years, this was the first and only time that he felt like he was actually at the scene of the crime – as it happened.

"She saw the whole thing," Autumn continued, breaking the monetary silence.

"Who?"

"April. She watched her brother get murdered. She had followed them outside. She was right there when he shot him in the back. She ran over and knelt beside him... holding him." Autumn paused. "Then he took her. He put his hand over her mouth and just carried her away back into the house. She bit his finger, but he said if she did that again she would end up just like her brother. I can feel her. She's so scared – so terrified."

"Ask her if she can see the man's face?" Henry knew he wasn't supposed to talk while Autumn was under – it might snap her back to consciousness – but could not help it.

Dr. Pallance politely reminded Henry of the rules by motioning him with her hand. "Autumn, can you see the man's face?" she asked for a second time.

"No. I don't know why? He's right there – dressed in all black. But his face is just a blur."

"Is he white, black? Is he tall? Fat?"

Autumn shook her head negatively. "No, he's not fat. He's tall. He's so strong." Then, abruptly, Autumn changed her line of narrative. "I'm back in the house. He's taking April back upstairs – back to the bedroom. Oh, no. No."

"What is it?" Dr. Pallance asked hesitantly.

"He's found Lilly. She's still in the closet hiding. Why didn't she run?" At this point, Autumn was narrating with bated breath. "He's pulling her out of the closet. She's so scared that she can't even scream. Her pajamas are soaked. She must have been so terrified that she peed in her pants. He threw her on the bed with April." Henry and Don looked at each other. This detail they *both* remembered: a puddle of urine was found inside the closet and traces of urine were also found on one of the beds. Through the corner of her eye, Dr. Pallance could see them gazing at each other in disbelief. That's when, for the first time, she thought that this may not be some show after all. But then again – how could it be for real?

"He's pulling something out of his pocket," Autumn continued. "His pants are baggy and has lots of pockets – like army pants. It's tape. He's going to tape them up. Both Lilly and April are crying. They're so terrified."

There was a four to five second pause where Autumn just suddenly stopped talking. "Are you still there Autumn?" asked Dr. Pallance. "Are you still in the room?"

"He's taping up their hands and feet." Henry tapped Dr. Pallance on the shoulder and quietly asked her to ask Autumn if she could see what kind of tape it was. Dr. Pallance asked. "It's silver," Autumn readily answered. Henry jotted down: *duct tape.* "April's trying to resist. Her nightie is covered in her brother's blood. She's yelling 'what did you do to my parents?' She's trying to escape," Autumn continued in a highly excited voice. "She kicked him and is running for the door." There was another pause and the feeling of air being let out of a balloon. For everyone in the room knew that April did not escape. "She can't get away," Autumn said as her voice quickly changed from excited to disenchanted. "He grabbed her by the hair and pulled her back on the bed. He's pulled a knife from his waistband and is threatening her with it. He's climbing on top of her on the bed." Autumn's voice began to tremble. "He's putting his hand up her nightgown."

"That's it, stop!" Joanne yelled as she lept from her chair. She simply could not bear to hear another word. "Just stop it! Stop it now! Wake her up!" She went on hysterically.

Dr. Pallance excitedly – and quickly – explained that she would wake Autumn up, but Joanne had to either calm down or leave the room. "Please Mrs. Grace. This has to be done right." Dr. Pallance then pulled Autumn out of her hypnosis.

As Autumn snapped back to the "real" world, she had no conscious recollection of anything she had said while under the hypnosis. In fact, for a second, she didn't think that it had worked at all. However, as she looked around the room at everyone's faces – he mother was still crying – Autumn realized that something had transpired. Immediately, she asked what had happened, what she said. At first, all the adults just looked at each other. Then Joanne, without saying a word, abruptly stormed out of the room.

As Sheriff Harrelson went out to comfort Mrs. Grace, Henry solemnly explained to Autumn, what she had told them under hypnosis. Dr. Pallance, in a rare moment of feeling that she was not in control in her own office, simply listened. But she was surprised by Autumn's reaction. She had naturally thought that Autumn would be disturbed upon hearing what she had divulged under hypnosis – even if she was pretending to be upset, as part of an act. However, Autumn seemed excited, almost elated. That's because Autumn was by now well accustomed to the shock and horror of the Pentagram Murders. Unbeknownst to Dr. Pallance, the sixteen year-old had already had numerous, detailed visions of that unspeakable night. Her purpose in coming to Eugene to be hypnotized was to learn more; to somehow be able to see the missing frames of this real-life horror film. She had no idea if it would work – but now she knew that it did. True, the most important questions – what happened to April and Lilly and who did it – were still unanswered. But Autumn believed – hoped – that that was only because she had been woken-up too soon. That's why she begged Dr. Pallance to put her back under, right away.

Dr. Pallance, still trying to wrap her mind around if what she had just witnessed could possibly be "real", explained that she could not do so without her mother's permission. Autumn did not like that answer and pressed Dr. Pallance. That's when Henry, who was obviously just as anxious for Autumn to go under again, suggested that maybe it was time to take a break and digest what they had just learned. "I have some calls I have to return, anyway," said Dr. Pallance.

"Well can I just speak to you for a moment first, please?" Henry then glanced at Autumn and she realized what the look meant – if she could leave him and Dr. Pallance alone. She really had no desire to go out and face her mother, but knew that she should oblige. Autumn knew that Henry just wanted to appease any reservations Dr. Pallance had about going through with another session.

Once Autumn left the room, before Henry could even utter a word, Dr. Pallance preempted him. "Henry, I know how close you are to this case. And I know how badly you want to believe that this girl somehow holds the answers. But really Henry, this isn't... well, I just don't think..." her sentence trailed off without an ending.

"Are you telling me you think all this is some kind of act?" Henry then explained about the Wonder Woman nightlight and the traces of urine they had found in the closet and bed.

Dr. Pallance, who despite being a hypnotist – what many people would consider mere smoke and mirrors – was a trained scientist and could still not fully let herself believe that Autumn could somehow recover memories that did not belong to her. And to Dr, Pallance, Autumn knowing so many details, including the nightlight and urine, was not proof. "Come on Henry, she could have known about the nightlight from... maybe she had seen a crime scene photograph somewhere. And as far as Lilly wetting herself, that's just a logical assumption. I mean so many of the details of this case were leaked by the media." Dr. Pallance paused. "I'm not saying that Autumn is *trying* to put us on. These might actually be her memories, but not in the way you think. Maybe she read about the case... saw a documentary on it. And now she learns that she is the separated twin of the girl who was abducted... it's quite possible that that triggered memories about the case that she doesn't even remember reading or hearing. The mind works in mysterious ways – especially when it's under stress."

Henry didn't correct Dr. Pallance in that Autumn started having these "memories" before she knew about being April's sister. He was not there to split hairs with the doctor – or to maker her see the light. To Henry, it was not essential whether or not Dr. Pallance believed Autumn. It was just essential that she put her under hypnosis again.

By this time it was close to 4:00pm and Dr. Pallance had a busy practice in which to tend. She explained that to Henry; that she had agreed to do the one session as a favor. She also reiterated that Mrs. Grace would have to give her approval and that was "very unlikely". She also, for the first time, suggested that they could be causing psychological damage to Autumn – not by the hypnosis itself, but by feeding her beliefs about being visited by her long, lost sister. "In fact Henry, I think I'm going to suggest that when they get back to Arizona, they find a psychologist for Autumn."

Henry Foster had come too far to simply go back now. As he had done originally, he played on the good doctor's conscience. "Listen, what if – just what if – April Glass is still alive? You said yourself that there have been cases…"

"I know what I said."

Henry pressed on and through a mixture of conscience and just realizing he was not going to take no for an answer, Dr. Pallance agreed to put Autumn under again. But there were three stipulations: Autumn's mother had to consent; they would have to do it that afternoon, preferably as soon as possible; and this was it – no matter what transpired, there would be no third session. Henry gave Dr. Pallance a hug, practically smothering her with his oversized arms and hands.

Next it was time for Henry to work on Joanne. Joanne, Autumn and Don were all outside, near the entranceway to the building in which Dr. Pallance's office resided. Sheriff Harrelson was still trying to console Joanne. Autumn, was off sitting by herself by a concrete fountain. With time wasting, Henry went over and tried to delicately explain to Mrs. Grace why Autumn needed to be further hypnotized. Before Joanne could respond, Don interjected: "Can I talk to you alone for a minute."

Grudgingly, Henry walked with Don out of Joanne's earshot. He was surprised to learn that he also had to convince Donnie – or at least that Don was not automatically on board. How could he not be after what he had just heard, just witnessed. But like Dr. Pallance, Sheriff Harrelson was finding it too hard to believe: Autumn being able to recall exactly what happened the night of the murders as if she was there – even though she was not. It was just too strange to be real. It was like a science fiction movie. It was like an episode of The X-Files. Henry pleaded with Donnie to open up his mind. "You know me. I'm the last person to believe in this kind of shit," Henry correctly asserted. "But it's not just even what she said in there. It's other things she's told me – things that there's no way she should know. "Henry put his meaty hands on his old friend's shoulders and looked him straight in the eyes. "Do you really want to go home now and have Autumn go back to Arizona? Are you really willing to live the rest of your life wondering – and I know you will – what if we only would have hypnotized her one more time? What if she could have told us everything? We're right here Donnie. How could we live with ourselves if we just turn back now?"

Don bowed his head towards the ground, unable to look his old mentor in the eyes. Part of him knew that Henry was right. "It's not up to me anyway," he said in a faded voice, pointing to Joanne.

"Let me talk to Mrs. Grace."

Surprisingly, Mrs. Grace was the easiest out of the three to convince. That did not mean she was thrilled about the idea. In fact, the thought of Autumn going through that hell again made her shudder and nearly become physically sick. But unlike Dr. Pallance and, to a lesser extent Sheriff Harrelson, Joanne was now a believer. No one knew Autumn better than her own mother – and having raised her since infancy, Joanne was her mother – and seeing and hearing Autumn during that first session was all Joanne needed to know that this was no parlor trick. Nor did she believe it was merely Autumn recalling some long lost memories of something she had read or seen on TV. Henry did not have to lay the "what if" question on Joanne. He didn't have to ask if she would be able to live with herself without knowing what else Autumn could have revealed. Joanne knew that she would not be able to live with herself if they simply turned back now. In fact, the one condition to her consent was that she not be in the room this time during the hypnosis. She did not want to cut short the hypnosis as she had before.

At 4:45pm, Henry, Don and Autumn were back in Dr. Pallance's office. Joanne fretfully waited in the receptionist's area. Sitting on a single couch, both the Sheriff and Henry had pads in their hands, ready to take more notes. Autumn, apprehensively eager, reclined back down on the same over-sized, leather chair. Just as effortlessly as the first time, Dr. Pallance put her under. "Autumn, can you hear me?"

"Yes," answered a somnolent voice.

"Autumn, I want you to go back to the night of October seventeenth, nineteen eighty-five. I want you to go back to the house where…"

"I don't want to go back to the house," Autumn snapped, not letting Dr. Pallance finish her sentence.

Henry could feel his body tense up. What was going on? He gestured Dr. Pallance to press Autumn. But Michelle could not force Autumn to take them back to the house. That's not how it worked. "Where are you now?" she calmly asked.

"I'm in a dark place."

Dr. Pallance waited several seconds for Autumn to elaborate, but she did not. "Is there anybody there with you?"

"April and Lilly," Autumn's voice crackled. "They're just cowering in the corner, holding each other… crying." Dr. Pallance asked if there was anyone else in the room. "I don't see anyone. But I can feel… I can feel it."

"Feel what Autumn?"

"Evil."

As skeptical as Dr. Pallance had been, a cold, tingling chill ran down her spine. She looked at Don and Henry and they stared back at her. All three had the same expression on their face: like children being told for the first time about the boogeyman. "Autumn," Dr. Pallance continued in a noticeably less stable voice, "I want you to look around where are you are. What else can you see? Are you in some sort of a room?"

"There's no windows. It's dark. I can barely see April and Lilly. It must be some kind of basement. It's a small room." Then Autumn abruptly paused. "Wait. The door's opening," she said in now tremulous voice. Dr. Pallance, Henry and Don all fretfully waited for what was coming next – but for several seconds, all Autumn did was breathe heavy, as if she was too frightened to speak.

"Are you ok, Autumn?"

"It's him."

"It's who Autumn?"

"The man who took them." As Henry and the Sheriff waited to put pen to paper, Dr. Pallance asked – once again – if Autumn could describe what he looked like. "He's standing in the doorway. A light's shining behind him. Lilly and April are clutching each other, crying for their mommies. They're so scared." After clearing a lump in her throat, Dr. Pallance asked yet again if Autumn could describe the elusive man, especially his face. "He's tall." Henry and Don took note. "His hair is short... straight. He looks like a regular man... but his eyes are so cold...like two black holes. I don't want to look at him anymore," Autumn pleaded.

"It's ok Autumn, he can't hurt you."

"He's gone over to April and Lilly," Autumn continued. "He's smiling at them – but it's such an evil smile." Autumn's face visibly winched. "Such an ugly smile. He's telling them that if they just do what he says, he'll let them go. They're both crying. April's asking about her parents – what happened to them?" Henry wrote on his pad with a shaking hand: *girls must have been blindfolded – did not see the parents' bodies...didn't see them get butchered.* "He says that they're fine, but she knows he's lying." Henry put a question mark at the end of his last note. "He says he won't harm them as long as they just do what he says. But if they don't, he'll slit their throats."

Dr. Pallance, still not quite sure what to believe was glad that Mrs. Grace had decided to stay outside. Sheriff Harrelson was feeling sick to his stomach. Autumn spoke with such conviction that he had forgotten that he was not supposed to accept her narrative as fact. Henry, who originally met Autumn's bizarre tale with angry cynicism, now took her words as gospel, and as such, was sweltering in a mixture of rage and disgust. It was as if the fear and terror Lilly Flowers and April Glass had felt was flowing from Autumn's mouth, straight into his soul.

"They're trying to stop crying," Autumn continued. "Because they're afraid of what he'll do to them. He's standing right over them… in the corner of the room. He's unbuttoning his pants," her voice shuddered. "He's pulling them down. April looked away, but he turned her head so she's looking straight at him – straight at the demon. He's telling her to… She doesn't want to, but she's scared he'll kill her." Autumn began to cry. "So she does it. She has her eyes closed, but he orders her to open them. All she can see is the face of the demon. It's so ugly!"

At first, everyone in the room assumed that the "demon" was just a euphemism for penis. However, her last statement confused Henry, who though repulsed, was astute enough to ask Dr. Pallance to press Autumn for clarification. "When you say demon Autumn…"

Dr. Pallance didn't even have to finish her question. "It's the face of a demon: green with red horns. It's right above his… It's so ugly." It was a tattoo! It was the first real, identifiable mark of the perpetrator. That was of course, if Autumn's narrative was "for real".

Autumn started crying more profusely and Dr. Pallance announced that she thought it best that she brought the teen out from the hypnosis. Henry begged her not to. It tore at him to see Autumn in such distress, but it was a necessary evil. And he found some solace in the fact that last time she was hypnotized, she did not seem to remember anything once she was brought back. Reluctantly, Dr. Pallance continued with the hypnosis, but knew she had to do something. "Autumn, can you hear me?"

There was no answer, just crying. "I want you to look away. Can you leave the room?"

Within a few moments, Autumn's crying fizzled to a sniffling. "It's different now."

"What do you mean, Autumn? Are you somewhere different?"

"It's the same room... but it's different. There's a light in the corner – a lamp. And there's an old wooden table and two mattresses. There's even some toys strewn on the ground."

"What about Lilly and April? Can you see them?"

"Yes, they're there," Autumn immediately replied. "They're sitting together on one of the mattresses. They're in different clothes." Henry scribbled in his pad: *how long have they been down there?* Don wrote: *Seems girls were held captive in basement for quite some time.* "They're talking to each other," Autumn went on in an eerily calm voice. "I can't hear what they're saying. They're whispering... but they seem to be arguing. April's saying 'no', but that's all I can make out. Wait... the door's opening." Autumn paused. "It's him. He has... he has food with him... a plate of hot dogs... and two cans of soda. Lilly's telling him that she has to go to the bathroom. He's putting the hot dogs and sodas on the table and taking Lilly with him. I mean she's following him. As she walked out of the room, she turned and looked at April. They're gone now, but he left the door to the room open." Suddenly, Autumn's flow of speech stopped.

"What is it?"

"It's April. She's starting to cry. She's just sitting there by herself on the bed, with her arms around her knees." Again, Autumn stopped talking. Once more, Dr. Pallance asked her what was going on. But for another forty seconds or so, Autumn just sat there, speechless. Dr. Pallance was about to try another line of questioning when Autumn finally spoke. "Something's wrong."

"What? What's wrong, Autumn?"

"I don't know; I can just feel it. April's getting up. I think she wants to look outside the room, but she's too scared."

Suddenly, Autumn tightly clutched the armrests of the recliner. "There's screaming... It's Lilly! What's going on?! There's all this noise – like things are being knocked over and thrown around." Autumn's voice raced with trepidation. "What's going on?! April's screaming for Lilly. She's standing by the doorway. 'Lilly! Lilly!' There's heavy footsteps. Someone's coming down the stairs. April went back to the mattress. It's Lilly! The man – he's standing in the doorway with Lilly. He's holding her by the hair... and he's got a knife in his other hand! He's closed the door behind him, but he's still holding on to Lilly. 'This is what happens if you try to escape!' He's putting the knife to her throat! Oh God no!!!" Autumn screamed as she nearly jumped out of the chair. "No! Lilly! Lilly!"

Hearing Autumn scream through the walls Joanne, who had been in the receptionist area, burst into the office. But she did not have to tell Dr. Pallance to stop the session. Autumn was now hysterical and Michelle knew when enough was enough.

As Autumn woke-up, she was still shaken, still crying, but she did not know why. Neither did Joanne, who frantically asked what had transpired. Instinctively, Dr. Pallance consoled Autumn, assuring the teen that she was now safe. After trying to placate Mrs. Grace, Henry walked with Donnie to the other corner of the room, where the two conferred. As Joanne stood watching Dr. Pallance still comforting Autumn, she happened to glance at Henry's notepad, which he had left on the desk. Inconspicuously, she started reading the open page. Suddenly, something in particular caught her eyes. Joanne picked-up the pad to make sure she had read it correctly. "Oh my God!" Everyone else in the room now turned their undivided attention to Joanne.

Henry cursed himself for leaving the pad on the desk, figuring that Joanne was reading the details of what Autumn had said. "I'm sorry. I shouldn't have..."

"No, you don't understand," she interrupted in a ghostly voice. She then went on to explain something that would change everything. It was the scribbled words *Demon-face tattoo, green with red horns, just above penis* that had entranced her; that she could not believe she was reading. For Joanne had seen the same tattoo before – in real life. It belonged to her ex-fiancée, Carl.

Though veteran lawmen, Henry and Sheriff Harrelson were speechless – as was Dr. Pallance and Autumn. As Joanne tentatively flipped the page on the notepad, she then went on to explain that he also fit the general description: tall and slender, with short, straight hair. Before anyone could break the overbearing silence – they were all still in shock – Joanne dropped the pad on the ground and ran out of the office and straight to the ladies room, where she vomited.

Somehow, this nightmarishly, unbelievable case had become even more bizarre.

15

D r. Michelle Pallance was now a believer. She had heard, seen and felt too much not to believe. Yes, she felt it; felt in her gut that somehow, beyond practical explanation, this was the genuine article. Unbelievable as it sounded, Autumn Grace was channeling the dark, long-kept secrets of a twin sister she never knew she had. So although the psychiatrist had previously drawn a line in the sand – that there would be no more hypnosis sessions for Autumn – she now readily, in fact eagerly, agreed to another session. What more could Autumn tell them? Though working with the FBI and local law enforcement throughout the years had taught Pallance never to get her hopes up – for so many times an investigation seemed on the verge of being solved, only to have it fall apart and have to start at square one – she had this undeniable sense that they could actually be on the cusp of finally answering the decade-old heinous riddle that was the Pentagram Murders and the abductions of April Glass and Lilly Flowers.

Besides maybe Autumn however, no one was more overwrought about the possibility the infamous, cold case could be solved than Henry Foster. It had become a cancer living inside him, metastasizing with each passing year. There were so many false leads, so many shattered hopes. But now, despite the frailty of the evidence, Henry was certain he had a name – and a face. Now he had to track down this elusive Carl, a person he never knew existed up until a few days ago.

As Dr. Pallance walked Autumn across the street to get something to eat, Henry and Sheriff Harrelson questioned Joanne about her estranged fiancée in Michelle's office. Only this was no normal interrogation. Joanne eagerly complied; for she wanted to find out what happened to the two girls just as much as anyone. However, after having some time to think about it, she now refused to believe that Carl – someone that she had lived with and intended to marry – was capable of such evil. There had to be some mistake. "Carl could never murder anyone or hurt a child," she assured them. "I mean you're basing all this on a tattoo. It could just be a strange coincidence." Joanne paused as she searched her strained mind for answers. "Maybe Autumn had seen his tattoo when she was a baby and somehow remembered it."

Joanne's last sentence seemed plausible to Donnie – at least as plausible as a teenage girl receiving visions from a sister she never knew she had. Maybe this Carl even abused Autumn when she was young, he wondered to himself. Maybe that's how she had seen the tattoo. But supposedly, Autumn was not even a year old when Carl left for good.

Henry explained that serial killers and predators often blend into society. Most of the time, even their spouses and children have no idea of their secret life. Wolves in sheep's clothing, Henry called them. "You've seen it before. They interview neighbors, co-workers and even family members and they all say what a nice guy he was, how they could never in a million years imagine he could do something like this. Meanwhile, the guy's confessed to killing a dozen prostitutes." Joanne had heard the story before, many times, in one form or another.

"Can I ask," Henry said in his calmest, most gentle voice, "I mean I'm just curious; do you know why he had gotten that specific tattoo? Did it have some significance? I mean I realize that lots of people have sinister tattoos – devils, skeletons, demons – but it seems an odd place to put the face of a demon – right above your genitals."

"Well to tell you the truth, Carl always had this thing about the occult. But it was just a curiosity," she quickly added as a disclaimer. "You know, just a stupid thing. I mean he just had some books and stuff. It's not like he sacrificed animals or performed any rituals or stuff."

"Did he have any other tattoos? And what about pentagrams? Did he have any fascination with pentagrams that you remember?"

Joanne looked at the ground and then slowly back up at Henry and the Sheriff. "I don't know. The only other tattoo he had was on his shoulder; a picture of the Taraus bull, his sign." Joanne then paused, before breaking down again. "It can't be. It just can't be."

Saying nothing, Don Harrelson handed Mrs. Grace a tissue from a box that was on Dr. Pallance's desk.

Over the next forty minutes – until Dr. Pallance and Autumn returned – Joanne tearfully told Henry and Don all she knew about her one-time fiancée. She had met Carl Justin Donaldson while they both were working at K-Mart. She was 18 and had just graduated high school. Her mother had died of cancer when Joanne was only 12 and her father was an alcoholic. Wanting so badly to get out of the house, instead of going to community college – Joanne didn't have the grades to get into a university – she went to work fulltime in order to get her own apartment. At the time Carl was 20 and had recently served 9 months in jail for stealing a car. She would soon learn that he also had prior arrests for DWI and possession on marijuana. "But he was never arrested for anything violent," Joanne explained. "I mean he was a little rough around the edges." Joanne paused. "I guess that's what attracted me to him. You know… the 'bad boy' image. But he had this soft side about him. In fact, he was rather shy. I remember I had to actually ask him out the first time."

Joanne went on to explain that they seemed to "instantly fall in love." After only a month, Carl moved out of his parents' house and in with Joanne.

Eventually, Carl was fired from K-Mart for nearly coming to blows with the store manager. He bounced from odd job to odd job, but for much of the time, was unemployed. Then, when Carl was 22, both of his parents died in a car accident. "That must have had a dramatic affect on him," Donnie commented.

Joanne thought for a few seconds before answering. "He never had a close relationship with his parents. His younger brother killed himself when he was seven – Carl was ten. He shot himself with their father's gun. He said after that it was like his parents just didn't care about anything anymore... including him. I mean Carl never liked to talk about what happened to his brother, but I'm sure it had to affect him. Anyway, after he moved in with me, Carl lost all contact with his parents." Joanne paused. "I mean I guess it was a mutual thing." She paused again, this time for nearly ten long seconds. "Then one morning he got a phone call from his Aunt saying that his parents were in a car accident. They were hit head on by a truck and killed instantly." Joanne rubbed her hand against her mouth as her eyes stared right through the two men. "I do remember that he was crying. Carl, I mean. Despite their estrangement, he *was* very distressed."

"Anyway, Carl was their only son – their only living son –and was the sole beneficiary of their life insurance policy. At the time of their death, his parents were in debt and the bank took the house. But they couldn't touch the money from the life insurance, which was about seventy thousand dollars. To us, back then, it was like a million bucks. Suddenly, we went from struggling to get by to being rich. At least we felt rich. Carl made me quit my job at K-Mart. He said I wouldn't have to work anymore ever again. He said he was going to invest the money in the stock market and triple it."

"Did he know about the stock market?" Henry asked.

For the first time that day, Joanne let out a fleeting laugh. "No. But we were young and dumb. You know how it is." Both

Henry and Donnie smiled and shook their heads. "In fact we thought that it was the perfect time to have a baby. I had always wanted a child, but knew that I was infertile. Carl also knew about it. I told him everything. So we decided to adopt. But we quickly learned that that was a dead end."

Joanne had already told Henry and Sheriff about meeting Peggy Glass and how she "acquired" Autumn. Right now, they were more interested in Carl Donaldson himself – particularly, where they might be able to find him. As she did the day before, Joanne explained that after Carl "took off" she tried to track him down, but could not find him. She never heard from him since. He had an aunt that lived in San Francisco – at least she did years ago. Other than that, he had no immediate family of which she knew. The only close friend he had, had been friends of both Carl and Joanne – all of whom she had lost contact with some time ago. In fact, when she moved to Arizona, with the exception of searching for Carl for those first few months, Joanne had cut off all ties with the people she had known in Oregon. She then gave Henry and Donnie, at their asking, other details about Carl: he much preferred the country to big cities; he had good hygiene and cared about his appearance; his favorite beer was Miller Genuine Draft, his favorite liquor, Johnnie Walker; he was a devoted Seattle Supersonics fan; and so on.

Around 8:00pm, Henry, Don, Joanne and Autumn returned to the hotel they were all staying at for the night. Henry paid for both rooms. The agreement was to go back to Dr. Pallance's office in the morning so Autumn could undergo another hypnosis session.

As Henry and Don went into their room, Autumn was left alone with her mother. She was no longer filled with a surging sense of resentment towards Joanne. Now, she just felt extremely uncomfortable being around her. The two used to be close, but now everything had changed. What were they going to talk about: how much money her mother had to pay the Glasses; what was Joanne's serial killer ex-boyfriend like; describe all the times April had visited Autumn in her dreams; ask how her mother could have lived with the secret so long? Autumn already convinced herself that she would never feel comfortable around her mother again – but especially not now. But what was Autumn to do? Where was she to go? She felt relatively at ease around Henry – at least she could talk to him about what was going on – but he was with Sheriff Harrelson, and she did not particularly feel comfortable talking about her situation with him. Autumn wished that Molly was there. Though only knowing her for a week, Autumn felt a kinship with Molly; it was like she was a big sister. But Molly was over a hundred miles away, back in Dewey. Dewey. For a town that Autumn never knew existed several weeks earlier, it had become an integral piece of her life; a part of her DNA that she would never be able to detach.

Autumn told her mother that she was going to "walk around". Joanne said she would go with her, but Autumn pleaded that she needed to be alone. Understandably, Joanne was worried about her daughter, afraid to even let her out of her sight. But Autumn was persistent and promised that she would not go far. So reluctantly, Joanne relented.

Autumn walked around the hotel for about fifteen minutes. There was a bar in the lobby and Autumn could really have used a drink, but figuring there was no way they would serve her, she grudgingly walked on by. Eventually, the teenager wandered outside. The air was cool and there was favonian breeze blowing through the night. Under a vast, still darkening, star-speckled sky, Autumn aimlessly wandered around the parking lot and then down the block. It was not a congested area and though it was not yet nine o'clock, she did not run into a soul – which was fine with her. Autumn needed to alone with her thoughts. The soon-to-be high school senior was conflicted with tumultuous emotions. Understandably, she was afraid. But she felt not only fear for herself, but what April – her twin sister – and Lilly had gone through. She felt excruciating angst for what happened to the girls – and April's family. She also felt an obvious rage for the perpetrator – a person she was now convinced was her mother's long-time ex-boyfriend. On the other hand, Autumn felt a sense of elation that this nightmarish journey could be reaching its terminus. The pieces of the puzzle, it seemed, were finally all falling into place. Autumn also felt a sense of gratitude to Henry Foster, a great sense of gratitude. She knew that if it was not for him, she would have never gotten so far. Without him taking her to Gillian Flowers, Autumn might never have known that April was her sister – and that Joanne and Bill were not her biological parents. Without Henry there would have been no hypnosis and the plethora of clues that it unearthed. Thinking about this, Autumn remembered that she was not on this journey all alone. And in that, she felt a glimmer of solace.

As Autumn solemnly wandered outside, Henry and Sheriff Harrelson conferred in their hotel room. Their first step was obvious: track down Carl Justin Donaldson. The fact that he had been through the system – meaning he had been fingerprinted and should be in the National Crime Information Center ("NCIC") database – would be helpful. But then again, many ex-cons had gone incognito. However, their problem was not just finding Carl Donaldson; it was what to do with him after they found him. No judge was going to issue a search warrant – let alone an arrest warrant – based on dreams and vicariously recovered memories. And what jurisdiction did Sheriff Harrelson have anywhere besides Dewey? The answer was none. Henry was just a private citizen. In order to really move further, they needed the help of other law enforcement agencies – most likely the FBI. But who was going to believe their story?

From working the Glass Case, Henry had a friend in the FBI, Special Agent Mark Mullen – who had been a lead agent on the FBI's taskforce dedicated to the Pentagram Murders –who he and Donnie decided to go through. They knew that Mark's first question was going to be how they came into the name Carl Donaldson. After much brainstorming, they agreed to start with a version of the truth: a girl named Autumn Grace had contacted Henry saying she had information about the Pentagram Murders; it turns out that she is the fraternal twin sister of April Glass, separated at birth; Autumn's mother, Joanne, "bought" Autumn from the Glasses, along with her then-boyfriend Carl; though Autumn was young at the time, she somehow had suppressed memories – possibly things she had seen or overheard – that for whatever reason she was now recovering that suggested Carl had something to do with the crimes. Carl also had a prior record (though supposedly not for anything violent). Both Henry and Donnie realized that this was far from enough – especially after all these years – to arrest or possibly even interrogate Carl. But at least he should be considered a "person of interest". At least Mark should track him down and look into his background.

Neither Henry nor Donnie wanted to waste any time. But it was pushing 10:00pm in Oregon and Mark worked out of Virginia – unless he was on assignment elsewhere – which was three hours later, so they decided to wait until the morning to call.

"I'll tell ya Henry, I could sure as hell use a drink," Donnie said in a weary voice, as he dragged his hand along his forehead. "I saw a bar downstairs in the hotel."

Henry paused before answering. "Na, that's ok. You go down. I'm gonna stay up here and try to get some rest. We're gonna have a long day tomorrow."

Donnie's jaw just about hit the floor. Henry Foster turning down a drink?! Don waited for a few seconds, sure his old mentor was going to follow-up with "What are you kidding me; I was just fuckin' with you. Let's go get hammered!" But he didn't. "Yeah, you're probably right," Donnie replied softly, with a half-smile. "I should probably get some sleep too."

Early the next morning, Wednesday, June 9th, from the hotel room, Henry placed a call to Agent Mark Mullen's office. He had not spoken to the agent in several years and hoped that it was still the right number – hoped that Mark was still on the job.

As it turned out, Mark was still with the FBI and still at the same number. However, the person answering the phone explained that Agent Mullen was already out on the field, working a case. Henry left a message for him to call back – and that it was urgent.

While Donnie had breakfast with Joanne and Autumn, Henry waited in the room for Mark's call. It never came. Not wanting to put all their eggs in one basket, Donnie called his deputy back in Dewey and asked him to run a check on Carl Donaldson to see what he could find.

As scheduled, Joanne, Autumn, Henry and Sheriff Harrelson arrived at Dr. Pallance's office at 10:00am. As soon as they arrived, Michelle told Henry that a Special Agent Mark Mullen from the FBI had called for him (before leaving the hotel, Henry called Mark's office again and left the number of where he could be reached). Using a vacant office, Henry and Donnie called Mark back. It was not the first time Henry had enlisted Mark's help in tracking down a supposed lead for the Glass case – though it was the first time in several years – so his first inclination was to take this new information with a grain of salt. But that is why it was good having Donnie there, who over the speaker phone explained that "I think this time we may really have something". Still, the evidence – if you could call it that – sounded flimsy at best (if only they had told Mark the whole truth about how they had found out the information).

"Listen Mark, I know you can't go out and pick up the guy. But just run him through NCIC," Henry pleaded. "See what other troubles, if any, he's been in. Just check him out, see if you can find out where he's been living."

"All right, all right." It seemed simple enough. Mark would do – or have someone from his office do – the basic research on this Carl character. But if there was nothing there, which Mark didn't expect there to be, he was not going to dig any deeper. He didn't see how he could. Besides, he was already inundated with his own, current caseload.

Autumn, once again, found herself reclining in a chair in Michelle Pallance's office. Just like before, Henry and Donnie sat on a nearby couch, pads and pens in hand. This time, however, Joanne insisted on also staying in the room. She needed to hear what Autumn would say first hand. She needed to know if the unthinkable was possible: if the man she had lived with for years could be a pedophile-serial killer. But it was much more than curiosity; it was guilt. Were there obvious signs she should have been able to read? Is there anything she could have done? Did her long, dark secret about her connection to the Glasses help Carl from being a suspect?

Just as the day before, Autumn easily fell under Michelle Pallance's hypnotic trance. And also just as before, she did not need to be prodded hard for information, it just flowed. "I'm in the basement. Lilly's gone," Autumn's voice strained slowly with pain. "But there's another girl with April." Henry and Donnie looked at each other as their ears perked up.

"Can you tell me what she looks like Autumn?" Dr. Pallance asked in her usual soft voice.

"She's a little taller than April; maybe a little older. She has long, straight reddish hair and... and slight freckles." Henry and Donnie jotted down every word. "She's so scared. April's trying to comfort her."

Over the next forty five minutes, Autumn provided Henry and Donnie a wealth of information to put on their respective pads. Like narrating a story, the teenager depicted a chillingly, harrowing tale of April Glass; an insight that by all reasonable accounts should have been impossible for her to know.

At first, Autumn's narration was confined to the basement. With a trembling voice, she told of the unspeakable things that "The Man" – under hypnosis Autumn always simply referred to the perpetrator as "The Man" – did to April and the other girl; sometimes together and other times separately. Often, he would take pictures or even videotape the acts. The repulsive sexual details were too much for Joanne, who had to excuse herself from the room. In fact she had to go into the ladies room and vomit, as she had the day before. But she let the session continue, knowing – hoping – that the ghastly means would justify the end.

In between raping the girls, Autumn explained – as though she was watching a movie of it – that The Man would bring them food and actually try to befriend them. Once every few days, he would walk the girls to a nearby bathroom and give them a shower – always together – where he would videotape them, molest them, or both. If either girl had to use the bathroom, he would take her there. Autumn explained that he made April tell the other girl what happened to Lilly when she tried to escape.

Locked in a cellar together, often twenty-four hours a day, April no doubt got to know her new cellmate. "Her name is Jill," Autumn said, to the surprise of everyone in the room. However, though Autumn said she could see the two talking, most of the time she could not hear what they were saying. Then came an unsettling revelation. "The Man... he's come for Jill. Jill and April are looking at each other. He usually never takes one of them out of the basement unless they have to go to the bathroom. Jill is asking where he's taking her. He doesn't answer as he closes and locks the door. April is curled up in a ball in the corner of the room crying." As happened when Autumn talked about the sexual encounters, she was becoming quite emotional; her breathing accelerated, her body began to shudder.

"It's ok Autumn. I want you to take a deep breath." Dr. Pallance waited for Autumn to breathe. "Now I want you to tell me the next time you see Jill."

"He's come back to the basement – without Jill. I don't know... I can't tell how long he's been gone for." Autumn seemed upset at herself for not being able to provide this detail.

"It's ok Autumn."

"April asked him what happened to Jill." There was a foreboding pause. "He said that he let her go. That he decided to free her." Henry wrote on his pad: *killed girl*.

Suddenly, without any cue from Dr. Pallance, Autumn started to tell about the day her captor let her outside for the first time. She described being outside in the bright sunlight; The Man closely escorting April through a field of long grass. She described seeing what appeared to be a small abandoned church and a distant backdrop of jagged mountains. There was a swing set, which April's captor gently pushed her on and next to it a seesaw on which they teetered back and forth. But upon Dr. Pallance's asking, Autumn explained that there were no other kids – no other people – around. There were not even other houses that she could see. It was if they were in the middle of nowhere. Asked to describe the area further, Autumn explained that beyond the field, was a running rivulet with small trees around it. Then she volunteered that "he" would take April there sometimes to try to catch "tiny fish".

Being investigators, both Henry and the Sheriff suddenly noticed a strange change in Autumn's narration. When the hypnosis session first started, she revealed a tormenting tale of rape and fear; details that would make even the most harden detective sick and want to cry. But for the past ten minutes or so, it was almost as if Autumn was describing a father and daughter, playing in the backyard. Henry wondered if the captor had forged a bond with his captive.

Looking at her watch, Dr. Pallance noticed that the session had already been going on for forty five minutes and suggested they call it a day. Henry and Donnie agreed, so Michelle brought Autumn back from under the hypnosis. "What happened? Did it work?" Autumn eagerly asked. "What did I say?" Dr. Pallance told Autumn to relax for a few minutes and offered to get her a glass of water. It was not long though, before Henry recounted what Autumn had told them – though sparing her some of the graphic details.

The fifteen minute car ride back to the hotel was shrouded in silence, each person submersed in their own thoughts. Don

Harrelson, who was driving the rented sedan, was planning to call his deputy back as soon as they arrived at the hotel, to see if he unearthed any information on Carl Justin Donaldson. He tended to believe Autumn's hypnotic tale, but did not wholeheartedly buy into the fact that the only reason Autumn knew these things was because April had come to her from beyond the grave, like some kind of ghost from Christmas past. Sheriff Harrelson had found himself a new theory: that Autumn knew about what happened because she saw or overheard something from Carl or even her mother. Donnie no longer blindly accepted as fact that Joanne and Carl parted ways as long ago as Joanne asserted. He now believed that Autumn was older than just eight months when Carl left the picture. And he also believed that Joanne knew more than what she was letting on. In fact the small-town sheriff now found himself looking at Joanne Grace with suspicious eyes.

In the front passenger's seat Henry, ironically usually the biggest skeptic of the bunch, took everything Autumn had said – both under hypnosis and to him personally – as fact. And he did not believe that Joanne was hiding anything. Unconceivable as it seemed, Henry Foster believed that April Glass had telepathically communicated with her twin sister and it was for the purpose of finding the perpetrator as well as April and Lilly – and now even this girl named Jill. However, he was now letting himself think something that he dared not mention to the others: the chance that, against all odds, April Glass was still alive. Of course part of it was just plain wishful thinking. But he read much into the fact that Autumn never mentioned April being killed. Henry did remember that Autumn told him about the dream of being buried alive. But he also remembered that in the dream – at least what Autumn told him – Autumn herself was being buried. She did not actually see April being buried. Maybe the dream was about this girl Jill. From Autumn's latter hypnosis-induced testimony, she paints a picture of April's captor trying to befriend her. What if he *did* forge some strange bond with her? It wouldn't be the first time a kidnapper had bonded with his/her hostage. What if April even bonded with him, ala Stockholm syndrome? Could she actually still be alive?

Joanne sat in the backseat, her head staring aimlessly out the window. She wanted so much to cry, but had no more tears left. There was that enormous sense of guilt. It was overbearing, crushing her very soul. Her heart bled for April and Lilly – and for her own daughter. However, she also thought about Bill, her husband of sixteen years. Where was he? What was he thinking? Could he ever be with her again – especially when he found out the whole story? How could anything ever return to normal again, she wondered?

As for Autumn, she found a strange, almost surreal sense of comfort in focusing on the goal. And that goal was to find the girls and finally bring this monster to justice.

As soon as they arrived back at the hotel, the receptionist at the front desk said that there was a message for Don and another message for Henry. Both the deputy and Agent Mullen had called back. Excitedly, Henry and Donnie rushed up to their room where they could call back in privacy. However, Autumn and Joanne insisted on being there for the calls. Henry agreed before Donnie could even answer.

Henry made the first call, to Agent Mullen, who answered the phone at his office. "Hey Mark, I just got back to the hotel. They said you left a message for me. You find anything out?"

"Well you were right about this guy Henry – he's a real winner," Agent Mullen replied in a dry, cynical tone. "He recently served three years in Montana State Prison for molesting his girlfriend's eight year-old daughter."

Everyone in the room watched as big Henry Foster's jaw dropped and they knew right away from his expression that he was just told something crucial. "What? What is it?" Autumn pleaded. But Henry just put up his oversized, chubby hand.

"Three years? That's all he got?" Now everyone's curiosity peeked even more.

"Some goddamn liberal DA's office cut him a deal: five years. You believe that?! Anyway, he was paroled after just three years. He just got out six months ago. I guess the good news is that he's still on parole, so we can have the local P.D. bring him in for questioning and check out his place without having to get a court order." Agent Mullen paused. "But he's no longer in Montana."

A sinking feeling overcame Henry. "Whadya mean? He skipped?"

"No. I actually got a hold of his original P.O. According to him, Mr. Donaldson requested a move to Arizona; supposedly he had a cousin there that he could live with and get him a job."

"And he approved it?"

"Yeah, but he was assigned to another parole officer down there and periodically has to check in. I've got his address – it's in Tempe."

Blocking out everyone else in the room, Henry looked directly at Autumn. He knew that Tempe was right next to Chandler, where she lived and instinct told him that this was all more than a coincidence.

Autumn could feel Henry's cold eyes piercing right through her. What was it? What was the person on the other end of the phone telling him?

"Henry, if you really think you have something concrete linking this scum bag to the Glass case, then maybe we should rendezvous in Arizona and talk to the local P.D. down there and the D.A. and formulate some kind of a plan."

Henry agreed to meet Mark in Arizona. Henry wanted to interrogate this Carl himself, but knew that he was now just another ordinary citizen. He had no legal authority to interrogate anyone. But Mark Mullen did. And Henry knew that having been an integral part of taskforce on the case, Mullen wanted to catch this son of a bitch as badly as anyone. He also knew that Mark, a seasoned FBI man, was damn good at his job.

After getting off the phone, Henry explained everything to Donnie, Joanne and Autumn. Joanne sat down, nearly collapsing, on the bed and started crying profusely. At the very least, she now *knew* that the man she was going to marry was a pedophile. And because of that, the dots leading him to the killing of the Glass family and the abduction of April and Lilly were all the easier to connect. Instinctively, Autumn went over to console her mother. At that moment, she no longer thought about the lie her mother had upheld over the years. She no longer cared that Joanne was not her biological mother. At that moment, Autumn just knew that her mom was in pain.

16

It was Thursday June 10th, 1992. It was Autumn Grace's 17th birthday. But instead of planning an evening of celebrating with her friends, she was on a flight from Eugene to Phoenix with her mother, Sheriff Harrelson and Henry Foster, embarking on what she hoped was the last leg of a journey through the darkest caverns of mankind. Both mentally and physically drained, she gazed out the small oblong window at the settling dawn. So many thoughts twirled through her heavy head. Was this nightmare really reaching a conclusion? Who was this girl Jill? What happened to her? Were there yet other victims? Autumn also thought about Dewey. Would she ever be back there again? Would she ever see Molly and Mary again? Leaving from Eugene, she did not even get a chance to say goodbye; to thank Molly for all she had done.

Their flight arrived at Phoenix's Sky Harbor Airport at 10:00am. They were met by Special Agent Mark Mullen, who had taken the red-eye and arrived in Phoenix earlier that morning. After a round of introductions, Mark, a slender, balding man in his fifties – he could have already retired from the FBI, but was too dedicated to the work – ushered his party to an awaiting

Suburban he had rented. From there, it was off to the Grace residence. (The night before, Joanne called Bill, who had already gone back to Chandler, to fill him in on what was going on. Though still undecided if he wanted to remain married to Joanne, he said he would be there.)

As they pulled up to the house, tears swelled in Autumn's eyes, though she tried not to let anyone else see. There it was: the only home she had ever known. And looking at it filled her with overpowering melancholy as she reflected on simpler times. Autumn could almost see herself as a child, playing in the front yard; could picture herself helping her mother carry groceries into the house. She could visualize Kelly – oh, it felt so long since she had been with Kelly – waiting out front to pick her up for school. It wasn't so long ago that she had the same worries of any "normal" teenager: boys, grades, meddling parents, what to do on a Friday night.

As promised, Bill was waiting at the house. Henry introduced him to Mark. Then, Mark, Henry and Donnie were off to meet Carl Donaldson's parole officer – and Carl himself. Mark had arranged with the parole officer, Jim Klein, to have Carl come in for an unscheduled meeting (which was within Jim's authority). Jim called Mark back only an hour and a half earlier – Mark had a cell phone – to say that Carl would be at his office at noon.

Getting there twenty minutes early, Henry, Donnie and Agent Mullen introduced themselves to Jim Klein. As he was over the phone, Mark was upfront with the parole officer, saying that Carl has become a person of interest in a cold case in Oregon that involved multiple murders and kidnapping. He did not go into details; did not say that this was the infamous Pentagram Murders. Mark explained that he just wanted to ask Carl some questions, to "feel him out". Donnie Harrelson, who was the sheriff of the town where the crimes had taken place, might also want to ask him some questions. Perhaps no one wanted to interrogate him more than Henry, but being a civilian, it was agreed before they even met the parole officer, he should not be in the room during the meeting.

As they waited for their man to show up, Jim Klein, a short, pudgy man of middle age that looked like he had had enough of his job, gave a synopsis of Carl Donaldson. Per the terms of his parole, Carl had to check in once a month, which he did. But he had only been in Tempe for six months, so Klein had only seen him six times. Jim also made a point of explaining that the visits were always short. Since his charge – the one he was most recently incarcerated for – was not drug related, he was not subject to drug tests. The only other terms of his parole – it being the early '90's, Carl did not even have to register as a sex offender – was that he hold down a job. Having seen his pay stubs, Jim vouched that Carl worked as a supervisor at Home Depot.

"His P.O. in Montana said that Carl was living with a cousin?" Mark commented.

Jim reclined back in his aging, metal chair as it let out a metallic squeak. "Yeah, well that lasted about two weeks." Mark asked what happened. "According to him, he found out that his cousin and his old lady were into drugs – he swears he didn't know anything about it before – so he found his own apartment. He had two thousand dollars in his bank account, I guess he had saved up when he moved here," Jim said as a side note. "So as far as I know, he's living by himself – at least that's what he told me. Of course, I have the address. It's an apartment by ASU."

"He's a very unassuming guy," Jim continued. "Kind of shy, very polite; well manicured. His clothes are always neatly pressed. You wouldn't know he was an ex-con."

At one point, as Jim Klein was talking, Mark looked at his watch. It was 12:13 PM. Carl was late. Jim said that he had never missed an appointment before, but after fifteen more minutes, the consensus in the room was Carl Donaldson was not going to show up. Mark and Henry feared that Carl had been spooked, sensing that something was up; he had never before been called for an unscheduled check-in with his P.O. Jim called Carl at home, but no one answered. He then – after finding the number – called his job.

Mark, Henry and Donnie could all tell instantly by Mark's face that something was amiss. Then it came: "what do you mean?" Jim asked over the phone. "Are you sure?" As Jim went silent for over a minute, listening to the person on the other end, the others in the room watched his face grow red. Finally he hung up the phone, nearly slamming it down on its base. Before taking a breath, he explained to his guests that apparently Carl had been fired from his job nearly a month ago. He was supposed to notify Jim immediately upon any change in his job status. But that was not the worst of it. Carl had been fired when his boss overheard him saying inappropriate things – of a sexual nature – to a preteen, female customer.

At the very least, Carl Donaldson was in violation of his parole for not reporting that he had been fired. Everyone in the room agreed that they should go to Carl's residence. (Jim Klein was livid, feeling Carl had made a fool out of him. After all, Jim had just been making him out to be a model citizen). Wanting to make sure to dot all the "I"s and cross all the "T"s, Klein called the local police to dispatch an officer to go with them. If Carl *was* their man, the last thing anyone wanted was for him to walk because of some legal technicality.

In a police cruiser and an unmarked Suburban they pulled into Carl Donaldson's apartment complex: Henry Foster, Don Harrelson, Agent Mark Mullen, Jim Klein and two uniformed Tempe police officers. Though Carl did not answer his phone – Jim called again from the parking lot – a collective decision was made to see if he was in his apartment anyway. While Henry impatiently waited in the Suburban, the rest of the group walked through the complex; they parked on the other side of Carl's apartment so he could not see them in their cars from his window. They walked to the second floor, Apartment 34B, trying to make as little noise as possible. As soon as Jim approached the apartment – he was in the lead – he could see through a thin slit in the closed curtains that the television was on. Then, almost instantaneously, he saw someone moving inside. "He's in there," he whispered loudly as they all came to the front door.

As Mark and the two officers took-up defensive positions near the door – Donnie, who had no real jurisdiction, stood behind the two officers – Jim Klein gave three hard knocks on the door. "Carl, its Jim Klein!" he hollered. "I know you're in there. I saw you through the window! I have two police officers with me! If you don't open the door right now, we're coming in!"

Within seconds, the door opened. Standing in the entrance was a slender man, about six foot with short, thick black hair and an unremarkable face. His brown eyes hardly looked like that of a killer – whatever that looked like – or even someone that had spent several years in prison. Carl was cleanly shaven, stood upright and was wearing unwrinkled blue jeans and a grey t-shirt. Jim Klein walked right into the apartment; the rest of the team followed. Before Jim even said anything, Carl apologized for not making the appointment, saying that he had been battling a stomach virus. However, besides being nervous, Carl did not appear to be suffering from any ailment. "How come you didn't call," Jim asked while scanning around the apartment. "And how come you didn't answer your phone?"

Looking at his parole officer's companions, no doubt wondering why such a big party was needed, it took Carl a few seconds before Jim's questions finally registered. "Oh, I'm sorry. My phone's been on the fritz."

Standing by the kitchen phone, Jim picked it up. "Seems to be working just fine."

"Yea…Yeah… it's weird. Sometimes it works, and other times it doesn't. It's been like that for the past two days. I called the phone company and they said they've been havin' trouble with the lines in the area." Carl knew that Jim and the authorities could easily check to verify his assertion, but hoped that they would not. He didn't know what else to say.

As Jim asked Carl about being fired from his job, Don Harrelson noticed something on one of the shelves of the small entertainment center. As he walked over to the framed photograph, he could not believe his eyes. It was a picture of Autumn Grace – and it looked to be recently taken. She was standing by what was clearly a school, with books in hand. But it was obvious she had not been posing. In fact she appeared to be walking somewhere and even the layperson would have concluded that she did not realize her picture was being taken. As Donnie studied the picture, which he was now holding in his hands, Carl noticed and abruptly stopped talking to Jim Klein.

Trying to contain his anger – Donnie wanted to run over, choke Carl and make him talk – he approached the middle-aged parolee in a controlled manner. "Who's the girl in the picture?" he asked in a cold, stern voice.

"That's my daughter," Carl answered without hesitation, though it was clear he was unnerved by the question. Right at that point, Agent Mullen looked over Donnie's shoulder at the picture. As soon as Carl saw his face, he knew that they already knew who the girl was. But he tried to explain. In affect, Carl told the truth: he and Autumn's mother had parted ways when she was only a baby and had been estranged from both his daughter and ex ever since (he left out the part about "buying" Autumn from the Glasses). He went on to explain that the real reason for moving to Arizona – he apologized to Jim for not being up front before – was to try and reconcile with his ex and have a relationship with Autumn. "You guys are probably fathers. You can understand that." He pleaded.

Mark Mullen asked Carl the obvious question: "How did you take this picture? Have you been stalking this girl?"

"Stalking, come on... I'm her father." Carl paused, looking nervously at Agent Mullen. "Do you mind if I ask who you are – and what this is all about?" he asked in a subdued voice.

Mark introduced himself as an FBI agent, saying that he had led a taskforce in Dewey Oregon regarding the deaths of three individuals and the abduction of two little girls. He then quickly introduced Donnie as the Sheriff of Dewey. He just wanted to ask Carl some questions he explained. Obviously, Carl asked why they would want to talk to him about such heinous crimes in Oregon – but his eyes and demeanor gave him away. At that point, staring Carl Donaldson straight in the eyes, Agent Mullen knew that he finally had his man – after all these years. But he also knew that proving it was going to be another story.

"You don't mind if I look around, do you Carl?" asked his parole officer.

It was a loaded question and Carl knew it. Since he was on parole, Jim did not need a search warrant to look around the apartment. If Carl said "no", he would only peak everyone's curiosity even more. So, knowing he didn't have a real choice, he agreed. "Sure, go ahead. I don't know what you're going to find." It did not take Agent Mullen, a seasoned law officer, who had interrogated countless suspects over the years, to notice the stress in Carl's voice. Everyone noticed it.

As Jim "asked" Carl to stay in the living room with one of the officers, Mark, Donnie, the other officer and he all casually walked into the bedroom. Mark, being with the FBI, was cautious of his jurisdiction and let Jim Klein and the Tempe police do all the snooping around. Donnie, also cognizant of his jurisdiction, did the same. The room appeared very well kept; the bed neatly made, no clothes strewn on the floor. With nothing incriminating in the wide-open, Jim Klein started rummaging through Carl's chest of draws. The police officer, who looked to be a veteran of some years, started almost casually, searching the bedroom closet. In the top draw, Jim found an open box of condoms; certainly nothing against the law or in further violation of Carl's parole. On the top shelf of the closet, underneath some sweaters, the police officer pulled down a stack of several pornographic magazines. "Whada we got here," he proudly proclaimed. Mark, Jim and Donnie huddled by the officer, in front of the small closet. The first two magazines were Hustler – something that any male might have around – but the next two were magazines on bondage; the first one, having a picture of a young, perhaps twenty-something naked girl being whipped on the cover.

As Mark and Jim flipped through the pages of the bondage rags, the uniformed officer continued his search of the closet. Donnie watched as, after another minute or so of searching, the policeman pulled something out of the pocket of a coat hanging in the closet. It appeared to be a thick, letter-sized manila envelope. "What's that?" Don asked. Instantly, his question caught the attention of Agent Mullen and Jim Klein.

As the officer began to open the envelope, Agent Mullen quickly grabbed his hand. "Wait. Do you have gloves?" They all looked at each other. None of them had brought gloves. "All right, just be careful," Mark instructed. Using the tips of his fingers, the officer opened the envelope – it was not sealed. Inside was what they all thought it was from looking at the outline of the envelope: photographs. There was a whole stack of them. The first one was a picture of Autumn, standing in font of a house with another girl (it was Kelly). It must have been taken by a powerful zoom lens, because only the girls' faces and upper torso were pictured – and it was obvious that Carl did not snap the photo up close. Ever so delicately, holding the picture by its thin edges, using the tips of his fingers, the officer flipped it to the back of the stack. All vying for a view, Mullen, Klein and Harrelson looked on. The next photograph was another close-up Autumn, but by herself. The next picture and the next and the next were also of Autumn, in various settings. They were about to put the pictures back in the envelope, figuring they were all of her. However, halfway through the stack there it was: the snapshot of a young girl posing on the bed wearing only her panties. Wasting no time, the officer flipped to the next picture: the same girl with her hand down her underwear (it would later be discovered that the girl in the pictures was Carl's girlfriend's daughter – the one he had gone to prison for molesting). The men looked at each other, repulsed, but at the same time, excited that they might be holding evidence to put Carl Donaldson away for a long time.

Without looking through any more of the pictures, Mark announced that it was probably time to take Carl down to the station, notify the Tempe detective's department and have a crime scene unit do a full, thorough search of the residence. Everyone agreed. The officer delicately placed the pictures on the made bed.

As the men walked out of the bedroom, Carl, who was sitting silently on the couch as the other officer stood guard, was sweating bullets. The group had been in the bedroom for a good fifteen minutes and he had overheard them talking. He was not sure what exactly they found, but knew they found something. However, he didn't have to guess for long. "You wanna tell me about the pictures of that little girl, Carl?" Jim Klein asked. (Agent Mullen was not particularly happy about Jim's question. Being a salty veteran, even though Carl was on parole, Mark felt it prudent that he be Mirandized and have a local detective present before any interrogations took place.)

Carl's face turned pale and he grabbed his heart. "Are you ok?" Agent Mullen quickly asked. "Do you need medical attention?"

"I'll be all right," Carl replied with bated breath. "I have high blood pressure. I just need my medication – my Sotalol."

"Ok, where is it? The officer will get it for you."

Carl gripped his heart even tighter and started breathing even heavier. "It's… it's in the…" he said, pointing to the bathroom. The younger officer, who had been watching Carl, hurried into the bathroom and opened the medicine cabinet. The cabinet was full with toiletries, ordinary medication, such as aspirin and Alka-Seltzer, as well as several prescription bottles. The officer could be heard fumbling around. "Make sure it's not the expired one," Carl yelled out, still grasping his chest. "And… and... I should take a calcium tablet too."

"Just go in there," Jim instructed just as the officer was coming out with two prescription bottles in his hand. The last thing anyone wanted – though he deserved it – was for Carl Donaldson to die and take his secrets with him to the grave.

Acting like he had just run a marathon, Carl quickly shot up from the couch and met the officer by the bathroom door. After snatching the two bottles from the policeman's hand he instantly announced that "these aren't the ones." He then went into the bathroom – leaving the door open – into the medicine cabinet and found what he had been looking for. After splashing some cold water on his face and taking a moment to regain his breath, Carl walked back to where his P.O. and Agent Mullen were standing. Jim then had the veteran officer read him his Miranda Rights. As soon as he did, Carl "invoked", saying he wanted a lawyer. With that, he was handcuffed and taken away. One of the officers stayed behind in the apartment, to make sure the area was kept secure.

As Henry, who had been waiting impatiently in the blazer saw the men returning with Carl in handcuffs, he had two thoughts: first, *this is the guy – this ordinary-looking guy – who committed the Pentagram Murders?;* and second, *I wonder what they found in the apartment?*

Just as Carl was about to be placed in the patrol car, he started convulsing out of control. Unable, to tell anyone what was wrong, he was rushed in the back of the police car to the nearest hospital. But it was too late, he died en route. Carl Justin Donaldson was pronounced dead at Phoenix Memorial Hospital at 2:45pm, June 10, 1992. But he did not die of natural causes. The doctors immediately were able to tell from the white foam around his mouth that this was no heart attack. In fact, one of the veteran doctors on the scene did not have to examine him for long to suggest some kind of poisoning. Test would later confirm the doctor's suspicion. Carl Donaldson had died of a cyanide overdose. He had swallowed the capsules – capsules that he had kept with him at all times – when he went into the bathroom at the apartment. Unbeknownst to Jim, Mark, Donnie or the officers – unbeknownst to anyone – Carl had made a vow to kill himself rather than go back to prison, especially if he felt it was going to be for a long period of time.

While Agent Mullen talked with Tempe detectives as well as his supervisor at the FBI, Henry and Donnie went back to the Grace's to break the news.

Joanne, Autumn and Bill had been wondering what could have been taking so long; why they had not heard back from Henry. As far as they knew, Henry, Sheriff Harrelson and Agent Mullen were just supposed to meet Carl at his parole officer's office. That was at noon. Here it was, after five o'clock. Something had to have happened, but what?

Despite the un-believability and unpredictability of everything they had been through, the news that Carl had taken his own life was like a bomb dropping out of the clear blue sky. Joanne's immediate reaction was to cry. It was in no way because she felt bad for her one-time fiancée. Rather, it was all just too much.

Autumn didn't cry, but was in shock. Everything was happening so fast. After all, it was only two days earlier that through her hypnosis, Carl Donaldson was put into the crosshairs. Less than a week ago she had never even known the man existed. Less than a week ago, no one but Joanne knew about Carl. He was certainly never questioned in the Pentagram Murders. Autumn had tried to prepare herself for a drawn-out game of cat-and-mouse between Carl and the authorities. In fact she wondered, because of the lack of evidence – there was no evidence besides what she had said under hypnosis – if he would ever be prosecuted.

If the news of Carl's suicide was shocking, what came next was earth shattering, as Sheriff Harrelson told them about the photographs of Autumn – the recent photographs – that Carl had in his apartment. Bill's reaction was understandable for a father: "That motherfucker!" It was the first time he had ever cussed in front of Autumn. "That son-of-a-bitch took the easy way out! 'Cause if he was alive, I'd torture him to death!" Joanne simply went from a controlled sob to hysteria.

As for Autumn, a freezing-cold sensation flowed through her body, as if someone had injected ice into her veins. She immediately thought back several weeks earlier, when she sensed someone was following her. It had to be *him*, she now convinced herself. And she was left alone with a gripping, haunting thought: was this the reason why April had come to her now, after all these years? Was this Car Donaldson on the verge of abducting – on the verge of raping and killing – her? Was all this April's way of warning Autumn? Was she trying to save her sister's life?

Naturally, Autumn was relieved that this monster was dead. (Donnie also told the family about the pictures of the other little girl they found). He would never hurt another person again. But at the same time, like everyone else involved, she knew that this macabre story was not yet over. They had to find April Glass and Lilly Flowers – or at least their remains. They had to find what happened to this other girl, Jill, and the possibility if there were others. Carl Donaldson would never be able to divulge his dark secrets, but that did not mean that they died with him. Autumn urged to go back to Eugene, to be hypnotized again. "We have to find out where this place is – this house by the field, where he kept the girls. I know I can tell you more details. A few more sessions and I'm sure I can find out exactly what happened." To anyone else it would have sounded absurd – science fiction or the claim of a delusional person. But everyone in that room knew that it was because of Autumn's words – of memories that didn't even belong to her – was how they had arrived at this point. For them it was past the point of believing Autumn; past the point of trying to find some logical explanation of how she knew what she knew.

Henry had no doubt that Autumn *could* give them more information if needed. However, he explained that the first step was to do a full search of Donaldson's apartment – not him, but Agent Mullen and the local authorities – and delve further into his background; his previous residences; if he was ever a suspect in other unsolved crimes.

Carl Donaldson was obviously no longer a danger to anyone. But the authorities prudently wondered if he could have had a live abductee hold-up somewhere, an accomplice, or possibly both. So to them, even though Carl was dead, time was of the essence. Besides, there was no reason to go slow with their investigation. In particular, Mark Mullen, who had been a lead investigator in the Pentagram Murders, had waited long enough. Like Henry Foster, not only the crime itself, but the fact that it was never solved, had haunted the FBI agent throughout the years (though not on the same scale as Henry, where it overtook his entire life).

Early that evening, Agent Mullen, along with detectives from the Tempe Police Department, several deputies and a 2-person crime Scene Unit returned to Carl Donaldson's apartment. To be extra prudent, the detectives easily obtained a search warrant. Henry and Donnie stayed with the Graces. Mark promised to call to inform them of anything they had found.

The first thing that was looked through was the stack of photographs that were still lying on the bed where the deputy had placed them. Originally, Mark, Donnie and Jim Klein did not look through all the pictures. So Mark was surprised when the last five photographs revealed yet another girl. She looked to be about thirteen and was lying on a mattress, undressed, posing in several different, vulgar positions. They placed the pictures in a Ziploc bag and marked as evidence, for a case against a corpse. (Originally, Mullen and the others assumed that Carl had taken his life because they had found pictures of the first girl. But unbeknownst to them at the time, the girl was the same one that Carl had already been convicted and served time for molesting. However, Carl reasonably assumed that they had gone through all the pictures – and would also find anything else incriminating he had in the apartment.)

The search was far from over. As a photographer – somewhat ironically – snapped picture after picture, his flash lighting up the room with each shot, officers opened every draw;

looked beneath every cushion; behind every painting; inside every nook. It was one of the two detectives, however, that took special notice of a set of keys on the kitchen counter. Looking through the keys, he realized that one of them looked to belong to a safety deposit box. After alerting the others, he called someone to run a check on Carl's banking records, particularly to find the location of the box.

About an hour into the search, one of the crime scene technicians had the wherewithal to unscrew an air-condition vent cover and look inside the duct. From it, she retrieved three, unmarked VHS tapes. Apprehensively, Mullen and the detectives looked at each other wondering what sick, nefarious acts were contained on the tapes. At the same time, however, they knew that there was a great likelihood that they might hold some much needed answers.

From the time Mullen and company first went to the apartment to question Carl, seeing uniformed policemen, curious neighbors – it was an apartment complex – naturally poked behind windows and cracked doors to see what was going on. But by now, the yellow crime scene tape and army of lawmen had attracted scores of nosy pedestrians. But it was not just the locals who were curious. Before long, word of "something big" was going back and forth over police radios. Having police scanners, news crews picked-up on the chatter and, coupled with it being an otherwise slow news night, rushed to see what was going on. By 8:00pm, the area around the complex was a circus. Reporters aggressively pressed anyone wearing a badge to find out what was going on; it killed them that they did not know exactly what all the hoopla was about. Always cunning, they were able to rather quickly ascertain not only who lived in apartment 34B, but that he had served time for child molestation in Montana.

"Does Mister Donaldson have any connection to Anne Kudlow, the little girl that was kidnapped in Tempe last year?" one reporter asked a rookie officer who was there solely for crowd control. The policeman gave the reporter a perplexed look;

she obviously knew more than he did. He had no idea who Mr. Donaldson even was.

Eventually, an attention-craving police sergeant, who had only just learned the details of the case (and only knew a piece of the whole picture), granted a brief on-air interview. "Earlier this afternoon, detectives [which was incorrect] went to the residence of one Carl Donaldson to question him about an out-of-state cold case. Right before he was put in custody, Mr. Donaldson took his own life."

A veteran news reporter, who was usually always on her feet, was taken aback by the Sergeant's revelation. But only for a second, before she hit back with a barrage of questions. "How did he kill himself?"

"I'm unable to divulge that at this time."

"What is the cold case? Have you uncovered anything significant in the apartment?"

The portly, mustached Sergeant put up his hands. "I'm sorry. The facts of the case are still… everything is unraveling very fast. That's all I can tell you at this time. Once we've learned more, I will let you know." The sergeant had gotten his fifteen minutes of fame.

If news crews were probing before, they were now whipped up into frenzy. Fingers raced in a blur against keyboards. Phone lines were clogged. Boots hit the pavement.

17

In her bedroom, for the first time in what seemed like a year, Autumn called Kelly. Upon hearing her best friend's voice, Kelly started crying – she had not heard any news about Autumn since she had talked to her parents, before they left for Dewey. "Oh Autumn, I was so worried about you."

Hearing Kelly cry, the straining concern in her voice, made Autumn start crying. "Oh Kell, you wouldn't believe everything that's happened. No one would." Autumn paused for a second. "It's so good hearing your voice." For a moment, though in tears, Autumn felt a great comfort. In talking to Kelly, it was like a piece of her life had been returned to her.

"What the hell did happen? Where have you been? Are you ok?"

"Yeah, I'm ok. Listen, I can't really talk now. I'll tell you everything soon, I promise. I just wanted to let you know I was ok." Autumn let out a deep sigh. "But Kell... everything was real."

"What do you mean?"

"It was all for real." Then Autumn dropped the bombshell of all bombshells. "The little girl in the woods... the girl in my dreams...well...she's my sister. We were separated at birth."

Kelly was beginning to think that Autumn was lying about being ok. Obviously she had lost her mind. *Her sister?!* What the hell was she talking about?! "Autumn..."

"Listen, I now it sounds crazy, but it's all for real. The Sheriff of Dewey...Oregon...is downstairs with my parents right now. Those murders that took place...the Pentagram Murders...remember? They went to arrest the guy today and he killed himself. They're searching his place right now. But it's even crazier, trust me. Listen, I'm sorry. I'll call you later or probably tomorrow and tell you all about it, but I gotta go now."

"But..."

"I gotta go. I'll call you later."

Kelly was still holding the receiver, listening to a dial tone for nearly a minute, before she finally hung it up. She was afraid for her friend, afraid that she was delusional. Kelly sat on her bed, with endless questions running through her mind. Why couldn't Autumn talk? Should she call Autumn's parents? For half an hour she just sat there, deep in thought, while blindly staring at the TV. Then it happened: "Next on the Eleven o'clock news: a Tempe man who had served time in prison for molesting an eight year-old and is the prime suspect in a notorious cold case takes his own life as the police close in."

Kelly's jaw dropped. It couldn't be?! Could it? Was what Autumn had said for real? Kelly could not help herself and called her friend. "Autumn, I can't believe it!"

"Believe what?"

"The news. Are they talking about..."

"Hello," answered Joanne. "Who is it?"

"Mom I got it. It's just Kelly. Kell, I've got to go."

Autumn immediately hung up the phone and turned on the TV; she had been sitting in silence. One station had the local news on, but it was sports. She turned to CNN, but there was nothing. What was Kelly talking about? Autumn looked at her clock: it was 10:55 pm. Her heart racing, she ran downstairs. "Turn on the eleven o'clock news! I think it's on the news!"

Autumn, Henry, Donnie, Joanne and Bill all huddled around the living room television set. Sure enough, to their surprise, Carl Donaldson was the lead story. Somehow, the media had already been able to ascertain that Carl was linked to the Pentagram Murders and the disappearance of April Glass and Lilly Flowers. They did not know however – and what they were trying their damndest to figure out – was, after all these years, what lead the authorities to this individual. They had no idea about Autumn. And fortunate for her, they never would know the full truth about what happened (and a good thing – how would they have explained it to their audience). Besides ridding the world of his monstrous presence, the greatest gift Carl Donaldson gave by taking his own life was that the powers that be did not have to prepare a case against him (it was rather quickly determined that Carl did not have any accomplices). The prosecution never had to prove to a judge or jury – or the public at large – that it was a teenager's dreams and visions that led them to Donaldson.

It was getting late and Sheriff Harrelson and Henry said they were going to check into a hotel, but Bill and Joanne would hear nothing of it. Now faced with the thoughts that their daughter could have been in eminent danger from Donaldson, they both felt a great sense of gratitude to the men – especial Henry Foster – for possibly saving her life. As for Bill Grace, too much was happening too fast for him to remember how hurt and furious he was at Joanne. But he realized, after learning that Carl had been stalking Autumn, how much he loved his daughter.

Autumn spent the last remaining remnants of her seventeenth birthday up in her room, by herself. She was of course overwhelmed by a sense of relief that this whole ordeal seemed to be nearing an end. But the journey had been incomprehensively taxing on her mind, body and psyche. Though as mentally and physically drained as she was, Autumn could not sleep all night, staying up until the sun rose.

Agent Mullen, Sheriff Harrelson, local detectives and an agent from the FBI's Phoenix office, who had been called in to assist, worked through the night. Back at Police headquarters, a select group of about seven individuals watched the videotapes recovered in Donaldson's air-condition duct, in full. The first tape, which was about a half hour long, featured the eight year-old girl that Carl had been charged with molesting (apparently, the authorities in Montana had never known about the tape – or at least couldn't find it). It seemed to be taken over a period of several days. The first ten or so minutes was of the poor girl posing and performing self-sexual acts; Carl could be heard directing her on what to do. The rest of the tape, the camera was apparently put on a tripod, and actually showed Carl raping the girl. Needless to say, everyone in the room was repulsed. In fact, one male detective, a veteran, who had worked numerous murder cases, had to excuse himself from the room. As sickened as they were however, the lawmen knew that they had to watch the other two tapes.

Both other tapes appeared to be taken in the same location – though different from the first tape – a windowless, brick room that everyone watching assumed was a basement. The second tape contained similar revolting acts as the first one, but with a different girl. She looked to be about twelve years old, skinny, with short black hair. Then, after about half an hour, yet another girl appeared (and the previous one was gone). "Oh my god, how many girls did he do this to?" bemoaned someone. By the time the third girl appeared on the tape, there was not a dry eye in the room. Veteran FBI agents and detectives were wiping away their tears. Two more had to excuse themselves from the room.

The one thing that stood out on the tapes, besides the shear evilness, was that when another girl appeared, the one that preceded her was never seen again. Everyone surmised what this meant (except for the first girl – by this time, the authorities already had a picture of the girl Carl had been convicted of raping in Montana and knew that she was still alive).

The third tape, started off with two girls. Agent Mullen and Sheriff Harrelson looked at each other and then back at the screen, not believing their eyes. One of the girls was April Glass. She was with another girl: she looked to be about ten or eleven, with long, straight red hair and freckles. Immediately, Don Harrelson recognized her to be the same girl as Autumn had described under hypnosis: Jill. But he kept it to himself. It was just too unbelievable.

Lilly Flowers was not on any of the tapes. Agent Mullen took this to mean that either Donaldson killed her shortly after her abduction or that he didn't start filming his despicable acts until after a period of time. If the latter was true, there may be even more victims out there, who just weren't on the video tapes (or at least not these tapes). After watching the tapes Mullen did not think he could feel any more sick to his stomach, but the thought of there being even more girls was able to squeeze his gut even tighter.

Though there was no suspect to prosecute and though the authorities now believed that there was no live girl being held captive, the case took on an urgency for two reasons: one, to find out who the other girls on the tapes were; and secondly, to recover the remains of all the girls, so they could be given a proper burial and their families, given some kind of closure.

As the morning broke, many things were happening simultaneously. One group of officers and agents were going through still-open abducted/missing children files, trying to put names to the faces on the videos. Another group was tracking down all of Carl Donaldson's previous addresses. Agent Mullen and two detectives were paying a visit to the cousin with whom Carl had briefly lived. Another detective was trying to track down the safety deposit box that went with the key the authorities had found in Carl's apartment.

After about an hour of research, a safety deposit box in Carl Donaldson's name was located. By 10:45am, with a court order in hand, Agent Mullen, another FBI agent and two Tempe Detectives were at the bank to open the box. Inside was only one item: a letter-sized envelope. Agent Mullen carefully opened it and pulled out a single piece of paper – a handwritten note. As Mullen held it up, everyone looked on with silent, utter enthrallment as if they had just found the Arc of the Covenant. It read:

> *If you are reading this, hopefully I am dead. You're also probably wondering what kind of monster would commit such heinous crimes. You probably want to blame it on devil worshipping or the music I listened to or that my parents abused me as a child (which they did not). But the truth is – a truth more unbearable than any dark theories you can come up with – is that I don't know why I did the things I did. Yes, I dabbled in the occult when I was younger, but the pentagrams I left at that murder was merely to throw off the police – to make them think that a band of Satan worshippers did it. That's also the only reason I mutilated the bodies of that family. I killed them just because they were witnesses.*
>
> *No, the devil did not make me do the things I did – nor did any other outside forces. But if the thought that a normal-looking guy – someone that could hold down a job, someone that you might have even been friends with – can murder and rape for no other reason other than to derive pleasure, makes your stomach churn with fear than consider this: there are many more like me out there. Thousands! They might be your neighbor, your bank teller... your kid's teacher.*
>
> *It would be easy for me to say I'm sorry for the things I've done – and a part of me is – but what*

does "sorry" get anyone. Sorry doesn't change
the past.

Eternally,
Carl

Needless to say, every man in that room felt a sinking in the pit of their stomach after reading the letter. But as chilling as the words were, much was left out. It seemed as though Carl had intended the letter to be found by someone who already knew all the details of his crimes. Whatever the case, besides the reference to the "…mutilated bodies of that family" – which could have been somewhat easily traced to the Pentagram Murders – the letter was rather ambiguous. It did not name or describe any of his victims, how many people he had killed and/or raped, or where he had disposed of the bodies. The authorities did not know anything from reading the letter – besides that Carl didn't blame the devil or his parents – which they did not already know (luckily though, they already knew plenty).

At the same time Mullen and his crew were at the bank, detectives at Headquarters had found out that Carl Donaldson owned a house outside of Glendive, Montana, near the North Dakota border, which was left to him in his uncle's will. Calls were made to the FBI's Montana field office, as well as the appropriate persons at the state and local levels of law enforcement. The calls were placed for two reasons. The first was to ask local authorities if they had any unsolved abductions and/or murders of young girls in the area; if so, they might want to look into one Carl Justin Donaldson. Secondly, to notify them that a delegation of lawmen were on their way from Phoenix to search a house that supposedly belonged – at least at one time – to Donaldson.

By 2:00 PM, an assembly of officials – including Sheriff Harrelson – was on a flight, chartered by the FBI, to Dawson

Community Airport. Once there, they met up with other various law officers from Montana: state troopers, deputies and the sheriff from the local police, several Glendive detectives, a crime scene unit and an FBI agent from the Billings office. After a short briefing, right on the tarmac of the small airport, the convoy was on its way to the Donaldson house. Everyone – even the ones who had just found out what this was all about – was pumped up and ready.

The town that they drove through to get to the property reminded Sheriff Harrelson a little of Dewey – besides the landscape – a small town that had probably seen better days. The property itself – a small, ranch-style dwelling – was about two miles from the "center" of town, in an expansive, overgrown field. There wasn't much in the vicinity, besides the house, a miniature playground... and a small, wooden, apparently long-abandoned church. Don Harrelson could not believe his eyes. For he was the only one there that knew of the swing set and church Autumn had described while under hypnosis. And as he looked at the area and imagined what the field would have looked like ten years earlier, it fit Autumn's description to a "T".

Donnie found himself in a slight predicament. He felt the need to tell at least Agent Mullen that this *was* the place that Donaldson had kept numerous victims, the place almost certainly on the video tapes. But he did not want to sound crazy; didn't want to say *how* he knew this was the pace. But he could not keep it to himself. He had to make sure that every stone was unturned in the search of the house and surrounding property. So he simply told Mark that Autumn had described this exact place. "What are you saying," the agent asked. "Autumn has been here? Donaldson had her here?" Things had moved so fast that – probably luckily – Mullen was not yet told the whole, true story of how Autumn had lead Donnie and Henry to Carl.

"No, I don't believe so. I'm not sure exactly how she knew about this place," he lied almost instinctively. "I just think that we should make sure to thoroughly scour this whole area."

As it turned out, Donnie probably did not have to say anything. Upon entrance to the house – which was run-down and boarded up – the crew quickly found themselves downstairs in a cellar. It was a small, brick room with no windows. In one corner of the room was a rickety, old, wooden coffee table. Those that had watched Donaldson's abhorrent videotapes knew that this was the place. (The two mattresses depicted in the tapes were not there, but everyone assumed that Carl, knowing they probably contained forensic evidence, had gotten rid of them.)

The team of Feds, detectives and local police officers wasted no time in starting their search of the premises. By the next morning, cadaver dogs, excavating equipment and a ground-penetrating radar device, borrowed from the military, was on the scene.

Under an overcast sky, a pale light filtered through the soft, ubiquitous clouds. On a green but sullen lawn, in front of her old house, stood April Glass. There she was, just standing there silently, her bare feet against the short blades of moist grass. She was wearing her, thin, white nightgown. Only it was no longer covered in blood. In fact it looked as clean as if she had just taken it home from the store. For what seemed like minutes she just stood there. Then, a subtle breeze swept across the land, gently blowing her long, golden hair. Autumn too, could feel the breeze as she stared mesmerized at April; could feel the breeze inside as if it was passing through her very soul. Then, without saying a word, April Glass smiled.

Autumn had never seen April smiling before – except maybe in a few old photographs. She had always been so tormented. There had always been such sadness and fear in her eyes. But now those eyes, they seemed at peace. Autumn wanted to run to April, to hold her tight in her arms. But she was frozen in place. She wanted to cry out to her – there were so many things Autumn wanted to say – but she could not speak.

Suddenly, as April stood there smiling, her hair and nightgown flowing ever-so gentle in the breeze, the light began to change. Autumn could no longer see the sky above or the woods in the background. All she could see was April Glass and the house as a growing bright light blocked everything else out. Then, within seconds, even the house disappeared into a soft white background. All that was left was April, standing within a blank, three-dimensional canvas. She seemed so close that Autumn could touch her without even extending her arm – but she could not. Then, the girl who she had at one time simply known as "the little girl in the woods" started becoming translucent, as the growing light began to fade her into the white background. Second by second, she began to slowly disappear, until all that was left was her face. And though she uttered not a word, her eyes and smile spoke for her. They said both thank you and goodbye. Then, just like that she was gone.

"Autumn. Autumn." The seventeen year-old slowly opened her heavy eyes, to find her mother standing over the bed. "Autumn."

Gingerly, Autumn propped herself up. "Mom? What is it?"

"Sheriff Harrelson just called," Joanne replied in a shaky voice. "They just found several graves on Carl's [how she hated even saying that name] property containing human remains."

Without exchanging another word, Autumn and her mother embraced and cried into each other's shoulder. Autumn did not need to wait for forensic test results. She knew – she knew from the dream she just had – that April had finally been found.

In all, the search team unearthed nine, crudely dug graves in Carl Donaldson's backyard. In each one, the remains of a child's body – some, mere skeletons. Through dental records and other forensic anthropology techniques, the bodies of April Glass and Lilly Flowers were confirmed within days. Also within days, one of the bodies was confirmed as Jill Frances Vanderman, a girl who had disappeared in Miles City, Montana in 1986 at the age of twelve. Eventually – through painstaking forensic and detective work – the remaining girls were identified. It was ultimately determined that three of the girls predated the abduction of April and Lilly.

Unlike most of the other girls, there were no visible signs of trauma to April Glass' bones. From that and other anthropological evidence, though it could not be proven with certainty, it was determined that there was a good likelihood that April was buried alive.

What was never determined – though thoroughly theorized – was how Carl Donaldson transported April and Lilly over a thousand miles. However, that seemed of little importance now. The murders of Peggy Suzanne Glass, John William Glass and John Jr. Glass and the abduction and murders of April Glass and Lillith Gillian Flowers were now officially closed.

18

Two weeks after the remains of April and Lilly were found, they were returned to Dewey Oregon for a long, overdue proper burial. Autumn, along with her mother and father, made the trip. Waiting for them at Eugene was Molly. Autumn had thought Henry was going to pick them up and when she saw Molly, she ran into her arms. "Oh Molly, I'm so glad to see you."

Molly, who had never stopped worrying about Autumn, squeezed her tight. "I'm glad to see you too. How are you doing?"

Autumn took her head off Molly's shoulder and smiled. "I'm ok."

Next, Joanne and Bill said their hellos to Molly. They also thanked her profusely for everything she had done for Autumn.

Conversation on the long drive from Eugene inevitably focused on April Glass and Lilly Flowers. They discussed how horrible a fate befell the two girls. But the dialogue was not all misery and woe. They talked about the sense of closure that could now finally be brought; how the girls were "finally back home." The relief that Carl Donaldson could no longer torment another child was also not lost in the conversation.

Joanne and Bill also took time during the drive to tell Molly that they had decided to work things out. As Bill put it, "the family has been through too much together to split up now". Molly was happy, not so much for Bill and Joanne, as for Autumn. The way she figured it, the dark secret of the past had been exposed and could no longer hurt them.

As the car rolled into Dewey, Autumn stared out the window in mesmerized sight. If she lived to be a 100 years old and never stepped foot inside the town again, it would still always be a part of her. Or perhaps more appropriate, a part of her would always be left there. But as she looked at the small town, soaking under a blue, summer sky, it seemed much different than when she had first strolled down its streets. The stores and house, the surrounding woods and mountainous backdrop all looked the same. But it was as if a dark, ever-looming shadow had been lifted from it. And that shadow was the Pentagram Murders – and the abductions of April Glass and Lilly Flowers. Solving the once seemingly unsolvable macabre mystery – and brining the remains of April and Lilly home – brought closure not only to the dead, family members and those personally entwined with the case. It brought closure to an entire town; a town that had endured not only the unanswered questions, but also the rumors and ridicule that came with them. And Autumn was certainly aware of this.

That evening, Molly (with the help of her Aunt Edith) prepared a home-cooked meal for Autumn and her parents. Henry and Mary were also there. Like a family, there was a bond that would hold them forever together. Molly insisted that Joanne and Bill stay the night at her house, but they appreciatively declined. After dinner, Henry took them to the Davison Motel. However, Autumn did stay. That night, she, Molly and Mary finally watched their movie. There was no talk of Carl Donaldson, what happened that fateful October night or even the girls' funerals, scheduled for the next day. They just enjoyed being with each other, watching a movie.

Though Autumn had only known Molly and Mary for such a brief time, she felt at home sitting there with them. In fact, with everything that had transpired, at the moment, she felt more comfortable with them than being with her own parents. Autumn saw Molly as a friend – maybe even a big sister. Despite only meeting her less than a month earlier, Autumn felt she could tell her anything that she would tell Kelly, her lifelong friend. And then there was Mary. In between watching the movie, Autumn could not help inconspicuously glancing at the nine year old. Even in her darkest moments Mary had been a beckoning light of hope. Mary had – and always would have – a special place in Autumn's heart.

Later that night after the movie, the teenager from Arizona and nine year-old from Oregon talked. Knowing that Autumn would be leaving in a day, Mary asked, with a solemn voice and tears swelling in her eyes if she would ever see Autumn again. Smiling, Autumn made a promise to keep in touch and visit Mary when she could. It was a promise Autumn would keep. They not only stayed in touch, but their friendship grew. In fact, once a year, Autumn would make the trip back to Dewey. In later years, both Molly and Mary even visited Autumn in Arizona.

The next day was the funerals for April and Lilly. It was decided to lay them both to rest on the same day. Even the idea of burying the two girls next to each other, in side-by-side lots was put forth. In some ways, it did seem fitting. But it was ultimately decided that April should be buried with the rest of her family. And Lilly would be buried next to her father and the brother who died at only sixteen months old. However, both were in the same cemetery – the only cemetery in Dewey. Each of the girls' headstones was donated by a well-known monument company in Eugene. The local mortuary also donated their services.

Though April and Lilly would not be buried next to each other, in the viewing, which was held that morning, their closed caskets were placed side-by-side. It seemed all the townspeople came to pay their respects. Some people actually knew the girls. Others felt as though they had known them. Some parents brought their children. Some by themselves, others with a spouse or even child, walked up to the small, closed, black caskets. Tears flowed freely as though water through a faucet that had finally been unblocked. A few people fell to their knees shouting things like "why, God why?!" or "It's not fair!" But most wept silently; either gently touching the casket or even placing their lips on its smooth, cold surface as if to kiss the girls goodbye.

Lilly's funeral was held first. Under a clear, blue, mid-summer sky twenty or so people stood by the awaiting grave. Some were people that had actually been friends with Lilly from school, or the family. Lilly's uncle and his family had come. There was also another member of the family there: Lilly's mother, Gillian. Her brother had picked her up from the hospital and brought her for the funeral. Autumn did not see her at the viewing and had not expected her to be there. But as soon as she saw Gillian, sitting there in her wheelchair, Autumn put her hand up to her mouth and started crying. Then, after trying to gain some composure, she walked over to Mrs. Flowers.

"Mrs. Flowers, I don't know if you…"

"Of course I remember you," Gillian said in a frail voice. She then grabbed hold of Autumn's hand. "Thank you for helping find my little girl."

Tears streamed down Autumn's soft face, as she knelt down besides Lilly's mother. "I'm just glad she's finally home now."

Gillian shook her head. "And I'm so sorry about what happened to your sister. But she's with Lilly and her family now, in a better place."

It was the first time that anyone had ever referred to April as Autumn's sister. "Thank you," Autumn replied as she buried her head in Gillian's lap and cried.

In the eulogy, the priest echoed Gillian's sentiments that Lilly was in "a better place" now and how God worked in mysterious ways. Autumn tried, but could not pay attention to every word. Her head was filled with too many thoughts: *how could a god allow these poor girls to be taken at such a young age – and in such a way; what would Lilly and April be like, look like, if they were still alive; what feats could they have accomplished, what experiences could they have known; how could someone do such terrible things; was there really a hell – if there was, at least Carl Donaldson would be tortured there for eternity.*

As the time inevitably came to lower Lilly's casket into the ground, Gillian, tears streaming down her weathered face, cried out: "Lilly, baby, I love you!" Everyone's stomachs churned with anguish at the sight of a mother bidding her daughter eternal farewell. Joanne and Bill both put their hand on Autumn's shoulder.

Next came April's service. The same people attended as had been at Lilly's.

Before the priest started the ceremony, Autumn walked over to the casket and touched it. Autumn's heart and soul went out to Lilly – and all the other victims of Carl Donaldson. But April was different. Though Autumn never really knew her in life, April was her sister, her blood. And Autumn was the one she had come to… to help her find her way back home.

As the priest began to speak, Autumn could not help but fixate on Henry Foster. No one's eyes were dry, but Henry's tears flowed down his large, hardened face like a waterfall. But she knew that they were not mere tears of sorrow. For Autumn knew that she was watching Henry being released – released once and for all from the invisible prison that had enslaved him for eight long years.

As the casket was solemnly lowered into its final resting place, Autumn looked around. She had thought that April would appear to her one last time, at the funeral. Maybe she would even appear with her parents and brother; an apparition to let Autumn know that they were all together. But ghosts were nowhere to be found. Then, as the crowd began to slowly disperse Autumn realized why she had not appeared – nor ever would again. April's soul had finally been freed from the earth and released into haven. April Glass was finally home.